Penelope's Secret

BY THE SAME AUTHOR

The Human Paradise

Penelope's Secret
and Other Stories

by
Nicolas Ségur

Translated, annotated and introduced by
Brian Stableford

A Black Coat Press Book

ISBN 978-1-61227-733-2. First Printing. April 2018. Published by Black Coat Press, an imprint of Hollywood Comics.com, LLC, P.O. Box 17270, Encino, CA 91416. All rights reserved.
Printed in the United States of America.

TABLE OF CONTENTS

Introduction

Le Secret de Pénélope by Nicolas Ségur, here translated as "Penelope's Secret," was first published by Eugène Fasquelle in 1922. *Platon cherche l'Amour*, here translated as "Plato in Search of Amour," was first published by Flammarion in 1926. *Naïs au miroir*, here translated as "Naïs at the Mirror," was first published by Fasquelle under the aegis of the Bibliothèque Charpentier in 1920. I have arranged the three translations in the order of their internal chronology rather than the dates of their publication, as they are probably best read in that fashion. The three novellas represent different phases in a particular investigation whose central theme is the psychology and philosophy of amour, although all of them broaden out—as is inevitable in setting that theme in the context of ancient Greek mythology and philosophy, to a more general and penetrating enquiry as to what humans might require in order to live happy and fulfilled lives.

Le Secret de Pénélope is one of numerous "sequels" to Homer's *Iliad* and *Odyssey* produced by modern writers, picking up the story of the hero of the later epic where the *Odyssey* ends, following the slaying of the suitors who have been laying siege to the hero's wife while he has been away. The author, although he was Greek himself, calls that hero Ulysses rather than Odysseus, and almost invariably uses the Roman rather than the Greek variants of the names of the various gods of the Graeco-Roman pantheon. It might have been the case that the decision was not his and was forced on him by an editor, but whether or not it was spontaneous, the reason for it is that the French educational system strongly prioritized the learning of Latin, via exemplary texts by Virgil, Horace, etc., so French readers would have been much more familiar with the Roman variants at the time when the books were written.

Although no such consideration applies to modern English readers, I thought it better to remain faithful to the original texts rather than substitute the Greek equivalents, even though it is bound to seem jarring to sensitive readers to find the inhabitants of Athens routinely swearing "By Jupiter!" and referring to the temple of Minerva rather than Athene.

Ségur's novella begins with the revelation that Homer's account of Penelope's stubborn virtue was exaggerated, and tracks the effect that that revelation on Ulysses' attitude to his wife, which seems sufficiently puzzling to him to warrant an earnest investigation in which he seeks advice from Minerva, Menelaus—who has suffered a similar effect in respect of Helen—various shades of the dead and his old tutor, the centaur Chiron. Although the wise Chiron supplies him with a practical solution to his immediate predicament, that is merely a shelving of the issue, and the puzzling features of the mysterious ways of Amour/Eros with the human heart remain. The underlying enigma continues to intrigue the hero—although not so much as it continued to intrigue the author, who spent his entire literary career probing it.

The enigma still remains, of course, routinely shelved but never fully explained, so the attempted unraveling of Ulysses' predicament retains an ironic allegorical quality, addressed by the author in a light and knowing fashion, with a strong element of comedy—an approach echoed in two of the best-known sequels to the Iliad and the Odyssey by an author working in the English language, John Erskine's *The Private Life of Helen of Troy* (1925) and *Penelope's Man* (1928). Nicolas Ségur's further investigations included the two other ventures into the Classical world appended to the translation of *Le Secret de Pénélope* in the present volume, in which the author's imagination consulted other shades of the long-dead in order to obtain different perspectives on the issue.

In *Naïs au miroir*, the author had already published an observational account of the psychology of amour offered by the courtesan Naïs, whose self-examination includes accounts of her dealings with several of her lovers, but also extends to her observations of Athenian mores in general and the conduct of contemporary philosophers, most famously Epicurus. In the climax of the story, the courtesan is challenged to seduce the notoriously chaste philosopher Polemon, who believes that he has attained a state of being immune to the disturbances of Amour—a conflict of wills more complicated than any duel of heroes beneath the walls of Troy.

Platon cherche l'amour, on the other hand, goes straight to the summit of the great tradition of Greek philosophy, in describing the manner in which Plato, only just emerging from adolescence, feels the sharp impacts of Amour's arrows for the first time. Naturally, he seeks the guidance of his mentor Socrates—who finds himself, for once, at something of a loss, and has to hand over a crucial part of the educational process to the great courtesan Aspasia, but eventually weighs in usefully with memories of his own initiation into the mysteries in question.

The variety of attitudes and conclusions contained in the three stories allows them, when viewed as a set, to constitute a rich and colorful spectrum, brightened by deft ironic humor and dazzling erotic interludes. Although the philosophical reflections they contain could hardly be expected to exhaust such an intricate subject, they are certainly extensive, and always aim for profundity. Their narrative strategy is perhaps best described by a word apparently invented by Aristophanes—who appears briefly as a minor character in *Platon cherche l'amour*—in *The Frogs: spoudaiogeloion* [seriocomic]. Although the term never caught on, the strategy did, apparently used extensively by the Cynics, although so few of their works survive that it is difficult to be sure. What is certain, however, is that it is a strategy that has readily lent itself to misunderstanding, by virtue of its essential ambiguity, always tending to paradox; the allegory credited to Aristophanes in *Platon cherche l'amour*, paraphrased from the *Symposium*, is one of the most notable instances of the method and one of the most glaring example of its occasional misinterpretation by critics and commentators.

"Nicolas Ségur" was born Nikolaos Episkopopolous on the Greek island of Zakynthos in 1874; he began his writing career as a journalist in Athens in the late 1890s, and published a number of books in Greek. In the early years of the twentieth century, however, he moved to Paris and settled there permanently, eventually dying there in 1944, subsequently writing exclusively in French. He made the acquaintance of Anatole France not long after arriving in Paris and was taken under the latter's wing; one of his earliest French publications was a profile of the author published in *La Revue* in 1907. His conversations with Anatole France subsequently provided him with the material for three books, beginning with the best-selling *Conversations avec Anatole France ou Les Mélancolies de l'intelligence* (1925; tr. as *Conversations with Anatole France*), published in the year after the great man's death.

Ségur's first volume in French was *Pages de Légende* [Pages of Legend] (1918), recapitulating and commenting on some of the best-known stories surviving from the Classical Era, and his love of ancient Greek literature and myth was further reflected in *Naïs au Miroir*, his first short novel, which appeared with a laudatory preface by Anatole France. The author followed that up with the adventurous utopian fantasy *Une Île d'amour* (1921; tr. as "An Isle of Amour" in the Black Coat Press volume *The Human Paradise*), which addresses the question of how the psychological and social problems posed by human amour might best be addressed by political organization, in a direct but conscientiously light-hearted manner. Although *Le Secret de Pénélope* was published after those two novels, it might not be the case that it was the third to be written, and it could well have been the first; at any rate, it presents the problems by which the other two stories are preoccupied in a more straightforward and explicit fashion.

Both of the novels that preceded *Le Secret de Penelope* seem to have sold well—the prefatory matter in the copy of *Le Secret de Penelope* that I used for translation, which is adver-

10

tised as part of a third printing of a thousand copies, records that *Une Ile d'amour* was by then in its fifth thousand. That success was undoubtedly due to the intrinsic appeal of the subject matter, and reflects not merely the relative liberality of French literature but also the striking intellectual intensity with which erotic topics are routinely considered in France. Not only could no English language book of the period have manifested the frank eroticism of *Naïs au miroir*, but no English or American author would have between capable of inspecting that eroticism with such a sophisticated clinical eye. The Athenians of the Golden Age of Philosophy were not so coy, but Ségur's imaginative recreation of Plato's personal investigation of the subject makes the delicacies, hesitations and diplomatic evasions of the *Symposium* very obvious.

Following *Le Secret de Penelope*, and before turning to the shades of Plato and Socrates for aid, Ségur continued his personal quest for enlightenment by looking closer to home in *M. Renan devant l'amour* [Ernest Renan on Amour] (1923), a virtual monologue considerably less lively than *Plato cherche l'amour*, but even that book was subsequently advertised as having sold five thousand copies. From the publication of *La Belle Venise* [Beautiful Venice] (1924) onwards, however, the level of his success increased very significantly as he found his most profitable commercial vein, redeploying the philosophical insights regarding the role of amour in human affairs gleaned in his earlier works in a long series of contemporary novels that explore the problems and side-effects of passion in today's world, in a melodramatic and sometimes feverish fashion.

Ségur continued to write non-fiction alongside his novels, and he published a notable collection of essays on *Le Génie Européen* [European Genius] in 1926. He also attempted to continue writing more generalized philosophical fiction, producing *Le Cinquième évangile: Saint François d'Assise* [The Fifth Evangelist: St. Francis of Assisi] (1925), but the contrast between the limited commercial success of the latter volume and *Platon cherche l'amour* on the one hand, and the

11

far more voluminous sales of his contemporary erotica on the other, must have encouraged him, as well as his publishers, to concentrate on the more profitable enterprise; throughout the 1930s almost all of his fiction followed a pattern that became increasingly stereotyped, although never lacking in energy and virility. The element of *spoudaiogeloion* was gradually subdued, although it never entirely disappeared. Connoisseurs of that delightfully paradoxical art, however, will find it very abundantly displayed in the present volume, with a rare genius.

All three translations were made from copies of the original Fasquelle and Flammarion editions of the three books.

Brian Stableford

PENELOPE'S SECRET

Pan was the son of Penelope and all the suitors.
(Schol. de Lycophron)[1]

I

The day after the massacre of the suitors and the happy recognition, Ulysses quit his bed at dawn, gently moving aside the tapering leg with which Penelope was enlacing him familiarly, in the unconsciousness of sleep.

A host of anxious reflections clouded his mind, and the gracious spectacle of nascent spring that awaited him when he emerged from his dwelling could not distract him. Ulysses avoided old Laertes, occupied in tilling the soil, and scarcely cast a glance at his nurse, who had been the first to recognize him on his return to Ithaca.

Having arrived on the shore, he sat down on a rock green with algae and devoted himself to long meditations. The waves came to unfurl and die away at his feet, accompanying his thoughts with their mysterious music.

Joys are ephemeral, he said to himself. *They disperse and vanish like the marine foam that dies almost as soon as it is formed. Yesterday, after the bloody battle, finding myself king again in my reconquered island, I felt my heart inundated*

---

[1] This statement was allegedly attributed to Lycophron by Duris the Samian, according to the Byzantine poet John Tzetzes' *Scholiast* [i.e. Commentary] *on Lycophron*, but there might have been a mistranslation somewhere along the line. Pan is more commonly alleged to have been fathered by Hermes/Mercury.

with happiness and pride. But a suspicion has sufficed for my tranquility to be disturbed and for the poison of doubt to penetrate and corrode me.

Leaning toward Argus, his dog, who had followed him and appeared to be respiring delightedly in proximity with his master, he stroked him, passing his hand over his muzzle, and naming him in a tender voice. His thoughts having led him to suspect the sincerity of humans, it was pleasant for him to be able at least to place his confidence in that humble proven companion.

Gradually, while trying to untangle the thread of his anxieties, Ulysses became more confused. Aggravated, his suspicions attained a sort of baleful certainty. Soon, shadowed by sorrow, he thought that the sun was paling before him and that spring was darkening.

Suddenly, a hand posed on his shoulder and the hero, raising his head again, saw Penelope, who was smiling at him amicably, having arrived with slow steps.

"Why have you fled our bed so soon, valorous Ulysses? You have not even tried to renew in the morning the gentle and powerful caresses of which I have been deprived for so many years."

And, as Ulysses did not seem disposed to reply, Penelope, gazing at him attentively, perceived his sadness and the shadows of the preoccupations projected on his face.

"What's the matter, then?" she asked. "What dolor has transformed you so promptly? Yesterday, you were radiant with contentment, and youth seemed to be haunting your features again. Now you are dejected, as if plunged in darkness. I implore you by Minerva, your protectress, to confide your troubles to me, in order that I can share them with you." And as Ulysses raised his hand, sketching a mute and fleeting response, she added: "Have you forgotten our affection? How can you nourish cares jealously and, in a fashion, prolong our separation by hiding them from me?"

Then Ulysses, with the swift rapidity that always presided over his actions, made the resolution to speak sincerely. He therefore replied to Penelope: "O wife, it is you who are the cause of my preoccupations. Having heard your fidelity praised, and proud of your exemplary constancy, I trembled with emotion yesterday evening when, after having got rid of our enemies, I was finally able to resume my place in our bed and feel the soft warmth of your body. But how can I describe my surprise and my perplexity before the unexpected novelty of your kisses?

"I had visited, during my long voyages, the beds of many goddesses, and before that, I had already lavished my caresses on the beautiful captives of proud Ilium. However, I retained, vividly and brightly, the memory of your virginal modesty, your charming gaucherie. I had not forgotten the inexperience with which you once responded to the impetuosity of my desires, and when, before Troy, in the days of destruction, I saw the frail Cassandra emerging polluted and ashamed from the violent hands of Ajax, that sight reminded me of your chaste countenance, the timid distraction you showed in amour.

"Yesterday, however, climbing on to the high bed and enlacing you, I felt myself suddenly seized and forcefully imprisoned by your bold and intrepid arms. Your once-puerile body now showed itself expert and inexhaustible, drawing upon the voluptuous secrets of all the carnal artifices. The sensual Circe, who burned with inexhaustible fires and succeeded in rapidly drawing from me all my voluptuous sap, was truly only a schoolgirl by comparison with you. What she dispensed in passion and in charm in order to inflame me, you deployed yourself, as if in play, yesterday evening.

"Although your science and your experience fulfilled my body, they could not help awakening a great anguish in my mind. For I began to wonder whence came that marvelous transformation, and how, in your long and pure widowhood, retired to your cold bed, you succeeded in learning so many amorous artifices and acquiring such a warm and vibrant virtuosity."

At these words, Penelope's face was colored with the redness of the dawn. She avoided her husband's gaze and, bowing her head, she remained silent.

"Respond to my question," Ulysses went on, "and dispense with lies. All the Achaeans know that nothing remains hidden from me and that my subtlety thwarts the ruses of men. I can already see your confusion, and I hold it as certain henceforth, that you are culpable. Only sincerity can save you now and reunite us."

Then, trying to suppress the tumult of her heart, Penelope dared to raise her fearful gaze to Ulysses, and she replied: "You are right. Who would dare to deceive you? You are equal to the divinities and you visit the innermost recesses of the heart. I will therefore hide nothing from you, and I hope that you will recognize that Necessity was the only instigator of my sins, and that it was the will of the Immortals that prepared my defeat irresistibly. You can, moreover, punish me or absolve me as you wish, and everything coming from you will appear just to me. I only beg you to contain yourself until the end of my story and to listen to me calmly."

Not without uttering a long sigh, the queen continued: "It was during the seventh year of your absence that my courage received a first affront. Until then I had retained faithful to your memory and, imposing silence on my senses, I lived isolated, entirely attentive to following the vigorous growth of our son. The suitors, encouraged by the reverses of the Achaeans and believing you doomed, were emboldened. But they pressed me in vain, using flatteries and promises, to choose a husband; I believed unshakably in your return and avoided any pronouncement.

"One night, however, a dream came to trouble me. For I saw Minerva, your protectress, who predicted to me that a child, almost divine, would soon be born of my loins, and that all the suitors would contribute to it. When I awoke I tried to forget that dream and rebelled against the will of the goddess. I knew, in any case, that malign and deceptive spirits often usurp a divine aspect, and sow deceptive dreams in order to torment mortals.

"A few nights later, however, the irreparable occurred. It is necessary to tell you that I had adopted the habit of hiding myself, at nightfall, in the depths of my palace. I left the suitors banqueting noisily and gorging themselves on meat and wine in the rooms downstairs. My five maidservants, sleeping at the entrance to my apartments, guarded my retreat and ensured that it was respected. In taking those precautions, however, I had not thought of the impudence and cunning of the beggar Iras. In fact, that wretch, whom you have justly punished by breaking his jaw, had reached an understanding with my maidservants. Employing flatteries and corruption by turns, he succeeded in putting them to sleep one night by the usage of wine, and subsequently putting me at the discretion of the suitors.

"That night, therefore I was abruptly woken up in my bed, sensing a pressure and an unaccustomed warmth around my body. I believed at first, while still asleep, that a fly was prowling around and lingering on my lips. On opening my eyes, however, I perceived with stupor, by the light of a torch, that I was in the arms and beneath the body of a powerful warrior. I recognized him. It was Eurymachus, the son of Polybus, a man still young, well-proportioned and intrepid. The infamous Iras, his accomplice, was standing next to him, ready to support him in his enterprise.

"I had the intention then of crying out, struggling and defending myself; but the idea of your honor and my reputation, kept intact for so long and provoking the admiration of all the Achaeans, stopped me. In any case, the injurious attempt was already entirely perpetrated. Repressing my horror and my anger, therefore, and wanting to avoid any noise and outburst, I closed my eyes again. I pretended to be unaware of what, amid his joyous transports, kisses, sighs and tender appellations, the valorous Eurymachus was doing to my body. When he was satisfied, without my wanting to share his satisfaction, he left, followed by Iras.

"I remained alone, dazed, utterly stirred up, thinking about, trying to compose myself and console myself. Finally, the struggle I had endured enabled me to find sleep again. And it was with a new surprise that I woke up, again sensing a man in my bed, and then feeling arms, more ardent, if I dare say so, than those of Eurymachus. This time, it was the illustrious Agelaus, king of Zacynthus. Iras followed him. I saw that I was doomed, that Minerva's prediction was being realized, and that a second suitor was pressing irresistibly the body that I wanted to keep pure of all soiling, virgin of any foreign embrace.

"As, henceforth, I could only accept destiny, I consoled myself by thinking that there is always some advantage to be obtained from the worst misfortunes. *Since I cannot succeed in keeping my girdle intact for my husband,* I said to myself, *it is better if, at least, he cannot specify the object of his resentment, or have a determined rival. Serving several, my body will not belong especially to anyone, like a hostelry that, sheltering various individuals, can boast of having no master.*

"Thus, it was almost with joy and relief that I awoke again, still warm from the embrace of Agelaus, I saw the son of the famous Polyctor enter,[2] who was still beardless and had a divine form and strength. He slipped into the bed, very impatient, and embraced me with such a naïve and impetuous ardor that I could not help smiling at him......

"Why am I lingering, in any case, in this story? That night and the following night the visits continued. The hundred suitors succeeded one another. I always greeted them, I swear by the gods, with closed eyes and a modest attitude, making a semblance of being asleep. They did not have the satisfaction of seeing on my face the abundant joy that they were giving me.

---

[2] Two of Polyctor's sons are listed among Penelope's suitors, but this one is evidently Peisander, as the other, Eurymachus, was the father of Polybus.

"As they were from various countries, of different temperaments, and their demands were as various as their complexions and their habits, and as there were very lustful and very industrious individuals among their number, who revealed unknown secrets to me unintentionally, their obligatory commerce ended up transfiguring me and serving unwittingly as a voluptuous education. Nothing remained unknown to me of everything that Amour and Desire inspire in men.

"Such is my fatal sin, O Ulysses, and the dream that warned me of it proves to you that the gods were no strangers to it. Not only the perversity of Iras, but an Olympian design was to conduct that entire population of kings—and, I can say, almost every man carrying a scepter—to my bed. Now, judge me, and if you think that I failed voluntarily, and that my conduct was inappropriate to your interests and my reputation, apply to me the punishment that you think necessary."

While his wife was speaking, anger rose, dilating Ulysses' nostrils. He was on the point of becoming prey to dementia and imitating Ajax on the day when the latter killed the sacred flocks. When Penelope had confessed that a second suitor succeeded the first in her bed the hero had raised his arm to kill her, but he had killed so abundantly the day before and had steeped his hands so constantly in blood while exterminating the suitors and their concubines that the act of slaying had become insupportable to him.

In any case, during his long existence, Ulysses had seen so many men getting carried away, and accomplishing irreparable acts during their fury, that he had become prudent and had learned to dominate his anger. He therefore restrained himself.

Having need of calm in order to be able to behave appropriately in the new situation that was opening up before him, he turned to his wife and said to her: "Go away, bitch! Return to the palace quickly and await your salary."

At those words, accompanied by a terrible gesture, Penelope went away, sobbing. Ulysses began to wander aimlessly, and without respite, as if pursued by the Erinnyes. He passed unconsciously over the sandy beach where once, by sowing salt and feigning madness, he had tried to discourage the Achaeans who wanted to drag him into their expedition against Troy. Then he retraced his steps, pursuing his errant course at random, only desiring in reality to be alone, in order to be able to abandon himself to his reflections.

He had become just like all the rest—him, the most docile of the Achaeans, whose name was allied in human memory with skill and subtlety! Now he was like Vulcan and Menelaus, obtuse and wretched husbands whose conjugal misfortunes, sung by the aedes, enlivened the banquets of kings! His shame might even be judged incomparable, since neither Venus nor Helen could boast of having attracted and satisfied such numerous and varied lovers as the infamous Penelope.

I can say, he thought, *that all my glory is effaced and annihilated. All that I did admirably, in attracting Achilles and Philoctetes to Troy, inventing the Wooden Horse and visiting unknown lands, my wife has overtaken by means of the gigantic work of her bed. After having been the tamer of Ilium, the voyager supreme, the man who successively undertook all terrestrial labors and exhausted human knowledge, I will only remain in the memory of men for the excellence of my shame. The future will only recognize in me the husband whose fabulous misfortunes attained the summit of derision.*

Ideas of vengeance assailed Ulysses again, obsessively and tumultuously. He thought about running to the palace, dragging the infidel far from the hearth and, after having pierced her with a hundred wounds—as many wounds as she had experienced furtive joys—attaching it behind his chariot and delivering the polluted body to the impetuous ardor of his horses. Afterwards, he would abandon his disastrous kingdom, his rediscovered father and his faithful nurse, and he would go to resume the adventurous life in his hollow ship, braving the tempests and the pirates...

Ulysses was descending the hills of his island, fortified in his homicidal design, incessantly nourishing his unappeased anger. Already, the ancestral palace founded by Ithacus had appeared to his sight, reanimating his frightful memories. But at that moment, the air that surrounded him seemed to thicken and become colored, and the goddess with the blue eyes, Minerva, his faithful source of inspiration, took on a body of flesh and loomed up before him.

"Where are you going, Laertide, and what violent projects are filling your mind?" asked the daughter of Jupiter, in her clear and imperious voice.

On recognizing the redoubtable and propitious Minerva, Ulysses remained nonplussed, without having the strength to reply.

"I know what you have learned and the thoughts that are agitating in your mind," the goddess went on. "Beware, unhappy man, of behaving inconsiderately, and remember that it is the will of the Immortals that directs human action; Penelope was right to attribute her sin to fatality. If she has soiled your bed, it is in order that an almost immortal child would be born from her loins."

"One man would have been sufficient for that! Did it need a hundred to engender him?"

"That child, who will be called Pan—which is to say, *born of a total effort*—is destined to epitomize the fecund forces that animate the universe. It was therefore necessary that all human saps collaborate in his creation and be confounded in order to form him."

"I respect the will of the immortals; but it is cruel to think, O goddess, that my bed has groaned under the weight of an entire people."

"Of those men who have obtained Penelope's favors, not one remains alive. You have killed them all with your own hands. That supreme punishment has washed away the insult."

"And Penelope?"

"Contain the desire to avenge yourself on her," said Minerva, severely. "Otherwise, the secret of her sin, which has perished with the suitors, will burst forth and will be delivered to the knowledge of all."

"How can I bear to share my bed with that woman, who had welcomed there all the ardors of Dulichium, Samos and green Zacynthus? How can I resist repudiating her and shaming her?"

"Avoid even thinking about it," said Minerva, alarmed. "Penelope is sacred. Such as she emerges from the multiple embraces of the suitors, she still remains the symbol of fidelity. Helen, Clytemnestra, Andromache, Cassandra, all the queens and all the princesses, flying from lover to lover, have cast dishonor on their sex. The world laughs or turns away from their misbehavior, and only takes consolation from fortifying example in the virtue of Penelope. She is the one who incarnates Achaean honor. She must remain unsuspected. Cease, therefore, to nurture your insensate projects, and remember that the will of the Olympians protects your spouse."

Saddened, Ulysses remained silent for a long time. Then, softened, he said: "Your orders will be respected. Who would dare recklessly to oppose the decisions of the Immortals?"

"Go, then, and try to rise above human miseries," said Minerva.

She wanted to fly away, but Ulysses, tormented by a final suspicion, stopped her.

"Since you honor me with our favor and you protect me, tell me, O goddess, whether, in addition to the suitors, any other man has entered Penelope's bed during my absence."

"A god, taking the form of a goat, also enjoyed her favors,[3] but that was necessary in order that the child should be born with cloven hooves and able to participate in animal vigor."

Ulysses came through the door of his palace at the first approach of darkness.

---

[3] Hermes/Mercury is said by numerous Classical sources to have assumed the form of a goat in order to father Pan.

Penelope, anxious and humble, was waiting for him on the threshold, her complexion still animated by anguish and modesty.

"You are an honest wife, Penelope," said Ulysses, softly, caressing her chin, as was his habit. "Are the meats ready for the meal?"

"They are cooked to perfection, and I have even damped down the embers of the fires while waiting for you."

When Ulysses had appeared his hunger, avidly taking the best morsels and biting into them vigorously, Penelope drew a large cup of wine from a full skin, and offered it to him. It was then that he raised his eyes and, by the bright light of the torches, he contemplated his wife, who had come to sit down beside him, apprehensively.

And Penelope appeared new to him, and even more desirable.

Aided by the fumes of wines, excited by proofs and by emotion, Ulysses even had a strange vision. He thought that all the suitors, emerging from their tombs, came running, agile, active and attentive, each holding a chisel in his hand—a chisel like the one that Ulysses had seen in Crete in the marvelous hands of the sculptor Daedalus.

One by one, the suitors approached the motionless Penelope, and chiseled, labored and perfected her features, contributing to her transfiguration. Eurymachus, who came first, polished her arms and gave them a divine roundness. Agelaus turned her breast, in the image of Venus, and Peisander amplified her loins and ordered her curves in accordance with those of swans in flight and falling stars. The adroit Polybus widened her eyes and communicated to them the languid and charming softness that predisposes to desire, while another shaped her nostrils, according them a voluptuous palpitation, something that participated in flutters and sighs. All of them worked as perfect artists, divine sculptors, and under their amorous and expert operation, the known and familiar body of Penelope took on a new appearance in Ulysses' eyes, acquiring unknown perfections, and became an ark of desire, an ineffable nest, capable of enclosing all caresses.

The hero shook his head in order to expel the light dream. The suitors vanished then, but Penelope remained transfigured, splendid in beauty, young and troubling, full of unknown charms.

How can it be, Ulysses thought, *that having been kneaded voluptuously by foreign hands, that woman appears more desirable to me?*

And as he was incapable of fathoming that enigma, he summarized his thoughts in a single sentence, saying to Penelope: "You are an honest wife, Penelope, and you please me greatly. Is the bed prepared?"

"It's waiting for us. I've increased the number of cushions and covered them in Phoenician cloth."

"Let us go and repose there, then," said Ulysses, putting his arm around her neck and drawing her toward him.

II

The days passed without bringing appeasement to the insincere Ulysses, who wandered along the shores of his island, perplexed.

Am I awake, then, he said to himself, *or is the whimsical Ephialtes, a god fertile in ruses and resources, maintaining me in a deceptive dream?*

For the first time, his intelligence could not offer him any assistance, not clarifying at all the troubling enigma that loomed up before him.

Since I have discovered and specified the infidelity of Penelope, my delightful and wretched wife, I have not ceased to love her and desire her. I draw her to my bosom at nightfall, and I caress her again at dawn. I experience at every moment the imperious desire to go to see her again, and on seeing her again her charms seem new to me. The words she speaks to me have an immense resonance within me, and I judge them harmonious and inestimable.

"Do you love me, Penelope?" That is my perpetual question. And while interrogating her in that fashion, I sense that I am gazing at her as my unfortunate companions gazed at the Sirens, when their hearts and minds were already enslaved and doomed by the song. Then, during the brief moments that Penelope takes to reply to me, I cannot breathe and, all a-tremble, my future and my happiness depend on the words that are about to emerge from her mouth.

Lost in such perplexities, Ulysses evoked the past; and that evocation fortified him in the certainty that he had never adored and appreciated Penelope as much as he did at present.

He had been united with her on emerging from adolescence. She had dazzled him less by her beauty than the prestige of her family. Without loving her, he had judged it advantageous to obtain her. And as old Icarius, smitten with tenderness for his daughter, did not want to yield her to the caresses of a husband, Ulysses, stimulated by the difficulties, had employed every artifice and all possible charms in order to steal her from him.

He still remembered the decisive day when, making use of honeyed words, languorous gazes and the passionate silences that are more eloquent and more troubling than any words, he had succeeded in winning the virgin's consent and taking her to the shore. His ship was waiting for him there, its sails deployed, ready to travel the humid routes to Ithaca.

Old Icarius, stubborn, and having not yet lost all hope, followed his daughter at his uncertain pace and tried to move her to pity. Then Ulysses, to put an end to it, stopped his ship and left Penelope the liberty to choose between him and her father. With a modest and passionate movement, the virgin had lowered her veil, thus concealing the blush of her shame, and put her hand in the hand of the hero.

In the early days of their union, Ulysses had felt tenderness for Penelope, and later, amity, but he did not remember having loved her passionately. He had, on the contrary, taken pleasure in introducing captives into his bed during the adventurous siege, when the infidelity of Helen had kept the Achaeans assembled before Troy. Even more recently, sharing the bed of the lively and mobile Circe or holding the nymph of Ogygia in his arms,[4] he had completely forgotten his wife and savored without remorse or concern the varied pleasures that sensuality accords.

No, he had not loved her during the adversity, and he scarcely loved her any more when he saw her again on his return.

Far more than the possession of Penelope, it was vengeance, the recuperation of his kingdom, the enjoyment of the immense flocks and treasures guarded by the faithful Eurycleia, that had interested Ulysses and caused him to act. Even at the last moment, when he went after the carnage of the suitors to repose with his wife on the high bed, he had only experienced affection for her.

It is, therefore by virtue of having known her to be unfaithful and possessed by numerous lovers, of having divined and discovered the traces of other caresses on her body, that I now feel this devouring flame, this continuous haunting, this keen and unappeasable amour?

Ulysses thought that, with amazement, and it appeared to him incomprehensible and absurd. For his mind, open to reason and to logic, only thought of acting after reflection. Misunderstanding instinct, he believed that he only possessed what he understood, but he had given birth and originated within himself, for the first time, to the source of all refined woes and subtle torments: analytical intelligence.

So, unable now to explain than sudden sentimental deviation, that impetuous and sudden passion for Penelope, he was frightened by it.

The gods have pursued me with their anger for long time, he thought. *I am the man who has suffered from it more than any other. It could be, therefore, that the irrational evil by which I am alarmed comes from the gods, and that it is a final*

---

[4] Calypso.

26

vengeance of Neptune, the inauguration of a new series of ordeals and adversities.

And Ulysses wished incessantly for an enlightenment that would enable him to emerge from his uncertainties, which would guide him toward comprehension and aid him to attain the intellectual level-headedness indispensable to anyone who wants to render himself master of events.

Wandering and meditating in that fashion, he always ended up by finding himself back at his palace. For like consciousness, the unconscious—his obscure impulsions as well as his rational desires—drove him and led him to the places where Penelope was.

Having entered the palace, he searched for her impatiently, and discovered her in the nuptial and impenetrable redoubt to which only the faithful slave Actoris had access. His first impulse was to throw himself at her feet and say to her: "Why is it that I love you? What devastating force, what mysterious charm enchains me thus and attaches me to you, in spite of my resolutions, in spite of everything that could determine me to hate and destroy you? What new and active virtue is hidden in your flesh, then, what troubling and captivating flower has been born of your adulterous embraces?"

But he remained silent and restrained himself. In the course of his life, rich in experience, he had learned that spontaneous words habitually provoke disasters, and that there is a deleterious ferment in sincerity and truth that prepares baleful and tumultuous futures for us.

He contented himself with approaching his wife and taking her hand.

"Do you love me, Penelope? Do you love me?"

He posed that question with a dolorous precipitation, with a heated desire full of dread. It was visible that life or death, joy or torment, depended on the response that he was about to receive.

"Are you not my husband, and is it not my duty to love you, dear Ulysses?" said Penelope.

27

Her voice was calm and tranquil, without enthusiasm. And she added: "Why do you repeat the same question incessantly?"

Then Ulysses became conscious that nothing vehement or passionate filled or agitated Penelope's heart. A despairing equilibrium held it far from doubt, far from dolor, far from anxiety. And, in sensing how superior his wife as to him by virtue of that tranquility, how she would be able by a single word to render him equal to the immortals or precipitate him into darkness, Ulysses was afraid.

He replied: "Why, indeed, do I persist in always asking you the same thing?" He paused, and then went on: "Do I know? Do I know myself?"

He darted a distracted glance around him.

He saw then the bed that his powerful hands had constructed, and which dominated the room. He remembered the olive tree that had once blossomed in the same place, and around which, on the night of his wedding, he had first amassed and cemented stones, building the conjugal chamber. The trunk of the tree was destined to serve as the support of the bed. He had, therefore, cut off the bushy crown and the green branches, and had then placed the large planks on which he had subsequently lavished gold, ivory, and finally, crimson and soft hides that summoned slumber and caresses.

That bed, supported on the still-living trunk, whose roots went directly and profoundly into the earth, had once been for him a place of repose. He had savored tranquil and joyful pleasures there. Now it appeared to him to be redoubtable and terrible, more incomparably bewitching than those of witches and goddesses, as dangerous as the bed on which Vulcan imprisoned Venus, revealing her adulterous amours.

Not being able to retain or to master desire, wanting to drawn Penelope to him but fearful of forgetting himself once again in her delightful arms, Ulysses fled from the room like a madman. Once outside, he started walking, anxious and unhappy.

An irresistible need drive him to determine his woe and dominate it. It was necessary to end it.

Having arrived at the harbor, he perceived Noemon, the skillful pilot, who was in the process of preparing his curved vessel, the tall mast of which stood up proudly against the sky.

Making a sudden resolution, Ulysses then ordered Noemon to run to the palace and search there for sealed goat-skins full of wine, fine wheat, and everything necessary for a long voyage.

As he was habituated himself to the métier of mariner, he deployed the sail with his own hands, attaching it with two strong tethers. Finally, when Noemon returned, followed by two other companions, the hero embarked, without informing anyone, and allowed the wind to fill the noisy sail, precipitately.

Thus Ulysses drew away once again from his beloved island, and the vessel cleaved the waves rapidly.

The hero went forth, without any design, abandoning the known shores, seeing the liberating sea opening up before him.

III

In the beginning, Ulysses wanted to lower the sail before the harbor of fortunate Pylos, in order to ask the advice of the venerable Nestor, son of Neleus. Then he thought that Nestor had a heart chilled by old age. He must have lost the meaning and forgotten the range of passion.

He therefore allowed himself to be guided by the winds, the friends of vessels, and he soon reached the abrupt but fertile coast of Gythion. He disembarked there and, making use of impetuous horses, he arrived with his companions before the walls of superb Lacedaemon. His heart palpitating with emotion, he went into it and approached the palace of Menelaus.

The faithful Eteoneus, son of Boethous, saw him first and conducted him personally into the banqueting hall, resplendent in crimson and gold, where Menelaus, having been informed, was waiting for him with sculpted cups and bowls laden with meats.

The reacquaintance of the two heroes took place amid embraces, tears and the evocation of common memories.

They had parted outside the smoking ruins of Ilium, and each of them, borne by his destiny, had wandered far from his homeland in strange lands strewn with perils. It was Ulysses who first recounted to his host all the obstacles that Neptune had provoked on his route. He related his victory over the Cyclops, and his adventures with the King of the Laestrygonians, Circe, the Sirens and the isle of Ogygia,

In his turn, Menelaus told him how, the victim of tempests and the hatred of the winds, he had traveled in Cyprus, Phoenicia and Egypt, reaching as far as the land of the Ethiopians and the deserts of Libya.

In seeing how destiny had imposed similar peregrinations upon them at the time of their return, they felt the bonds that united them more narrowly.

Finally, when Menelaus, shedding abundant tears and tearing his hair had told Ulysses how his brother had perished under the perfidious blade of the adulterer Aegisthus, they broke bread together and, spurred on by hunger and emotion, they prolonged more than usual the satisfactions and contentments of feasting.

Ulysses was surprised not to see Helen appear, but Menelaus informed him that she was supervising the slaves who were gathering flax in the fields...

After the just repose that the fatigues of the voyage had summoned, the king of Ithaca found his host again by the portico, where he was respiring the freshness animated by the dusk.

"Now, valorous Ulysses," Menelaus interrogated, "you whose sagacity caused divine will to bend, who permitted the Greeks to accomplish all the fatalities necessary for the taking of Ilium, tell me what new design is drawing your steps away from your homeland. Why have you decided to tread foreign

30

lands for a second time? Scarcely victorious over your numerous enemies, here you are, breaking once again, voluntarily, the delights of the peace of your return."

For a few moments, Ulysses remained silent and hesitant. He gazed distractedly at the garment ornamented with golden plates, the rich brodequins dyed with Tyrian purple, and the sword engraved with a depiction of a lion-hunt—everything that heightened the splendor of Menelaus' natural aristocratic beauty. Then, desirous of relieving himself by communicating his trouble, he commenced:

"Alas, friend equal to a brother, you are mistaken in lending me your own happiness in believing that I have conquered peace and that I could render the enemy gods favorable and benevolent. Certainly, it's true that I finally landed in Ithaca with my vessels laden with booty. Similarly, I felled the enemies who were pillaging my palace gloriously. But the equilibrium of the soul I have not found.

"I would rather have been battling the Cyclops again or enduring terrible reverses in the land of the Laestrygonians; my lance and my cunning would have given me purchase over those enemies and I would have been sure of triumphing over them; whereas I am struggling now against an ardent and secret evil, like those that the gods sent to doom humans.

"Such as you see me, Menelaus, I am dispossessed of my former wisdom, my proverbial discernment. Like Ajax the Salaminian, I am acting against reason in loving someone that I ought to hate, in finding so much enjoyment and attraction next to a woman who ought only to be considered as my enemy."

And, under the seal of secrecy, Ulysses recounted the affront he had received from Penelope, his initial thought of punishing her, and the incomprehensible attraction that she exerted upon him. He described to his friend the passion that the woman inspired in him, a devouring passion that bound his hands, his senses and his understanding, as pirates bind the four limbs of captives before embarking them on their hollow ships.

He concluded by asking for aid and assistance.

"You, Menelaus, who have seen so many peoples, who have wandered in Egypt, which excels in all sciences, who have known the fires of passion, give me advice and dictate my conduct. Is it necessary for me to turn my blade against myself, in order to purge the earth of an insensate burden, or should I rather judge myself sick and have recourse to the healer Aesculapius, son of Apollo?"

Menelaus remained pensive for a long time, his head bowed, gazing at the dusty ground. Then he replied:

"How can I help and aid you, cunning Ulysses, since I have known the same slavery that you describe to me and I am still subservient to it? But I ought to add that I am not suffering from it. I am not naturally orientated toward reflection and the causes of the connections between phenomena have never occupied me. I savor with tranquility what every day brings me, and I leave to the gods, the governors of the Universe, the care and the trouble of thought. My mind, which is habitually somnolent—as is appropriate to anyone who wants to be happy—only awakens before danger. I only reflect in order to acquire, or to defend myself. Nevertheless, I will tell you what has happened to me, in order that you might obtain some appeasement and consolation therefrom."

And after a moment of silence and meditation, Menelaus went on:

"Having been among the first to depart, you only know imperfectly what followed the taking of Ilium. Discord burst forth between the leaders, whose unique occupation was pillaging and quarreling. Some readied their ships in anger, abandoning their companions, others wanted to remain in order to amass more treasure. All acted secretly and with suspicion. But I only want to confide to you what happened to me, personally, on the supreme day when, the gods of Ilium having deserted their altars, and the Trojans celebrating insensately our false departure, we emerged from the wooden horse, opened the gates of the city and sowed flames and carnage throughout the superb citadel.

"One sole thought, one single objective, had guided me until that day: vengeance. I saw incessantly before my eyes the absent and the dead, all the Achaean heroes who had punished, in seconding me in my enterprise, all those who had abandoned their hearths and their families and had come to expire on foreign soil. It was because of Helen, my unfaithful wife, that we had fought, wandered and suffered. She was the one who had provoked the great torment, by fleeing my bed, forgetting her oaths, and forcing that long and perilous adventure upon us.

"*When shall I have succeeded in getting my hands upon her?* I repeated to myself. *When shall I be able to plunge my sword into the depths of her bosom, sending her cruelly to the dark domains, in order that she will rediscover there, to her shame, Achilles and Patroclus, Hector and Troilus, the great Ajax and the superb Penthesilea, all those who died unjustly and lamentably, victims of her caprice?*

"To punish her, to see her at my feet, to spill her blood as the supreme expiation of the offense received—such was my unique aspiration.

"I had begged my brother Agamemnon for a long time to allow me to be the sole judge of my vengeance. 'Permit me to penetrate first into Priam's palace,' I had said to him. 'I will go straight to the upper rooms, where the women repose, far from any gaze. I shall not take captives there, I shall not raise an injurious hand to undo the girdle of virgins or take possession of their crimson robes. It is my wife that I want to seek there, in order to seize her by her hair, to drag her in the black dust, and to pierce her heart. Then I shall attach her abhorrent cadaver to a chariot before the eyes of all the Achaeans.'

"He permitted me that. Preceding you all at the moment of triumph, therefore, I penetrated into the women's apartment. They were lying down, weeping and trembling, for the noise of the supreme combat had reached their ears. They divined their fate and were lamenting it. On seeing me, old Hecuba uttered a loud scream and came to embrace my knees. She wanted to implore my pity, but for Andromache, who, pale and bleak, holding Astyanax on her knees, was waiting silently for the accomplishment of destiny.

"Any man who had known a mother, any man having the memory of having played tenderly in his childhood with his sisters, would have felt nothing but a great pity before all those unfortunates, once brought to the heights of felicity and now condemned to follow injurious masters, to share their bed and to serve them ignominiously. But I set aside all emotion. My objective was different. Pushing Hecuba away with both hands, I said to her: 'No one can set aside the fate that awaits you, unfortunate woman! And if you do not want me to pierce you incontinently with my sword, indicate the retreat of your son's adulterous companion, the infamous Helen.'

"Hecuba obeyed. She advanced so pitiful that I thought I saw Despair marching at my side. Through chambers covered in cedar and ivory she led me to a distant door and opened it. Then, as she quit me, she said, with a bleak expression: "Go avenge yourself, and avenge us. That is where the destroyer of cities is hiding, the scourge of the world, the woman who has spread mourning through my house and robbed me of five children, all the posterity of Priam, the pride of the earth.'

"Launching myself forward, I went into the room, and immediately, I saw a woman who, fleeing far from the couch where she had been reposing, went to hide behind the group of her slaves. It was Helen! Without even distinguishing her with certainty, I drew my blade and raised it. Anger and satisfaction filled my head and made it resonate like a cymbal.

"Then Helen, who recognized me, advanced her face, in which mute prayers were mingled with a surge of fearful modesty. The light was falling directly upon her, as if expressly to illuminate her naked body. The entire dawn was concentrated upon her. And in contemplating her thus, my hand fell back, as if a divinity were weighing with all its supernatural weight upon my arm to paralyze it. A charm operated within me.

"Do not believe, Ulysses, that I had forgotten Helen's beauty. I knew at all times that she was, corporeally, the most perfect of Achaean women. However, I sensed that I had the courage, and I had made the decision, to avenge myself. But it was not the same Helen who was now standing before me. It was an unknown woman, with enchanting features, a woman who delighted and dazzled me like wine or like the cherished voice of a mother returning from the tomb to speak to us. Her face, the lines of secret signification that her body formed, what I saw of her breasts and what I divined in the obscure profundities of her loins, troubled and confused my memories. That incomparable Helen I had certainly never had the good fortune to hold beside me in a bed. How, in any case, could that radiant new woman have a past? She only had a marvelous future.

"*To know her*, I said to myself then, *to touch her body, to draw her to me, to hear my name pronounced by her mouth...*

"I stammered: 'Helen!' And my heart was hammering, for I feared that she might only be a phantom, and that she would vanish at the sound of my voice.

"Then Helen smiled at me, still ashamed and already reassured. Oh, that smile! It seemed to me that I had been waiting for it anxiously, that it was to see it born on her cheek that I had left green Lacedaemon, that I had traversed the seas, and confronted death in the midst of battles. Like the unfortunate mariners who, having wandered in inhospitable lands, extend their impatient hands toward the natal shore, weeping, laughing and delirious, when it appears to them on the horizon, I leaned recklessly and avidly toward Helen.

"The sword fell from my rigid hand. I understood instantaneously that our suffering, the blood we had shed, our wanderings and our mourning, formed an offering that was due, like the victims, to the divinities.

"And I said to her, believing that I was expressing the truth: 'It is to see you and to hold you again that I have attempted so much and striven, O Helen. You are worthy of it! If ever irritation and anger came to lad me astray, when I saw my men perish and our ranks thinned, and malady and discord fell upon the Achaeans, it was because you were far away and

I could not realize the benefits of your presence. In any case, those who died for you would find their fate worthy of envy if they could see you. For myself, I would have endured further proofs, even harsher, to conquer you. For in you, as in a mirror, I see my homeland again, my dwelling, my fields, my flocks, experiencing in advance all the tumultuous emotions that await me on my return to Lacedaemon.'

"Thus I spoke, O Ulysses, and such was the magical reversion that the sight of Helen produced in me.

"I hesitated later to confess my clemency. I even departed secretly, without seeing my brother Agamemnon again. In order to taken Helen aboard my ship safely, I confounded her with the captives, in such a way that she passed unperceived.

"That was not so much because I was ashamed of my action; it was rather because I could not easily explain and make known to others the new and precious significance of my wife's beauty. Like the oak that one leaves paltry, slender and weak, prey to the winds, and finds again, after a few years of absence, majestic, tall and bushy, Helen's empire over me had increased during the separation and had been fortified.

"That is what I had to tell you, Ulysses, and in order to understand my story more fully, turn your eyes and see her coming."

The radiant Helen was, indeed, approaching, in the glory of the setting sun, distinct among her retinue. Very blonde and supple, she changed her rhythm and attraction at every step. She was like a sinuous wave, like a tenuous white cloud, like the pure and extreme flame of fire. Around her loins, one divined that she held, huddled and subservient, all the secret fatalities of the flesh, which attract the gaze irresistibly and wound the heart by planting the arrow of lust within it.

But Ulysses, filled and overflowing with the image of Penelope, looked at Helen without emotion.

He recognized her. She had not changed since he had conversed with her in Ilium, one night when he had penetrated the city secretly.

The same gaze of a shameless bitch, he said to himself, *the same lascivious bearing, the same perfidious gait. And she has aged!*

He deplored the fact that, softened by desire, Menelaus had not run her through with his sword.

And he added that: *One can see that he has not known Penelope, in order to find that woman beautiful.*

Helen came to sit down, and after an exchange of warm and joyful words of recognition, Menelaus, his eyes riveted upon his wife, spoke again to Ulysses: "You saw her once, when were disputing her, fighting against the man who had taken her to his palace. Confess that she was not as beautiful then! Look at her arms, so white, animated by the same tender life, the same gracious movement, as the doves! Harmonious is her flesh! Everything in her vibrates, and everything in her quivers. As for thinking of what she becomes when, in a bed, she opens her arms to the man she loves, how can I express it to you and how can I not faint in thinking about it?"

His eyes attached to the profundities of the vesperal sky, however, Ulysses, deaf to words, was evoking the massive bed attached to the earth by tortuous roots, in which the true enchantress lay, the diverse, troubling, incomparable Penelope, the object of desire.

IV

The days succeeded the nights, and aboard his ship, cleaving the waves, Ulysses interrogated the sky, prayed to the winds, and waited, vigilant.

When shall I cease to travel the humid routes, then, and how long will I continue to wander, a plaything of capricious Neptune? he asked himself.

Following the advice of Menelaus, he was, in fact, going to consult their former master, the luminary of Greece, the celebrated Chiron. At first, Ulysses had turned the prow toward the countries of the East, intending to go northwards afterwards as far as the savage and haughty Thessaly, the refuge of the Centaurs. It was there that Chiron studied the course of the stars, the secrets of numbers and the charms produced by harmony.

But Neptune, perceiving Ulysses' ship from the depths of his palace, inflated the winds, which drove it all the way to the foggy and tenebrous land of the Cimmerians.

Once there, Ulysses wanted at least to interrogate the shades regarding the matter that preoccupied him. Attaining, therefore, the rock where the two chthonian rivers met, near the black forest of Persephone, he immolated victims and evoked the dead.

They hastened and crowded around him, innumerably. Perceptible in the melee were the beardless faces of ephebes, the pale and clear faces of virgins and the ravaged and tortured bodies of aged individuals whose sex could no longer be distinguished. Ulysses allowed them to come to slake their thirst on black blood, and then he asked their advice.

"I was deceived abundantly by my wife, but I only love her more for it. How can I get out of that frightful situation."

Thus he proposed the problem.

Reanimated by the blood, and seized again by the memory of the past, the dead responded. But Ulysses remarked that they contented themselves with talking about their own amours, declaring moreover that, in passion, they had acted in opposition to reason, against all logic, as if a god had overturned their understanding and enveloped their eyes with darkness.

The majority of men confessed that they had been deceived by their wives. Some had known that while alive and, according to their temperament, either they had killed the infidels in the first boiling of anger, or they had spared them and ended up desiring them more. Others, who had not been aware of their misfortune until after their death, retained doubts in that regard in order to console themselves for it.

The hero consulted few women. He was fearful of their loquacity and their deep-seated penchant for lying.

A king of Egypt, who still bore the uraeus on his head and held the ankh in his hand, a sign of power, desolated Ulysses with his response.

"I lived," he said, "in the fortunate country irrigated by the Nile. One day, the gods, to punish me for a crime that I had committed, plunged my gaze into darkness. The oracle that I went to consult told me that, in order to recover my sight, my eyes had to be touched by the hand of a woman who had only had intercourse with her husband. I thought at first that my own wife, on my return to the palace, would promptly deliver me from my woe. Nothing of the sort. I then had recourse to my sisters-in-law, the spouses of the priests who lived in the sanctuaries, and then the wives of royal functionaries celebrated for their virtue. But I did not find a single woman who had the purity required to cure me. There were all adulteresses. My kingdom did not contain any others. I had despaired of seeing the light again when, after many years, I chanced to met a beggar-woman on the road to Thebes who had only known her husband. She confessed afterwards that on the very day of our encounter, she was going to an amorous rendezvous for the first time. I had found her just in time, and she rendered the light to me."

One last apparition was floating in the thick darkness of Erebus. Ulysses summoned him. It was the shade of Cephalus, the son of Aeolus,[5] who, after having listened to the hero's request, said: "Unfortunate Prince, no one can be as interested as me in your anguish. Handsome once, until being abducted and seduced the delightful Aurora, I was united by the bonds of marriage to Procris, daughter of Erectheus, king of Athens. I loved her and was jealous of her. Wanting to prove her, therefore—for that is the constant occupation of the jealous—I pretended to go away. Then, returning unexpectedly and disguised as a merchant, I tempted Procris' virtue by offering her sumptuous robes and rich presents.

---

[5] Cephalus is usually said to be Aeolus' grandson and the son of Deioneus.

"She resisted those dishonoring propositions at first, but her resistance was weak and did not last long. Soon she seemed ready to succumb, forgetting the memory of her husband. Fortified by that fatal and shameful certainty, I abandoned my disguise, had myself recognized, and expelled the infidel from my house. She fled, disappeared into the woods, and from then on, no longer possessing her and knowing her to be prompt to seduction, I regretted her until death. Know, O Ulysses, that one scarcely loves that which one holds securely, but adores that which has ceased to belong to you and which others have appreciated. That is the fate of the living, the sad law of amour."

As a last resort, Ulysses evoked the shade of Tiresias, the diviner of Thebes.

"What, unfortunate man, you are still traveling?" exclaimed the latter when he appeared. "Can you not remain tranquil for a while in your house, far from the uncertainties of the sea? After having run after warrior adventures, you are wandering now in order to clarify amorous problems. Instead of simply feeling, you exhaust yourself trying to dissect and analyze your own sensations. Well, go and consult Chiron, since destiny is driving you there. Still living, he knows the agitations that passion provokes in the human heart. As for me, I am dead, and such concerns seem trivial and vain to me."

*

Ulysses, finally aided by Notus, the favorable wind, was approaching Thessaly.

One morning he saw Mount Pelion, the summit of which was confounded with the clouds. The ship was hauled on to the shore, and the hero, mounting one of the celebrated horses that are nurtured in that country, headed toward the lair inhabited by Chiron.

A strange emotion had taken possession of his soul, conquered by distant memories. He recalled the inimitable Centaur distinctly, the son of a god, whose immense science had caused wonderment in his youth.

Chiron knew secrets forbidden to mortals. Favored by haughty Diana, hunting with her in the forests, he had learned to discern the virtue of simples and decipher the mystery of the stars. The supreme arcana of knowledge were opened to him by the skilful manipulation of numbers, by the true penetration of celestial movements, by the usage of redoubtable or salutary substances elaborated in plants. He knew how to cure the sick, to prevent crimes, to deflect evil influences and divine the future. Young Achaeans, avid for instruction, flocked toward him.

After having tempered and sharpened the indomitable soul of Hercules, Chiron had organized the expedition of the Argonauts and had then brought it to a successful inclusion. All the noble heroes who had risen to the luminous summits of glory and left an imperishable memory among the peoples— Aesculapius, Castor and Pollux, Theseus and Hippolytus, as well as the majority of those who had perished before Troy— had emerged from his school. But his dearest disciple, after Bacchus, was the son of Thetis, his beloved godson Achilles, the swift runner.

Ulysses recalled the powerful and unforgettable aspect of the master. With his robust hindquarters and his equine legs, which posed forcefully on the ground as if they were drawing their strength from the earth, the Centaur had a slender and noble bearing that his mortal disciples envied him. If the extremities of his body still plunged into the mystery of animal instinct, his head, on the contrary, equaled the wisdom that of the omniscient Apollo.

Impatient to see his master again, Ulysses penetrated into the shady forest that he had traveled so often in his youth, initiating himself in panic fear and experiencing the first and gripping admirations that nature inspires.

The Centaur's grotto came into view. It was entirely covered by the tortuous vine that seemed to be playing with it, suspending its clusters of grapes everywhere and going to mingle with the branches of the poplars and elms that shaded the surroundings.

Ulysses stopped in order to listen to the cadenced murmur of springs; and that familiar sound recalled a thousand memories, causing many charming and forgotten images to surge forth before his eyes.

Finally, he went in.

By the light of the odorous cedar that was burning in the middle of the grotto, he distinguished Chiron, lying on the ground, his tawny breast projected forward and his head reposing meditatively against a stone.

As he moved closer, however, he scarcely recognized the Centaur's features, so much had the years and sadness altered them. Ulysses was surprised by that, for he knew that Chiron was immortal and did not understand how the insults of old age and the movements of dolor could have affected him.

The hero did not have time to make himself recognized. The Centaur extended his forefeet, the extreme elegance of which came to him from his mother, the mare Phylira, hugged him cordially to his breast. It was evident that a great pity dominated the joy that had assailed him at the sight of his disciple

"My son, unfortunate and estimable Ulysses, I've been expecting you," he said. "There's no need to recount your life to me; I know exactly what has covered you with glory and what has heaped woes upon you. Your actions before the impregnable city are familiar to me, and I also know how you have suffered during your return. I am not unaware, finally, of the cause of your latest voyage, nor what you have come to ask of me."

He looked at him again; his eyes, which appeared to have penetrated definitively into the profound and forbidden regions in which everything is intelligible, were moistened tenderly by tears.

"You want me to enlighten you regarding the problems that are troubling your mind. For the mind, granted by the gods in order to help humans, has been perverted in you to the extent of becoming a source of joy and a source of sadness. I experience keen regrets in that, all the more so because I recognize therein the fruit and the development of my lessons. Yes, I failed in your education and I repent of it bitterly. Seeing your understanding so alert and so exceptional, I allowed myself to go so far as to cultivate it and enable redoubtable reflection to flourish within you.

"In the same way that I oriented all the faculties of Achilles toward strength, appeasing and atrophying thought to the profit of the muscles, and caused to flourish in Bacchus and bring to their complete blossoming the tragic and uplifting instincts of enthusiasm, I nourished and fortified curiosity in you, the appetite to seek everything and know everything. Instead of a movement, I wanted every phenomenon to awaken in you a thought. I succeeded in that—and now look where it has brought you! Not content with thwarting the designs of your enemies, you want to enter into the torrent of the passions and take your soul, sacrilegiously, as an object of study.

"Furthermore, I have already learned by my own example how deceptive knowledge is and what a bitter aftertaste its deadly fruits leave behind. You are not unaware that the god who engendered me granted me immortality, considering it as a supreme gift; and, indeed, it is a fine and inappreciable thing to exist, while life brings novelty and provokes continual surprise. But when one knows and divines the play of things, when one pierces the veil of appearances, when one knows all causes, and one sees the present and the past united in a single plane with the future, life no longer offers anything attractive. Existence then appears to be a frightful, fruitless and vain waiting.

"Such is my case. Knowledge has poisoned my vital sources. I know what will happen, and for me, every instant contains, and encloses insupportably, all eternity. So, overwhelmed by that morose monotony, no longer able to tolerate my dismal science, I have begged the gods to cure me of the disease of living and to pass my immortality to another being. Jupiter has granted my wish. Prometheus is becoming immortal in my place, to his misfortune. As for me, I glimpse the end and deliverance henceforth, and I am savoring the sweetness of growing old, which is giving me in anticipation the first fruits of the happiness of dying."

As Ulysses was about to speak, he went on:

"Yes, my son, I understand that all of that is of scant relevance to you. One single question is enfevering you. You are in haste for me to tell you what you want to know. What can I tell you? You are dealing with amour, with stormy, anguishing amour, which scarcely spares the inhabitants of Olympus and equalizes, and confounds under its power, slaves and those who carry the scepter. Created to renew life and hasten death, amour nourishes itself on blood and suffering. One cannot curse it, however, for it is also what grants moments of perfect joy, of total rapture, and enables us to glimpse the blissful countries.

"Of that redoubtable and divine passion, however, no one can grasp the laws, so absurd, iniquitous and violent do they seem. It is necessary to declare oneself the prey of a scourge when one is in the power of amour, and it is also necessary to avoid darting an inquisitive glance at it, just as it is necessary to avoid looking into the terrible and divine face of Medusa, daughter of Saturn.

"I can, however, enable you to profit from my science by telling you that what has happened to you is routine and always comes to those who love. For our desire runs toward that which flees it, and only ever wants to possess that which it is going to lose. Vexation, jealousy, cruelty, violence and everything that pollutes the beloved object in adultery only serve to enfever passion. Cease, therefore, to plunge your gaze into that incomprehensible and deceptive abyss, and since, being intelligent, you can already attract nothing but dolor in every fashion, at least refrain from adding thereto the torments that an exact knowledge of passion imply."

"What if I were to kill Penelope?" said Ulysses, frightened by that speech and rolling his eyes. He appeared agitated, as if he were struggling between the claws of a lion.

"You would regret it eternally," replied the Centaur. "Your amour would crystallize, becoming immutable, no longer able to be subject to any alteration. You would conse-crate yourself to the memory of your wife and you would soon imagine that she was perfect. It is death that plays the greatest tricks upon us when we are amorous."

"What if I were at least to expatriate myself and go to live far away from her?"

"Like the magnet that summons iron in an occult fashion, she would attract you. You cannot flee her. It is futile to caress such a project. Why not rather resign yourself to entering un-der the common law and submitting to that which you cannot understand?"

"I'll resign myself to it," Ulysses sighed. "In any case, the mystery is clarified. I'm beginning to understand. Moist with other kisses, the woman we love appears to us more de-sirable, and she renews our passion. But that amour, which defies logic, frightens me. It will perhaps lead me where de-mentia led the unfortunate Ajax. For know, O my master, that Penelope could doom me with a single word, that in her hands I am an object more docile than her spindle, or the ball of cloth with which she plays by the river when she is resting after work. One of her smiles makes the joy of my days, and an irritated movement plunges me into distress—me, who killed Paris, made Ilium tremble and whose true name is Re-doubtable!"

Falling at Chiron's feet and embracing his knees, Ulysses begged: "Save me, you who can do anything. Annihilate the poison that is acting more powerfully in my veins than Circe's charms. Banish the frightful delirium from my understanding, in order that I can look at Penelope with indifference, as I looked at Nausicaa or the beautiful Calypso, who, although she was a goddess, could not retain me or distract me from the travails of life. Cure me! Cure me, O my master!"

"There is no remedy against amour. Penelope alone could open your eyes and accord you the exact vision of how little she is, and of her true and relative value." Then, prevent-ing Ulysses from replying, he went on: "I want to save you even so, because you are dear to me and I feel responsible for the misfortunes and difficulties that are accumulating over your head. I shall therefore accompany you as far as the rock of Ithaca and I shall remain there in order to accomplish your complete cure.

"As for you, do not cease to invoke the gods: Minerva your protectress; Jupiter who commands the clouds; and above all Venus, who weaves and unravels all the webs of passion. If they come to your aid, you will soon be able to savor life with measure, seeing Penelope clearly, and without the deceptive and transformative veil that Amour, the marvelous and perilous Amour, deploys before your eyes.

V

Throughout the voyage, solicited by Ulysses, the Centaur talked about amour. Having professed for a long time, he had acquired the art of simplifying explanations and rendering them clear and striking.

Thus, in the autumn of life, after having learned to guide himself and defend himself, to conquer cities and deceive men, Ulysses was instructed in the difficult sciences of the heart.

"There are two sorts of amorous desires," the Centaur told him, "those which produce dolor and those which engender crimes. Both throw disarray into the human soul."

He also said to him:

"The first effect of passion is to steal the sight of the beloved object, which, having penetrated into the intimacy of our substance, escapes any examination henceforth. There is nothing in common between the real woman that we love and the image that we have of her. That is why the amorous malady offers no purchase to any remedy. Penelope dwells in a forbidden region, in the depths of your heart.

He also said:

Amour expels us from ourselves. It empties our imagination and our mind of any foreign object, and then it installs itself there and remains the master. Conquered by an intrusive and omnipotent image, we feel alienated from ourselves, dispossessed of our past, of our cares, our joys and our aspirations.

And the Centaur added:

"We have no influence over the person that we love and who makes us suffer. We are the defenseless flesh and she is the trenchant blade. She wounds us without our being able to protect ourselves from her."

Then he continued:

"A ferment of hatred is at the foundation of every amour, and without that ferment no true passion can arise and prosper. Ordinarily hidden beneath a flood of tenderness, the hatred only becomes perceptible and evident at the moment of the caress. Anyone who has seen people making love on a bed cannot forget that there is a contest, a loss of control and a cruelty in the sensual attitudes. A destructive intention seems to be the nub of lust, which is, to tell the truth, a sacred fury that partakes as much of the bite as the kiss."

And he went on:

"We demand of the object of our amour to be paid in return, but in reality, if she obeys us, we never forgive her. What we always forgive her is making us suffer."

And he concluded:

"To judge by appearances, amour uniquely seeks intercourse. Fundamentally, it only acquires substance and aliments itself on cries, tears and blood. It creates life incessantly with torn and palpitating flesh. That is why we can say that every being brought into the world, every child that is born, is a product of hatred, dolor and violence."

Ulysses protested: "Gods! Why then do mortals run after amour?" And he tore his long hair as a sign of fear, despair and perplexity.

But the Centaur replied to him:

"Mortals know amour, and that is a special benefit of the divinity. For amour is the salt of life, its unique flower, and its excellent and inimitable ornament. Thanks to amour, the living person can be compared to the perfect eglantine, the modest violet, the splendid anemone, to everything that blossoms, becomes odorous and colored in spring, to iridescent nights and crimson sunrises. Blessed be amour!"

Agitating on the ship and striking his face with his hands, Ulysses was still moaning. "I am lost now! Everything seems confused before my eyes. I no longer understand...I no longer understand anything."

But, tranquilly stretched out on the vessel, Chiron replied:

"Life has not been created expressly for you to understand it. It laughs at your reason. Destructive and creative, it hastens toward its ends, easily accepting al the materials that fall under its hand, works in turn with smiles, with sighs, with blood and with joy, amid orgy, exaltation, cries and alarm. Very fortunate are those who never see the sunlight, also fortunate are those who die young, soon escaping the torments of existence. But thrice miserable are those who want to penetrate the mystery of things and reflect it in their poor and narrow reason!"

Discoursing in this fashion, they arrived in Ithaca.

Penelope rejoiced in Ulysses' return.

"Were you anxious about my precipitate departure?" the hero interrogated, hoping that she was and wanting to be assured of it.

"I wasn't at all anxious," she replied. "I've known your prudence for a long time. On learning that you had left the island I told myself that you could not have acted thus without necessity."

He sighed, disappointed. "But at least you missed me?" he said. "Did you wish for my return?"

"What wife does not wish for the return of her husband, and how could I have done otherwise? But I've employed the time during your absence in supervising the slaves picking olives and enabling the precious oil to flow from the press. Thus, the days seemed short to me."

Ulysses sighed again.

He had put Chiron in the hands of women who took him to the bath and offered him pure water and perfumes.

The Centaur's arrival was the marvel of all the hamlets perched on the rocks of Ithaca. The chiefs came to visit and salute that being, equidistant from a human being and a spirited horse, that master equal in wisdom to the Immortals, whose renown haunted the Achaean acropoleis.

Chiron sought the confidence and the commerce of Penelope, who took pleasure in his troubling aspect, his unexpected movements and his substantial and pondered conversation.

In order to captivate her, the Centaur told her marvelous stories. He told her about the misfortunes of his mother Philyra, smitten with Saturn, suffering the jealousy of Rhea and begging the gods to transform her into a tender floret in order to escape the evil of living. He also told her about the battles between the Centaurs and the Lapiths during the wedding celebrations of Pirithous, and then the latter's exploits in company with Theseus, their exemplary amity, and how they abducted the beautiful Helen, for whose favors they drew lots.

Those stories, which were familiar and familial, charmed Penelope and rendered Chiron indispensable to her. So, she gave him all her attention and all her confidence.

And the Centaur was satisfied.

Ulysses, who had not emerged from his desire and his preoccupations, asked him: "What should I do? You promised to cure me. How are you going to do it?"

He replied: "Let yourself live and don't nurture any worry. The enterprise is my concern."

After having captivated the ear and gained the consideration of Penelope, the Centaur began to converse with her about Ulysses' past. She knew about her husband's voyages, but she was unaware of the exact circumstances. Chiron narrated them to her, lingering above all over the erotic adventures, He gave her minute details of how easily women fell in love with Ulysses and how Circe, with lascivious forms, powerful philters and strange amours had kept and caressed the hero in her bed.

In the same way, he spoke at length and vividly about Calypso, the charming goddess whose arms had enclosed the sighing breast of Ulysses for years.

Soon, from the mouth of the Centaur, who strove to render all the ardor of the amorous exploits, Penelope learned that throughout the twenty years of his absence, her husband had been the tender object coveted by all the mortal woman whose beauty and grace were celebrated by Renown. She also knew that Ulysses responded ardently to the multiple passions he inspired. He had given amour for amour, caress for caress, and, untiring, supple and valorous, inflaming the modest Nausicaa, cutting a swathe though the captives of Ilium, and had even charmed and conquered the charmers, the Sirens.

For the Centaur exaggerated, deliberately adding fictitious adventures to the true ones. His intention was to create an impure and lascivious legend for Ulysses and surround him with a passionate aureole.

Penelope felt troubled by these stories and interested by them. Since her marriage, she had not ceased to believe in the fidelity of the king of Ithaca. As soon as he was her husband she had no longer looked at him, having fixed him in her imagination once and for all and being sure that he would always belong to her. But now, through the admirable narratives of the Centaur, Ulysses was transfigured in her eyes. The testimony of so many women victim to passion attested to Penelope that the king of Ithaca was ornamented by hidden attractions and triumphant gifts; and she ended up being proud of possessing such a husband.

And as soon as she considered Ulysses as an object of covetousness and desire, she feared losing him. Then, fearing to lose him, she paid attention to him, thought about him often, and pleased herself thereby.

Now she came to lean on his shoulder and, gazing at him proudly, she seemed to be saying: *This is the man that I have subjugated and who loves me, while all women sigh after him fruitlessly.*

"Don't be too sure of that," the Centaur suggested to her then, having divined her thought. "He is whimsical, changing, devoted to infidelity. One can never say that one holds him securely. He escapes incessantly, ready to fly to other beds."

And he gave her to understand that in his latest voyage, Ulysses had conquered and bent to his will the woman who had bloodied Greece and Asia: Helen, the ravishing Helen.

A cloud passed before Penelope's eyes. And the Centaur, lying on his back and rubbing his forefeet, said to himself: *She's ready; she's ready to love him.*

Then, changing enterprise, he went to Ulysses, who was still burning with the fires of passion. Feigning discouragement and despair, the Centaur said to him:

"In spite of my meditations and my efforts, I can truly find no means of coming to your aid. Not only does Penelope remain insensible to your amour, but she even lacks esteem toward you."

"Any hope of a cure is lost for me, then?"

"Not yet, provided that you will obey me blindly. You've declared to me that you felt that you were strong enough to kill Penelope in order no longer to sense the obsession of amour. I won't ask so much of you. But treat her rudely, show her hostility, in order to awaken her amour."

"How can I make her hate me?"

"By brutality, by violence. Create faults, forget your principles, be unjust, and don't hesitate to go as far as barbarity."

"And what good can that do me? Your design appears to me to be absurd."

"Carry out my orders without examining them and without understanding them. Have you not promised to submit to them blindly, and are you not convinced that I can see further than you?" And as Ulysses hesitated: "In any case, if you don't want to follow my advice, I'll go away, abandoning you to your destiny."

"I'll obey. Tell me more exactly in what manner I ought to behave."

"Repress for a while the amour that you have for Penelope. Disguise your sentiments, as the perfidious Helen, before the wooden horse, disguised her voice, imitating those of your wives in order to make you speak."

"But how can I behave harshly toward the woman who dominates my life?" groaned Ulysses, in a final protest. "A single disapproving gesture coming from her makes me tremble."

The Centaur remained unshakable and, in order to convince his disciple, he threatened to quit the island.

"For what can I reproach Penelope?" exclaimed Ulysses.

"Her conduct toward the suitors, her complaisance. Then too, you have no need to make her reasonable reproaches. On the contrary, be unjust, absurd, cruel, capricious, unpredictable and inhumane.

Ulysses obeyed, reluctantly. Under the insistence and in accordance with the advice of Chiron, he neglected Penelope and pretended to devote himself to other concerns. He spoke to her brutally and tried to make her ashamed of her past. As she fell silent, the hero, utterly loud exclamations, reproached her for her impotence to defend herself. He did not quit her until tears were steaming from her eyes.

"That's not yet sufficient," Chiron said to him. "You're soft; your long voyages have made you effeminate. Where are the impetuosity and rage of the valorous Ulysses of old?"

And in order to fortify him in violence, the Centaur made him savor a delicious wine, a gift of Bacchus, a divine liquor that enveloped and disturbed his senses. Under the influence of the stimulating drunkenness, spurred by Chiron, Ulysses had moments of cruelty. He covered Penelope with scorn, reminding her incessantly of what she had done that was reprehensible, and also what she might have done. He arrived at the point of being able to inflame himself seriously with anger, and to believe his own words. He maltreated her.

Finally, one day, having drunk beyond a measure and pliant to the suggestions of the Centaur, he brandished his dagger, a present from King Alcinous, and wounded Penelope slightly in the breast. Then, red with confusion, having sobered up, he left the banqueting hall, supported by Chiron.

Tears were flowing from his eyes.

"What have I become?" he groaned. "I'm a wretch."

"I'll go examine her wound," said Chiron, "and I'll cure her. Henceforth, I won't demand any more effort from you. Show toward your wife the sentiments that are natural to you. We'll see what will happen."

He went to care for the queen. Inanimate, pale and bloodless, Penelope seemed to be at the gates of Tartarus. She only returned to life slowly, as if regretfully.

Finally, her eyes opened, and were dazzled by seeing the daylight again. Her first question was: "Where is Ulysses?"

Chiron advised her not to talk.

"It's necessary that I see him!" she insisted. "I don't want to die far from him."

Ulysses came running then, still frightened by his own work of destruction.

"Forgive me, daughter of Icarius," he implored. "I acted like an insensate."

"I love you. Are you not my master, and ought I not to welcome as a precious gift everything that comes from you, even death?"

She had a pale smile on her lips; she was happy to see him, incapable of being sated by his presence.

The long convalescence was extended in a kind of marvelous ecstasy for Penelope. She cherished him now with all her might. On the day when she had learned how lovable he was, and what power of seduction he exercised over women, she had already conceived a passionate interest for him. When, subsequently, she saw that Ulysses had withdrawn his love, she was afraid, and her tenderness had been increased by it. Finally seeing herself scorned, she had admired him more and ended up fearing him.

With each dolorous tear she shed, her amour revealed itself to be greater and more submissive.

He no longer adores me, but he is adorable, she said to herself.

She loved him above all for his faults, which rendered him more human and brought him closer to her. Gradually, she ended up by finding a strange sweetness in suffering, and lent herself to it with a troubled and troubling mixture of sensuality and dread.

She became habituated to considering herself as his slave. At times, when, becoming violent, he raised a brutal hand to her, Penelope thought: *He's very cruel and he takes pleasure in doing me harm*.

But, far from irritating her, that thought appeared to make her tender. An irresistible desire to prostrate herself at Ulysses' feet took hold of her, and her amour became more vehement.

Finally, at the moment when he struck her and she felt that she was about to faint, she murmured faintly: "How happy I am to die for him!"

And from then on she was his, in a servile manner.

It was now her turn to think incessantly about Ulysses. She interrogated him, fearfully, about his affection, orientated herself toward his desires and prompt to satisfy them.

As for the hero, he could not get over his wonderment, and without fully understanding the amorous blossoming of Penelope, he responded abundantly to her effusions and her tenderness—with the consequence that ineffable days opened before them.

"How content I am," Ulysses said to the Centaur. "She loves me! What does the rest matter? Everything is smiling at me henceforth."

Penelope came to huddle at her master's feet. She gazed at him rapturously and rejoiced in cheerful thoughts that were reflected in Ulysses' eyes, just as she was anxious when a sad cloud appeared therein. Not allowing him to draw away for an instant, she attached herself to his footsteps, collected the most beautiful flowers for him and mixed the finest flour with perfumed honey, with her own hands, in order to prepare his favorite cakes. Ulysses did not have time to formulate his desires before she had already granted them. At every moment, radiant, enlacing her arms around the hero's waist, she said to him: "Is it true is it true that you love me?"

And when he had replied, she repeated the same question again.

VI

Long months had gone by, and the Centaur still remained on Ithaca. He did not appear content to have reckoned with the problem and, far from congratulating himself, one might have thought that he was cursing his science and his infallible clairvoyance.

Nothing is more disappointing, he thought, than foreseeing everything and always succeeding. *There is, in truth, no success or real triumph without preliminary effort, doubt and uncertainty. Always sure of attaining my goal, I am ignorant of divine hope, in the same way that, being able to foresee events, I am deprived of the sublime attractions of novelty. My science forbids me the unexpected that life brings at every momen*t.

One day, he went to post himself near Crow Rock, where the warrior Medon had his modest dwelling. He wanted to surprise Ulysses. He knew that the son of Laertes, neglecting Penelope's bed for some time, was secretly frequenting that house, attracted by the slave Amphylice. That Phoenician woman, whom Ulysses had ceded to Medon as a recompense for his fidelity and collaboration against the suitors, was coarse in her features and bronzed by the sun, but her tender youth and a sort of ardor typical of her race had awakened the senses and the curiosity of the hero.

Chiron had to keep watch until nightfall. Finally, he saw Ulysses emerging furtively from Medon's dwelling, and who, perceiving his master's presence, seemed disconcerted and tried to avoid him. But the Centaur ran swiftly to meet him and barred his way.

"Shame on you, my son," he exclaimed. "This, then, is how you respect the bed of the charming Penelope and how you honor Medon, your faithful servant. What does she have to bewitch you in this fashion, that plump Phoenician, and how can you prefer her to the daughter of Icarius?"

Taken by surprise and blushing with confusion, Ulysses dared not respond.

And the Centaur went on: "What has become of your amour? Not long ago you were begging like a starveling for a smile from Penelope. Intoxicated by her charms, you wanted her to render you caress for caress. Now your wishes are finally granted, you no longer appreciate that happiness. You flee your wife and even go as far as preferring vile slaves to her."

And, further inflating his voice, as if a great anger were carrying him away: "Do you find Penelope less tender? Does she love another man?"

"She loves me and cherishes me more than ever," Ulysses finally replied. "Attentive to my words and following my footsteps, she is more faithful than Argus. Then, when she holds me in her arms, she weeps, happy and swooning, wanting to die amid my caresses."

"For what, then, can you reproach her?"

"Far from having anything for which to reproach her, I judge her irreproachable and perfect. But she no longer has attractions for me, and sometimes her passion oppresses and overwhelms me. Sometimes I regret my errant life and have the desire to mount my rapid ship again."

And having relieved his heart at a stroke, the hero breathed in deeply.

"And your former amour, your urgent and servile affection?" said the Centaur.

Ulysses remained confused and silent, slowly becoming conscious of the changes that had taken place within him.

"In fact, what has become of my affection?" he stammered, finally. "What has become of that sharp emotion, the divine and beautiful anxiety that once took possession of my entire being at the appearance of Penelope? I often go back into the past without being able to recognize myself therein. No trace of the violent transports of old subsist in me."

And as the Centaur said nothing, Ulysses went on: "You must agree, my master, than in spite of your recommendations, you were not able to liberate me from amour; but now, hazard and time have succeeded where your science had failed."

"Insensate," cried Chiron, "do you not see that this cure is my work? Making use of you and Penelope as a potter makes use of malleable clay, I have lent you my impulsions, I have fashioned you in accordance with my intentions, and have forced you to accomplish my designs."

And he showed Ulysses the manner in which he had filled Penelope with illusions and had prepared and aided her to find her husband desirable. He told her how, by suffering, he had then fortified and magnified nascent amour within her.

"I knew that in granting your wish, your desire would be cured," he added. "That is the sovereign remedy. For passion only lasts as long as it finds no response and it burns in solitude. We love with constancy those who neglect us, but scarcely do we sense that we are loved and satisfied than the enchantment disappears. Surety leads to satiety, as if amour killed amour."

For a long time, Chiron continued speaking, clarifying the mind of his disciple.

Ulysses lent his ears avidly to that speech and seemed gripped and amazed by what he heard. Finally, he collapsed on a stone near the shore and began to weep. For, instructed by his master's revelations, he read his heart clearly, and that of Penelope—and the cruel and disappointing reality penetrated and reawakened his consciousness.

"What! Because Penelope adores me, she has therefore ceased to please me and to appear desirable to me!" he exclaimed, in a strangled voice. "And, on the other hand, is it for having raised a homicidal hand against her that she is definitively attached to me?"

Now following the movements of his heart, and consciously retreading the passionate road that he had traveled until then in tumult and distraction, he felt a sharp despair. And, reactions being vivid and violent in him, his first impulse was to run on to a rock in order to hurl himself into the sea.

But Chiron held him back.

"Why should I live?" moaned Ulysses, trying to liberate himself from the Centaur's powerful grip. "If only, thus cured of amour, I were at least happy! But no! Since I no longer aspire to anything, life is deprived of all its brilliance, and no longer offers me beautiful temptations. Once, in the ignorance of passions, I lived from day to day, taking pleasure in increasing my wealth or acquiring new glories. But since great fevers have burned my existence and have revealed the supreme interest of passion to me, I can no longer do without it. For want of amour I feel dispossessed of everything, impoverished and miserable. Everything seems obscure to me, colorless and tasteless. Nothing spurs me, nothing attracts me. On, the sublime woes of old, the atrocious sufferings of jealousy, anxiety and desire—how I regret them! In squeezing my heart, those dolors proved to me that I was alive, and the brief moments of joy that I felt then were worth a thousand times more than the monotonous flow of days at present."

"Do you remember, unfortunate individual," replied the Centaur, "when I told you that, baleful and redoubtable, sowing hatred and disarray, summoning tears and blood, amour is still the sole celestial light that transfigures life and renders it desirable? Good and evil, sweetness and bitterness, honey and absinthe, everything is contained in it, everything is in accord, in admirable, terrible, mysterious Amour."

VII

He work complete, the Centaur was getting ready to depart, without Ulysses trying to retain him. For nothing henceforth appeared to interest the hero, who, liberated from all anxiety, as he had wished to be, did not feel any happier.

One day, Chiron said to him: "Why are you sad, in sum? For what can you reproach Destiny? Your island is favorably situated, and the winds visit it without overwhelming it. One breathes a persistent perfume here that comes to vivify everything and which does not seem to emanate from flowers but to exist as a natural element in the air. As for the inhabitants, they all have smiling faces, since the generous earth furnishes them abundantly with everything that it necessary to them. And I'm forgetting the most powerful and the most likeable attraction of your kingdom, which resides in the ever-new aspect with which these beautiful shores dress themselves in the sunlight. What marvels in perpetual creation and what a wealth of pleasures there are in the rocks, the curved inlets filled with sand, and in the meandering streams! It seems to me that even if you no longer had a vehement interest in living, you could still tolerate existence with the sole objective of gazing at what this beautiful nature offers you untiringly."

But Ulysses did not appear to be sensible to that language. Nature was for him merely a favorable or hostile environment, aiding him in his enterprises or placing obstacles in his path.

And the Centaur, recognizing that such consolations were inappropriate to the hero's mind, fell silent, anxiously

On the eve of his departure, having discovered a new remedy for his disciple's woes, he came to find him at dawn.

Ulysses was sitting on a stone beaten by the waves, with a distracted gaze, empty of all thought.

"How despicable humans are, and how cruel the gods are in their irony!" he exclaimed, on seeing Chiron approach. "I desired ardently to inspire amour in Penelope, but scarcely was my wish granted than the success no longer provoked anything in me but indifference. That which, in spring, appeared to me to be a happiness for which I could scarcely hope, already gives me no joy in autumn. Have I changed my heart? Am I no longer the same man? How can it be that the realization of Ulysses' dearest wish does not give Ulysses the slightest pleasure? Is life nothing but a dream, then, nothing but a mobile shadow, a bitter derision?"

The Centaur replied: "Don't be completely discouraged, my son. Know that in their clemency, the gods have accorded to humans the faculty of attenuating their despair by embellishing it. They have granted them Art, which is capable of lending divine attractions even to suffering. You're unaware of the consolations and the appeasement that illusion gives. There is a final resource in that, which I have come in order to reveal to you."

And, encouraged by the interrogative gaze that Ulysses turned toward him, Chiron continued:

"Do you remember the origin of your anxieties, those shameful nights during which the suitors came to weigh upon your bed and take Penelope in their arms? A child was to be the fruit of those multiple embraces. That child was born, and grew up. I met him yesterday." And he added: "It's necessary that we go to see him together before my departure. Pan is his name. Although he is still young, I do not hesitate to offer him to you as an example."

Followed by his disciple, Chiron headed toward a grotto that he knew, and where he had encountered the child of adultery.

While walking, Ulysses though, with melancholy, that the existence of that child would once have inspired a great movement of hatred and anger within him, whereas now, it only awakened surprise and curiosity. He saw in that a new sign of his indifference toward Penelope, who appeared have been expelled and effaced from his heart.

The master and the disciple traveled in silence through the fecund and cheerful plains of Ithaca. They finally arrived on a solitary and abrupt promontory that looked out toward the isle of Samos.

"There is the grotto in which Penelope's son lives," said the Centaur.

As he approached it, he called to Pan by name.

A deformed young man of strange aspect, covered in a starry goatskin, emerged from the grotto. He saluted the Centaur; he seemed to be attracted to him by mysterious sympathies and natural correspondences.

Ulysses noticed two small horns growing on the ephebe's forehead, and a black pelt that shadowed his body from the navel downwards, and covered his cloven feet, like those of a goat, mere thickly.

"He is, in fact, ugly, and differs from humans," the Centaur said to him, divining his thoughts, "but don't hate him for that and conclude that he's inferior to them. By virtue of the horns and the pelt, he is allied more intimately than you with the nurturing earth. The healthy forces of animality, and its admirable instinct, live within him. And as he sometimes feels and acts in a human manner, without ceasing to enjoy animal plenitudes, one can say that he summarizes all creation within him. In any case, it is in order to bring humans closer to the earth that the gods decreed his birth."

And the Centaur told Ulysses how amour and its sufferings had led Pan to construct a lute and to draw a balm of consolation and a diversion from music.

"It was on a spring day," he said, "that Pan encountered the nymph Syrinx, who was bathing in the river, She was amicable and welcoming, and was able by her words, her movements and the profound science of attraction with which every woman seems to be infused, to charm and captivate the adolescent. Then, soon, obedient to her natural cruelty and fickleness, she cast him aside. Responding with mocking laughter to his language of passion, she disappeared among the reeds and left Pan prey to all the torments of ill fortune.

"The young man cursed his own ugliness, cried, wept and thought of dying. Finally, he perceived one day that Syrinx was following another lover and passed close to him indifferently, as if she did not know him. He felt that his heart was about to burst, since, accumulated for a long time within him, his dolor demanded an issue, required a prompt outflow. It was then that, instinctively or guided by an obliging god, Pan extended his hand, cut one of the reeds that hid Syrinx from him, and raised it to his lips.

"Sounds emerged from it. Undisciplined at first, pliant to the laws of chance, those sounds were gradually assembled, aided one another and accorded with one another; and from that resulted something superhuman and tender, which appeared to lend a consciousness and a voice to all the surrounding nature.

"Pan experienced a sort of appeasement; for that melody, which surpassed human speech in its sweetness, in the richness of its intonations, those chords, which contained the seed of all sentiments, all joys and all sadness, liberated and lightened the soul of the musician.

"Thus, with the reed between his lips, Pan saw himself as a creator. Gradually, he came to blow into his flute the emotions that that the rising morning, with its birdsong and its drops of dew, produced in his heart. He also celebrated the young shoots of spring, proud and straight, which come to renew and ornament nature, and then related the dying of the light at sunset, the soft palpitating silences of nights, and the vast moving expanse of the sea.

"Since then, scarcely have his lips touched the flute than ardent desires, pure amours and sweet regrets take flight around him. The sounds of the instrument recreate the world and organize it in accordance with Pan's intentions.

"And the young man was soon able to express, with the aid of his flute, his inexpressible passion for Syrinx. He revealed the intimate essence of the flame that was devouring him, the most secret of his dreams, and how beautiful the Nymph seemed to him, and the emotions that the sound of her footfalls provoked in his heart, and the tenderness that overwhelmed him with sweetness when, leaning over to pick a flower, Syrinx displayed the frail elegance of her figure.

"He rendered above all, by means of sounds, the splendors of the ineffaceable image that the cruel individual had left in his memory. He painted with the aid of music the real charms of his beloved and the others, the incomparable ones, with which his imagination adorned her and enriched her incessantly.

"Then, by virtue of a sort of miracle, in ornamenting his unfortunate passion and perfecting it, Pan finished up by delighting in it. His own creation, that portrait of the ideal Syrinx that he magnified without respite, caused him to forget the terrestrial one, the imperfect Syrinx. Scarcely had his hand taken possession of the flute than his heart already ceased to suffer, for music liberated him from all pain, and, bending the universe to his desire, elevated him above the real."

Such was the Centaur's story. When he had concluded it, he asked Pan to take up his flute and to play before Ulysses.

The hero was wonderstruck by it. He thought that he was transported into unknown regions. A mysterious voice, which was preexistent within him, it seemed, but which had previously been silent, awoke now in order to speak a divine revelatory language. The sounds of the flute resonated all the way to the most profound substance of the hero, putting his soul in communion with nature, and demolishing, as if by enchantment, the barriers that isolate beings.

So, before going away, Ulysses saluted Pan, looking at him with terror and admiration.

"Now you know how humans, aided by art, can cure their torments and escape from themselves," the Centaur said to him, after a long silence.

"Are we not sufficiently victims of illusion? Was it worth the trouble of the gods adding the lie of art hereto?"

Chiron replied:

"Unhappy man! Know that there will never be enough consolation for you, so glorious, but disastrous, are the paths into which your intelligence draws you. In growing old, humanity becomes more and more perverted. Already, it is no longer sufficient for you to explore nature and defend yourself against the ambushes of life. You start to interrogate the secrets of your heart, you fathom the universe and you claim to be stealing its secrets. And from all your acquisitions, dolor springs forth; for the truth is bitter, and the fruit of knowledge leaves a taste of ashes on the lips.

"It is therefore necessary to thank the gods if, alongside plaintive thought, they have granted you fiction, the consoler of human being. Penelope's child will leave you harmony as a heritage, while on another island, a man equal to the gods, Daedalus, is communicating to inert matter the face of things, fashioning it to such an extent that it offers to wonderstruck eyes a new and tangible universe."

The Centaur fell silent for a few moments. Already, the scintillating doors of Ulysses' palace were outlined in the distance. Then he resumed:

"Henceforth, mortals can escape their cruel condition. Reconstituting, with the aid of the creative intoxication of art, an imaginary world, and grating it the beauty that is absent from the real world, they will be able to support life and persevere without dementia to scrutinize the mysteries of the future."

"What you say is true," Ulysses acquiesced. "There is in the sound of Pan's flute a marvelous philter, analogous to that of the lotus. It is necessary to forget everything. The power of music is great!"

"There is an art even higher and more divine," said the Centaur, "an art victorious over time, victorious over humans, and akin to eternity. Someone other than me will reveal it to you."

VIII

"Why have the gods introduced so much illogic and dementia into amour? Would it not be simpler to love someone who loves us and hate someone who deceives us? Is it necessary that instability attaches us more than constancy, that vice charms us more than virtue, and that there is more attraction in suffering than in joy?"

Thus spoke Ulysses, while he was accompanying the Centaur to the port where the hollow ship, all sails deployed, was ready to depart.

"If things have been organized in that fashion," replied Chiron, "that is what is apparently necessary," Chiron replied. "Remember, Ulysses, that amour is primordial, that it plunges its obscure roots into the origins of life, and that, in order to create, it can only inspire a state of supreme exaltation, a sort of sacred delirium."

"Gods, gods! What misdirection and dolorous surprises there are in existence! However, I only aspire to feel the divine suffering again."

"To suffer is to rise in the hierarchy of beings," said the Centaur.

"To love also," said Ulysses.

"To love is already to suffer," said Chiron.

"I feel that I had wings, and that I no longer have them," complained the hero, again. "Without passion, life seems empty, one does not even perceive the flow of time."

"Your regrets and disappointments will calm down when, soon, you will be touched by the supreme appeasement of all woes: old age. I too, after having ceded my right to immortality to the insensate Prometheus, and on the point of being attained by the years, feel myself invaded by a kind of sensual mildness. Have you ever followed, Ulysses, my mysterious deployment of the dusk? Light goes away then. Everything that was life and brightness withdraws and disappears. However, one might think that the beauty of things becomes more intense, that forms gain in perfection, that a supreme repose, a sort of harmonious and gentle pacification visits the landscape. There is a tender charm in that, which inspires within us a melancholy more enviable than joy.

"The benevolent operation of old age on the human heart is similar. Life withdraws from us, along with the sublime and noisy cortege of the passions, which excuse and embellish existence. And one might think, however, that at that moment, a human being finds a new equilibrium, a secret and perfect measure, and that everything is compensated and accorded within him. You will know old age, Ulysses. You will see yourself live again in your children, you will no longer extract your pleasure from the uncertain future, nor from the blind present, but from the past, the unique treasure of human beings. Then Penelope will draw you to her again, for you will love her henceforth as a companion, as a witness to your life, as a living part of your memories, as an aspect of your destiny... Afterwards, death will come..."

"Death!" murmured Ulysses.

"Yes, death," the Centaur repeated. "Revelatory, liberating death."

But Ulysses felt a frisson. He saw before him the immense plain of Ilium, the warriors struck by fear and fleeing the homicidal iron. He heard once again the screams of women, the lamentations that rose up from the height of the ramparts, the gasps of those who fell, badly wounded. And he remembered the mysterious pallor, the strange appearance, calm and yet fearful, that covered the faces when the last breath had quit the lips.

"You don't find any savor in life, you curse it, you reprove it, and yet you're afraid of dying," Chiron said to Ulysses as he boarded the ship, which was bobbing impatiently, scarcely retained by its anchors. He added: "You're inconsequent, disordered, prey to all phantoms, habituated to all miseries—a man, in sum."

Drawing him powerfully between his feet and clutching him to his proud breast, he embraced him.

"We won't see one another again, my child; my end is near. Enjoy the savor of what each day brings you, and try to make the untiring curiosity that devours you into an ornament rather than a torment of your existence."

The ship drew away, driven by the wind, and was soon no more than an uncertain dot on the infinite azure of the sea.

And Ulysses returned sadly to Penelope.

IX

The years passed.

Ulysses attained extreme old age.

One day, sitting under a thick olive tree in front of the lair of Naiad Nymphs, daughters of Jupiter, he was gazing at the port of Phorcys. And it seemed that every wave that came noisily to die at his feet brought him the salutation of distant and nearby lands that had once seen him love, fight and suffer. His immense endeavors and his multiple troubles haunted his mind.

Yielding to the voice of memories, Ulysses invoked the lands of the Phaeacians, where Nausicaa, more beautiful than Diana, had beaten laundry near the benevolent river, and the isle of Calypso, and the high bed in which the mobile and ardent goddess had bound him by means of her charms, and the redoubtable lair of the Cyclops, and the land of the Laestrygonians, and the mysterious palace of Aeolus.

Lastly, he remembered his return, the battles and his disordered amour for Penelope

Marveling at the voluptuous regret that those memories stimulated within him, he came to be no longer able to distinguish the good from the bad, so much did he feel that they were equally attached to his life, like constant and proven friends.

And he began to think that no one, among the Achaeans, surpassed him in the knowledge of human mores and the science of the movements of the heart. He even understood, as the Centaur had once announced to him, that dolor and adversity had enriched his consciousness in forcing him to fathom mortal things.

And, sensing his superiority over other men and his insignificance before destiny, he became fearful of dying. He thought he saw once again the sacred wood of Persephone near the seething confluence of the Acheron and the Cocytus. The avid flock of souls, crowding around the black blood in order to taste once again the pleasures of the earth, reappeared to him, and he remembered the superb shade of Achilles, dominating the dead and proffering the bitter words: "Don't talk to me about death, illustrious Ulysses. I would rather be a laborer and serve a poor man for a humble salary, scarcely able to nourish myself, than command the population of the dead."

Thinking now about death, and overtaken by a strange melancholy, Ulysses knew the desperate desire for immortal things. A tall and beautiful woman stood up then before the infinity of the sea, and approached him.

He recognized the protective goddess Minerva, the daughter of tempestuous Jupiter.

The redoubtable virgin extended her hand, caressed his chin, and said to him:

"O Laertide, what do you desire, and why is your heart nourishing itself in torments? Are you not content and satisfied near your flocks, in your house, seeing your father, the venerable Laertes, smile at his posterity? If you have once known the evils of exile, your present repose is all the sweeter for it. You were among the intrepid company who doomed superb Ilium, you shared the bed of goddesses, you vanquished the son of the Lord of the Sea and no one can compare to you, except a god, for cunning or for strength. Even amour came in its turn to heap you with its rigors and its gifts. What more do you want, Ulysses?"

Thus spoke Minerva of the blue eyes, while Ulysses shook his head and smiled sadly.

Finally, he replied:

"I recognize you, goddess, not only by your resplendent visage, but also the wisdom of your words. In you resides the intelligence of Jupiter of the innumerable designs. Don't be irritated by my sadness. Far be it from me to bewail or to judge insufficient what the Immortals have wanted to accord me. Having found repose near my people, I no longer experience terrestrial desires, and I do not fear the jealousy of Nemesis, who is offended by excessively perfect happiness. It is rather from happy memories that I draw my melancholy.

"Sitting on the edge of groaning Amphitrite, I am thinking about my past life, the glories of yore, days full of travails, numerous joys and innumerable dolors. And while old age haunts me without respite, I do not have the courage, O goddess, to smile at the death that makes everything disappear. Is it not horrible to die at the summit of wisdom, rich in experience, without leaving any memory to generations to come?

"People repeat that it is dolorous to perish young, and that mortals ought to hope for a remote decease. My sentiment is entirely other. For, in sum, why have I collected the various spectacles of worlds, the sensualities of life and the sweet bitterness of passion, why have I harvested glory, if all of that must vanish when my eyes are closed by death? Is it worth the trouble of suffering so much, since the hand of the Fates will efface everything?"

And Ulysses looked at the daughter of Jupiter with such a great dolor that she was moved in her divine strength and replied:

"You are sad, sage Laertide, because of something inevitable. Mortal, you are subject to the fate of mortals. It is even necessary to thank the gods for being able to die, as Tiresias predicted for you, consumed by a long maturity and seeing your people prosper. As for your skill and your strength, they reside henceforth in your children. It is Telemachus who will continue your work and your race. Cease to lament, therefore, and formulate a more precise wish."

The wily Ulysses looked at the goddess with an imploring eye. Then, without being discouraged, he said:

"I confess, O goddess, that I have wished to sense on my lips a drop of nectar, the sublime nourishment of the Olympians, a drop that would preserve from death not only my body but he memory of the actions that I accomplished and the treasures of my experience, everything that my consciousness has accumulated of the great and redoubtable. No one, among the Achaeans, has done or suffered what I have done and suffered. I would like that to remain indestructible, O goddess. But alas, I am asking the impossible. How could I be worthy of the marvelous beverage that your handsome cup-bearer, the incomparable Ganymede, pours out for the Olympians?"

"O ingenious and subtle man," the goddess relied, laughing, "How belated you are in making your request, and how able you are to render it innocent. No, I cannot grant it to you. No one except for the gods may taste the delightful nectar that confers immortality, and in any case, whoever tasted it would feel his lips burning, consumed like embers. In spite of your wisdom and your travails, you are consecrated to death, and even the will of the Olympians could not save you from it."

Having spoken thus, Minerva remained pensive. She looked at the bitter earth, the liquid plain that was deployed, mysterious and murmuring, and the distant islands what were posed like black bucklers in the midst of the waves. Her blue eyes fraternized with the ether.

Then she lowered her eyes toward the man again, and she continued:

"I cannot grant you what you desire, but as you are dear to me, since your life was almost an immortal work, and you summarize in yourself generations of men, I will create in your favor a new nectar, capable of being savored by ephemeral lips and delighting them. It will be my last favor to you—and Chiron, moreover, has already announced it to you."

Having spoken, and taken on the aspect of a dove, she opened her wings, launched herself forth nimbly, and attained the inaccessible sky.

Ulysses remained pensive, with a leaven of vague delight in his heart.

X

He was returning now to his house, passing by Crow Rock, where his pigs were grazing on acorns. Near the spring of Arethusa, he paused to follow the women who were beating laundry with his gaze. His heart was wounded again by the memory of the Phaeacian virgin. He remembered the smile full of attractions, the beautiful arms and the marvelous complexion, all the graces of the body, comparable to those of Venus, which had inspired in those who gazed at Nausicaa the desire to repose with her on a bed.

He was still possessed by that vision when, as he drew away through the noisy wood, animated by the voice of springs, he perceived an unknown man coming toward him, wearing a garment unusual on the island.

"Venerable old man," the stranger said to him, "I approach you without dread, even though you do not know me. Newly arrived in Ithaca, I request hospitality for a few days. If you are sheltered from need, as your rich clothing leads me to hope, receive me generously in your house, and the gods will accord you in return all that you desire."

"Follow me to my dwelling and you will be my guest," Ulysses replied, "for it is not permissible for anyone to send away travelers protected by Jupiter. There are enough fattened pigs, tender ewes and woolen blankets in my house for your sojourn in Ithaca to be comfortable and amiable."

They arrived thus at the palace of the Laertides, and Ulysses asked the steward to temper the wine with water and to prepare the table, while Penelope took the stranger to the bath that reposes the limbs.

In the evening, in the hall brilliant with gold, Ulysses sat beside his guest, and uncovered the meats, offering him the best, after having burned the thighs in honor of the Immortals. When he had appeased his hunger, a need to learn new things came to him. He therefore addressed his guest and said to him:

"I do not think to offend you, stranger, in asking you the name of your homeland and the object of your voyages. Are you a warrior, a skillful navigator, or do you exercise the difficult and risky métier of thief, abducting beautiful virgins and heavy tripods? During my youth I knew all those métiers and, without boasting, I can affirm to you that I excelled in them. Now, it is my son who travels the seas in search of livestock and slaves. But times have changed and kings can no longer, as of old, gain immortal glory and amass riches in voyaging thus to distant lands.

The stranger, recognizing by the words and opulence of his host a pastor of peoples, rejoiced in that.

"I was born, O King, in Smyrna in Aeolia, built in accordance with the advice of Jupiter by the inhabitants of Phricon, celebrated for their horses. The waters of the sacred Meles bathed its shores. I am not a warrior and I have not distinguished myself in pillage. Destiny has given me the mission of guiding the learned virgins, daughter of Jupiter, who inspire songs and posses the marvelous and multiple secrets of music. Mentes, an honorable pilot, the son of the valorous Anchialus, left me here, wanting to go and send a few days in Leucadia. He will come back later to collect me in order to take me to Colophon and Cyma, which overlook the plains of Hermus."

"You rejoice my heart, my guest, in telling me that you know the secrets of song, but I cannot hide my surprise. How is it that, free to follow arms, you prefer to be a poet?"

"My eyes are weak, my sight is darkening. I fear going blind. Thus it is destiny that has chosen that métier for me. My name is Melsigene and I am the son of Phemius."

Ulysses remained silent, wondering privately, what purpose poets might serve. But he said nothing, because he was wise and to his innate prudence, old age had added mildness.

When the cup-bearer finally passed the bowl and the noble Penelope, once the object of so many desires and now touched by the years, came to sit down with the men, the stranger, obedient to his host's invitation, took the lyre in his hands.

"Would you like me to sing you the war of Jupiter and the Giants, or the amours of Mars and the noble golden Venus?" he asked. "I have also composed a new song about the admirable and already forgotten deeds of the Achaeans who fought against Ilium. One of the kings of this country, the subtle Ulysses, took part in that admirable war."

At his host's request, he sang the destiny of the Achaeans and the evils that they endured and the fatigues that they suffered, until the day when the divine Ulysses, making use of the horse that Epeius made with the aid of Minerva, toppled proud Ilium.

The son of Laertes, who was hearing his remembered glories harmonized for the first time by the human voice, felt moved. A violent trouble rose all the way to his nostrils, and he could barely hold back his tears.

"O singer," he said, when the stranger fell silent, "you are more worthy of admiration than any other mortal, and the Muses, daughters of Jupiter, have been singularly favorable to you. I visited multiple countries and saw marvelous things, but now you have just awakened impetuous and unknown emotions in me. Sing more of what you have learned of the adventures of the Achaeans and the return of Ulysses,"

"I have sung what I knew of them," said the poet, sadly. "Renown vanishes when harmony does not aid it to fix itself in human memory. I am traveling expressly to collect, among the descendants of the Achaean warriors, the traditions of the past, and I beg you to tell me what you know about the last peregrinations of Ulysses. Fate was hard for those heroes and their works perished with them. That is why, while singing about the gods, the labors of Hercules, the destruction of Thebes of the Hundred Gates, I can scarcely recount the recent combats of the Achaeans and their adventurous returns."

"O divine singer," the old man finally confessed, "I am Ulysses, still forgotten by the Fates, living and breathing in the innumerable memories of the past. If you wish me to talk to you about Troy and the fate of the heroes, and the death of Achilles and my return to the isle of Ithaca after my long wanderings, I will do so gladly. I would love the memory to be revived with the aid of the winged words full of rhythm that emerge from your lips."

Then the young man fixed his vague eyes on the old man, with amazement.

"Forgive me if, on seeing myself in the home of one of the kings of Ithaca, I did not recognize you immediately, you, the greatest among mortals. My sight is troubled and I passed an afflicted youth. I knew, however, that I was going to encounter you, for the divine Apollo revealed it to me in his sanctuary at Delphi. I sense now that it was the will of the Immortals that I know you. Speak, recount to me the unique things that you have accomplished, the immense travails of the Achaeans, all the dolor and grandeur that the Tyndaride stimulated when, fleeing from the bed of her husband, she followed the handsome Trojan to proud Ilium..."

And then, while the flames of the torches vacillated, obfuscated by the smoke of mats, and the high-ceilinged halls scintillated with gold—the bucklers and the bows standing out, formidable, on the walls enameled with colors—Ulysses evoked the past before the quivering soul of the poet.

But he omitted to recount the voluptuous transformation of his wife and the passion she had provoked in him. He no longer talked about that. Recalling the advice of Minerva, he respected the virtue of Penelope.

XI

The trees flowered, and then shed their leaves, and the days became short and cold. Every evening the old man talked about his momentous years, and the young man wrought those words with his genius and communicated an ideal perfection to them. Sometimes, he also took up the lyre, and then Ulysses sensed his past revive and thought that the Fates were weaving destinies before his eyes, He saw once again the forgotten countries, the dangers he had run, the faces that had inspired desire or amity in him, and the others at which he had gazed hatefully.

The words of the poet were so vivid and so vibrant, his tone recreated the extinct life so intensely, that the hero was frightened at times, thinking that he was penetrating recklessly into the luminous abode of the Immortals.

Finally, one day, the ship of the pilot Mentes appeared in the harbor and the poet got ready to depart.

Ulysses made him a present of a golden cup that the king of the Phaeacians had given him, as well as a heavy bronze tripod.

Then, on the eve of the departure, while Helios was inclining his chariot toward the west, he took him to the lair of the Nymphs, wanting to enjoy his words again.

"I will sing you, since it is the last time we shall see one another, a long rhapsody that I have just composed, on your return," the poet said to him.

And he sang the anger of Neptune, the tempest, and then the isle of the Phaeacians, and Nausicaa, more beautiful than Diana, and the arrival in Ithaca. It was all of his youth, and the grandeur of his exploits, and his sensualities, and his dolor, that loomed up before Ulysses, eternalized by the Word and as imposing as Mount Ithacos, which protected his isle. The hero saw himself, reliving an existence even more beautiful, and his heart filled with pride and joy, so great did those past things seem that had worn him away in passing, all transfigured by genius.

He had already wept when the poet had related the death of Alpenor falling from Circe's roof, and he had shivered when the redoubtable shades of the Black Dwellings passed before him again, and then had laughed at his own ruse against the Cyclops. Now that the poet was singing the joy of old Laertes seeing his son again, he could not retain himself.

Caressing the stranger's chin with his hand and kissing him on the cheek he stammered: "Where have you learned these things, divine aede?" For he could not believe that he had recounted them himself.

"Now," said the poet, "I am returning to my homeland, near devastated Troy and the shores that you knew. A great fatherland in dissolving in those countries, multiple races are uniting there, an entire people is awakening that seems to have inherited the merits and the cunning of the Achaeans. It is the youth of a new world. All of them are as avid to know as you, and in their hearts the appetite for great deeds is triumphant. I shall spread there the admirable things that you have told me.

Children will retain them, and young men and old. Thus, perpetuated by song, they will live in centuries to come.

And then, in the mind of Ulysses, the mysterious words surged forth of the promise that Minerva of the blue had once made to him in that same place. Then he sensed his heart becoming sated with tranquility, and a strange calm invading him, as if his end were approaching. And he knew that, although about to die, he was nevertheless savoring nectar, and that the stranger was founding his immortality with sonorous words.

"What you say is true, O poet," he exclaimed. "Your words will remain, and through them I shall live incessantly in human memory, for such is the will of the powerful goddess, daughter of Ceraunian Jupiter.

In a single instant, it was as if he were penetrated by the grandeur of the Art that the Centaur had revealed to him for the first time near Pan's lair.

Depicting the aspect of things by means of sculpture, moving and consoling souls by mans of music, Art could thus perpetuate the memory of men.

And, seized by a sort of panic before that whole new era of thought and harmonious edification, the era that was about to succeed years of mighty sword-thrusts and happy rapine, Ulysses turned to the singer again.

"Tell me," he said, "what the name is of the land that you are announcing to me, and where your songs will resound."

Then Homer extended his hand and, describing with a broad gesture the expanse of the unfathomable sea, he said: "It is Greece. Everything that is deployed before us is Greece."

And the hero was able to see, with his final gaze, that the places the poet was indicating to him were filled with light.

PLATO IN SEARCH OF AMOUR

Preface

Plutarch reports that the Botticeans, a people living in Thrace, but who pretended to originate from Attica, expressed their aspirations toward the primitive fatherland by a solemnly-intoned religious chant whose refrain was "Let's go to Athens."

That nostalgic cry of the Botticeans symbolizes marvelously the appeal of every well-born individual who loves beauty and the ideal.

Today, still, "going to Athens" means ridding oneself of any narrow or heavy thought, lightening oneself of all material and temporary cares, and reimmersing oneself in the eternal sources that ennoble and elevate.

It was in my desire to go to Athens for a while that I imagined, freely, this short novel.

To live for a few moments in the divine Greek maturity, to animate certain anecdotes that seem to me to characterize that perfect human spring, to evoke shades that are dear and familiar to me: such was my aim.

Anyone who wants to know Plato's exact ideas about Amour should read the *Symposium*. He will only find a feeble, altered and fictionalized echo here of the august words, once pronounced near the little hill on which the Parthenon rises, which transformed the consciousness of humankind and suddenly orientated its destinies.

I. The Crown of Athens

When Phaedo came back bringing figs he found Socrates sitting on the bank of the Ilissus near the lair of the Nymphs. He was dipping his feet in the running water and the river was caressing his ankles and crowning them with stripes of silvery foam.

"The coolness that rises from the water summons clear thoughts," said the master. "Sit down beside me in the shade of these agnus castus trees. The day is mild, and, because if the luminous quietude that surrounds us, while eating this beautiful fig, I believe I am communicating with the sun that ripened it."

It was the meditative and ecstatic hour when the star, finding itself in the middle of its course, envelops Athens in a gilded torpor. The light is insinuating then, saturating bodies with an obscure and muted sensuality and slowly enchaining the brain like the virtue of a generous wine.

Socrates and Phaedo kept their eyes half-closed, troubled by vague reveries, and only conscious of the cold caress of the water.

"I have a question to ask you that is soliciting my mind imperiously, like the enigma of the Sphinx," said the disciple, finally. "Yesterday I went up to the Acropolis to see Phidias' radiant Minerva again. At the back of the sanctuary, the austerity and meditation of her face struck me, and I remembered the ancient statues of the goddess, less perfect but smiling, with features as clear and joyful and the gush of a spring. The old masters of Sycion and Aegina were able to lend the deities that cheerful aspect, so typical of our ancestors, but which we judge inappropriate today. I wonder why Minerva lost her soft smile, and why sadness and cares invaded her and invaded us. We have now become like Pericles, who always appeared pensive and severe, studied in his movements and his stride, not consenting to laugh in front of anyone."

"Perhaps we differ from our ancestors by virtue of a graver conception of the meaning of life," relied Socrates. "In that case, we would simply have taken a step forward n the road of wisdom."

"Do you believe, Socrates," the disciple objected, "that there is anything wiser than living each day in harmony with natural things, savoring pleasure, conversing with friends and crowning the passing hour with the most beautiful flowers? You were anxious yesterday in seeing young Alcibiades intoxicating himself in the arms of Herpyllis. You criticized him for possessing vast stables, for maintaining a host of slaves and amassing in his home so many cloaks of byssus cloth and crimson sandals. I confess to you, however, that sitting next to the river now and seeing the Attic plain resplendent under the sun, like a cup filled with gilded wine. I am tempted to recognize the sovereign good in sensuality."

"The freshness of the water is communicating happy thoughts to you, friend," said Socrates, opening his eyes slightly. "In any case, I'm not as Spartan as you imply. I didn't criticize Alcibiades for possessing fine chariots and wearing rich cloaks. I only wanted him to occupy himself with other things as well."

"But, precisely, is it worth the trouble of occupying oneself with anything else?"

"By the Stars,[6] I believe so!" replied Socrates. "And in order to succeed in that, I judge it preferable to order one's life with simplicity."

"It was, however, exactly the opposite that our forefathers did, who vanquished the Persians," the young man remarked. "In those days, the citizens only went to do battle for the liberty of their hearths. On their return, they enjoyed the good things of life. The Ionian wind had blown its delightful softness all the way here, and the streets of Athens were per-

---

[6] In the original, Socrates swears in this instance "par le Chien" [literally, by the Dog], which I assume to be a reference to the constellation Canis Major, hence my translation.

fumed by the passage of beautiful slaves clad in Punic fabrics. Cedar and ivory, rare stones from the banks of the Ganges, Phoenician embroideries, peploi from Lydia and carpets from Ecbatana were abundant in the houses. The men were handsome. At the festival of the Panathenaia they were seen, slimmer than the stem of a palm tree, ivory scepter in hand, with majestic beards curled in stages in the Oriental style, their red tunics embroidered with flowers and their hair attached over the forehead by large golden clasps."

"Were they happier?" asked Socrates.

"At any rate, they savored life more. Themistocles had himself carried in his triumphal chariot by four naked women, and Cimon loved the large wineskins of Samos so much that often, on emerging from banquets, he could no longer distinguish Syrian maidens from young boys.

"Yes, Phaedo, but on the other hand, our ancestors' eyes reflected fewer thoughts. In the epoch that you admire, the Athenians were still superstitions. Don't forget that the priests succeeded in enabling Pisistratus to reenter the city by having him accompanied by a wretched wooden doll. The people believed that doll was Minerva in person, and no one dared attack a tyrant protected by the Olympians."[7]

"No, Socrates, you won't be able to convince me easily that the coarse tunics, simple mantles and trimmed beard of today, our sad expressions and our subtle thoughts, create a superiority over our ancestors, and constitute progress. I think, on the contrary, with the young Aristophanes, that our ances-

---

[7] The tyrant whose name was Latinized as Pisistratus was deposed twice during his reign, which lasted from approximately 561 to 527 B.C., returning the first time on a golden chariot accompanied by a tall woman allegedly mistaken by the populace for Athene—Ségur's Minerva. Socrates' allegation of priestly involvement is not unlikely, but Pisistratus appears to have been an early populist and proto-democrat who supported ordinary citizens against the aristocracy, and that probably had more to do with his reinstatement.

tors did great things, and that they equaled in splendor and in glory the most ancient peoples, the Egyptians and the inhabitants of sumptuous Babylon. You can say that we think better and reflect more on the aims of the universe, but others have done that before us, and Greece already possessed Homer and Orpheus, Heraclitus and Pythagoras. Can we lay claim to a greater splendor than that of those days?"

As he did not receive any response, Phaedo turned round and saw Socrates motionless, rapturous, in ecstasy, in one of the moments of intimate mediation in which consciousness seemed to quit his body. It was said that a mysterious voice spoke within him then.

Eventually, he seemed to wake up and replied:

"It isn't easy to demonstrate that we're better than our ancestors. Who, in any case, would dare to appear sure, except Apollo, who divines the future? He alone could see clearly into what we're doing. We are like the pieces of multicolored thread with which the virgins of the Acropolis weave the peplos of the goddess; we don't know what design we're going to form. Perhaps we surpass our ancestors by virtue of the very gravity and sadness for which you're reproaching us.

"While you were speaking I remembered the response that old Silenus made to King Midas when the latter, having captured him, demanded the secret of happiness from him. 'Why are you forcing me to tell you what you ought not to know, Midas?' he said. 'Happiness for you would have been not to be born. But since you exist, the only happiness that remains to you is to die soon.' That, Phaedo, is a conception of destiny that elevates life by giving it a profound and tragic significance, entirely contrary to the insouciance and levity that you propose as the ideal.

"In any case, don't worry. We can only continue what our forefathers did. But while they only gave a meaning to the joys of life, we also want to give one to its mysteries and anxieties. Our goal is theirs, by which I mean beauty. Except that the beauty that, for them, was external and naïve, we enable to penetrate into the soul. After having made it the law of our lineaments, we also want to import it into the rhythm of our sentiments.

"Athens, which you can see extended down there, under the intoxicating song of the cicada, is striving to ennoble its life. According the same severe harmonies to thoughts and forms, its genius composes, with the aid of all our creative aspiration, a hymn to the ideal. The old artists of Sicyon that you mentioned liked smiling faces, and were ambitious to give their statues a naïve expression of happiness. Phidias wanted more. He climbed Olympus and attempted to mingle the human with the immortal. Can't you see that he spread a spiritual aurora prodigiously over his metopes?

"His works are enlightened by intelligence. His adolescents and virgins appear to be conscious of the marvels that a generous soul inhabiting a beautiful body is capable of accomplishing. His Minerva is grave because, being conscious and nurturing beautiful thoughts, she wants to show the harmony that exists between her soul and her body and to become not only the plastic center, but also the moral ideal, of the universe."

"I think I understand what you're saying," replied Phaedo. "According to you, the ideal of our epoch ought to be the ideal that I once heard you assign to music and wisdom, the equilibrium of the beautiful and the good, the radiant alliance of physical perfection with moral grandeur. I'm beginning to grasp your thinking. And as usual, you're winning me over and becoming familiar to me. You believe, then, that it's Phidias who concentrates within him the consciousness of the new era, and will testify for us before the future. Isn't that your opinion?"

But Socrates was slow to respond, gazing in the direction of the Fountain with Nine Jets, which rose up in the middle of the road.

"Can you see over there," he said, finally, "an old man coming toward us surrounded by a cloud of dust. One might think that Boreas, who appears to be waking up and blowing violently, is attempting to take possession of him, like a new

Orithyia. Either I'm much mistaken or that old man is wearing the robe of a strategus. He's just passed the statue of Achelous and his daughters."

When the man had come closer, he went on: "Yes, it's one of the old strategi who were in command during the expedition to Samos. I recognize him. His name is Sophocles.

"Is he the one who once gave *Antigone* to the choregi?"

"That's right," replied Socrates. "We can go to met him. I know him, and his company is agreeable."

When they reached him, Socrates invited him to sit down with them near the Fountain.

From there, they could see the tranquil fields of asphodel whose rosy waves flowed all the way to the plain of Phalera. The sea seemed scarcely separate from the sky, so blue was the atmosphere and so resplendent were the horizons with an even light.

"Have you come from the Agora, Sophocles?" Socrates asked the old man.

"I've come from further away," the latter replied. "I've come from my house in Colonna. I don't know why all the Athenians don't go to shelter in those arbors of vines and ivy, where I can see the daylight and which the voice of the nightingale animates. The air of Colonna is so mild that one might think that Bacchus and his Nymphs stroll there every year. You know where I live, Socrates. The perennially murmuring waves of the Cephise meander there, fecundating the dear earth. And my little house, escorted by saffron and narcissi, is crowned by beautiful gilded grapes, in which celestial dew scintillates."

"I believe that the fruit of the vine of which you speak is also dear to Bacchus," said Socrates. Ion was telling us recently about the cheerful days that you spent in Samos when the battles left you a respite. The charm of Ionia is vivacious in Samos and amour blows over the shore of those fortunate isles. Ion was telling us in particular about your feasts and the joyful conversation that animated them."

Sophocles smiled in remembering the distant expeditions. Beautiful recollections caressed his memory.

"Yes," he said, "there were happy days and cheerful conversations."

"You see, Phaedo," said Socrates, addressing his disciple, "that the Athenians have always had an appetite for fine things. But tell us, Sophocles, what subject is haunting your mind at the moment, and what new tragedy is about to surge from your mind, as perfect and serene as Minerva's."

"The misfortunes of Oedipus are still summoning my verses and moving my thoughts. I would like to show Oedipus growing by force of dolor, to the extent of reaching and equaling the Olympians. That man marked by fatality, who unwittingly accomplished so many crimes, seems to me to be superhuman and sacred by virtue of the very extent of his misfortune. The mysterious links between dolor and wisdom: that, in sum, is the subject of the tragedy that I'm planning. I've already composed the choruses, but certain details still escape me..."

Socrates gazed at the poet and his eyes were veiled by emotion.

"Sophocles," he asked, finally, "can you tell us what the origin of tragedy was, in truth? It's a creation that no people prior to the Greeks knew. Its nature is troubling. Sad, it transports us beyond joy. Showing us crimes and dolors, it nevertheless purifies us and procures us noble emotions that our ancestors did not experience."

"It's by virtue of a miracle that tragedy has been revealed to the world," Sophocles replied, gravely. "Aeschylus affirmed that to me before dying. His story remains engraved in my memory."

"You can repeat it to us, then," said Phaedo, sitting down at Sophocles' feet, and embracing his knees,

"We ask you that as suppliants," said Socrates, with a smile, indicating his disciple's attitude.

Sophocles did not reply for a moment, his gaze lost in the direction of the silvery sea. His features, framed in the whiteness of abundant hair, respired a mild serenity. Then, in a sonorous and calm voice, he commenced his story.

"It was the spring day on which the Athenians vanquished the barbarians at Salamis.[8] During the previous night, taking refuge in their frail boats, they had followed from the sea the conflagration that consumed their houses and triumphed disastrously on the rock sacred to Minerva. They saw themselves wandering henceforth, with no fatherland and no hearths, deprived of their gods, prey to the inconstant Mediterranean. And yet, they were proud and felt light, for, deprived of everything, they had discovered in adversity the divine significance of Liberty, of which no other people before them had had the notion.

"Thus intoxicated by noble thoughts, they were determined to be victorious; and when, the following day, the fleet of Persian ships appeared before them, as infinite as an invading forest, the Athenians experienced no distress. Their blue eyes believed that they could see the shades of the ancient tutelary heroes Ajax and Telamon advancing resplendently to aid them from the shore of Aegina. And coming all the way from the terrain of Eleusis, aureoled by a distant light, they heard the sacred chorus of the god Iacchus, suing by the ancestors, who also came running to mingle their wild and tumultuous souls in the combat.

---

[8] The battle fought at sea between Athens and the island of Salamis by the outnumbered forces of the allied Greek city states, commanded by Themistocles, against the Persian forces of Xerxes, in 480 B.C., followed the opposition mounted by an even smaller Greek contingent that had interrupted the advance of Xerxes invading army at Thermopylae. Unable to maneuver effectively in the narrow strait, the Persians were decisively defeated at Salamis and Xerxes was forced to retreat, clearing the way for the subsequent development of Ancient Greek culture and thus making a vast difference to the history of the western world.

"Full of courage henceforth, proud of their ancient glory, the Athenians no longer held back. The oarsmen made the sea a vast frisson of foam, and the sacred paean, the harmonious battle-song, responded to the savage cries of Asia. 'Forward, sons of Greece,' said the paean, 'liberate the children, liberate the wives, take back the temples, save the tombs of the ancestors.'

"Then the sun rose, bronze truck bronze, the long bucklers opposed the winged arrows, and blood mingled its horrible color with the azure of the Bay of Salamis.

"The trireme that was carrying the poet Aeschylus, which his brother Amenias commanded, was the first to encounter a Phoenician ship and break it. The Athenian Lycomedes and the Naxian Democritus continued the combat. Prows plunged like darts into the curved flanks of the Persian vessels, oars broke, the sea mingled with men.

"Bows were seen quivering, and lances striking rapidly, while the reflection of blades was extinguished in blood, axes hesitated, blinded, and arrows disappeared into profound wounds.

"The intoxication of death soon confounded the vermilion prows of Athenian triremes and the somber Carian ships. The archers of Babylon, soldiers of Cilicia, whom the vermilion rendered sinister, and dark-complexioned Egyptians, fraternized in death with the hoplites of Greece. Agile and light, furrowing the water and the blood, Themistocles' trireme sowed victory everywhere.

"The sun, in its decline, was already reddening the foaming sea when Aristides, taking Psytalia, the last refuge of the Persians, put an end to the Dionysiac fury of the melee over which Mars and the Fates were hovering. And in the first anguish of the evening, Xerxes, superbly seated on his throne, posed on the summit of the promontory, saw a fleet that was fleeing, humiliated, which was his own.

"The Athenian bandaged their wounds and offered sacrifices to Jupiter the liberator. Now they watched the enemy flee far from Attica, and hasty and opulent Asia disappear in confusion and shame. The Bay of Phalera was no longer bristling with barbarian masts, and the Acropolis became once again the inviolate sanctuary of Pallas. Invoking the gods, the Athenians then took the road of return..."

Sophocles paused momentarily, and then went on:

"I too remember that day! With the other children, returned from exile, we were waiting for the Victorious. The air of Attica had an unfamiliar lightness, which the flame of liberty rendered as intoxicating as wine. As they approached the city that they had quit without hope, our warriors were weeping with joy.

"I followed them when they went up the sacred rock in order to kiss the maternal ground. While the sun spread gold over the somber olive groves, they sang, imitating the cicadas. I was handsome then, and Themistocles chose me and ordered me to dance before everyone, in order that victory would be crowned by beauty.

"Since then, I have often experienced the intoxication of success and have seen Athens acclaim me many times in the theater of Bacchus, but no emotion can compare with the triumph of that morning when, in dancing, I delighted the eyes of the Victorious by means of the cadenced movements of my naked body.

"And it was on that same evening of triumph that the miracle of the birth of Tragedy was accomplished, crowning the victory. Aeschylus, the victorious soldier of Salamis, returned after the rejoicing to Eleusis, his native soil. He experienced, he said, a kind of powerful intoxication, and his breast was swollen by the generous exaltation that floated over Athens. The liberty and courage that had germinated in that elect city inflamed him. The very soul of the homeland seemed to acquire consciousness within him, desirous of being transmuted into poetry.

"And in the middle of that night, in his sleep, Aeschylus saw Dionysus, the god of Eleusis, crowned with grapes, advancing on a chariot ornamented with all the gifts of renewal and drawn by lions and panthers. The god had a visage full of shadow, but his body was resplendent with an ardent beauty.

"He approached the poet, smiling, leaned toward him and put a kiss like a divine burn on his forehead. Then, penetrated by a sacred and supernatural light, Aeschylus conceived the idea of evoking on the stage, by means of a grandiose and harmonious dialogue, the disarray of the Mede and the triumph of the battle of Salamis. And he wrote *The Persians*.

"Thus, the veritable and, so to speak, primal tragedy, was born of the miraculous kiss that Dionysus placed on the forehead of the warrior, who felt the triumphant and exalted heart of his homeland beating in his breast. It was like the crown of merit that descended to circle the marmoreal head of victorious Athens..."

Sophocles fell silent.

A white cloud, obscuring the bright light of the sun, rendered the air more caressant, and the tranquility of things milder. On the island of Aegina a crimson-tinted aureole with opalescent fringes appeared, as if composed of the soul of the roses that were born in abundance on its plains. The purity of the air was such that it was possible to distinguish, on that distant soil, the temple of Minerva glistening with gold and marble.

"That is a unique conception!" said Socrates, in an emotional voice. And, addressing Sophocles: "That Tragedy, scarcely known to Phyrinicus,[9] which Dionysus revealed truly

---

[9] Phrynicus, whose work is only known via a few fragments, is recorded as the winner a drama contest in 511 B.C. and often cited as the originator of the tradition of Tragedy, in his play *The Sack of Miletus*. In 476 B.C. he celebrated the defeat of Xerxes at Salamis in *The Phoenician Women*, which Themistocles financed as a choregos. Contrary to the account rendered here, Aeschylus' *The Persians* is recorded as first having been performed in 472 B.C. and was allegedly modeled on *The Phoenician Women*. The titles of seven other plays by Phrynicus are recorded, and he is said, under the influence of

to Aeschylus, you have made into a more moral and more human work, and you have enriched it with unknown accents. And I see in that a creation that might perhaps survive in duration the marbles of Phidias, and which will be capable of recounting the glory of Athens, better that any other superb edifice, when our children's children are no more."

After a pause, he went on: "Sophocles, if you do not want me, quoting from memory, to alter the sublime verses in which Antigone sings the unwritten and imprescriptible laws, recite us a few strophes of your new Oedipus."

"I have to go to the agora," said Sophocles, without hiding the pleasure that Socrates' eulogy provoked in his heart. However, I'll recite a few lines on the death of Oedipus, which are prowling in my head and which mark the conclusion of my tragedy:

"...*A subterranean thunder was heard, and at that noise, which chilled them with fear, Antigone and Ismene fell at their father's knees, weeping, groaning and striking their breasts incessantly. He, meanwhile, had enveloped them in his arms and said to them: 'My children, it is finished. From this day forward, you no longer have a father; nothing of him any longer remains to you.' For a long time he held them in his embrace, weeping and sobbing together; in the end, fatigued by their dolor, their plaints died away, and there was no longer anything but a great silence. Suddenly, a voice burst forth, the terrible sound of which made the hair stand on end. That divine voice summoned Oedipus unrelentingly: 'Oedipus Oedipus,' it cried, 'why this delay? You are awaited...'"*

For a long time, Sophocles recited sublime lines in that fashion, and the Attic air was still quivering under those tones when he stood up.

"By Jupiter," Socrates said to him, "the gods must have been present at your birth in order to heap you with such gifts, and I can call you fortunate without hesitation."

―――――――――――――――――――――――――――

his mentor Thespis, to have initiated the tradition of theatrical dialogue by separating an actor from the chorus.

And while the tragedian drew away, addressing Phaedo, Socrates went on:

"See him fading way in the sunset. Yes, look at him well. The gods are forming a cortege for him! It might be that the ideal of Athens, which we were attempting to specify just now, will be realized by him. That harmony of the soul and the body, that divine measure in joy and in sadness, Sophocles eternalizes, as well as Phidias, but no longer attributing it to the divinities of Olympus, like the sculptor, but to earthly humans. And he adds thereby to liberty and ease of human thought, calm in the face of adversity, the wisdom in dolor and the domination of the passions that are the very substance of the Greek soul.

"There he goes, disappearing, with his white tunic agitated by the Phalerian breeze. He is immortal! The verses of Homer, magnifying the power of Art, come irresistibly to my lips: *As soon as you had tasted divine nourishment, Phoebus, golden loincloths could to longer retain your impetuosity, cords no longer stopped you and all your swaddling clothes were torn apart... Suddenly, the brilliant Apollo said to the goddesses: 'Give me a harmonious lyre and I shall henceforth reveal to men the certain oracles of Jupiter...'*"

And as they got to their feet in order to depart in their turn, Socrates added: "Man immolating himself, accepting dolor, dominating the passions, equaling the gods by means of virtue or the force of proofs, that, I believe, is the substance of the *Prometheus* of Aeschylus and the *Oedipus* of which Sophocles has just given us an idea. It is the very substance of tragedy. And I think that the new morality of goodness and renunciation that is forming us and kneading us with its hands us so great that it will be capable in future of giving birth to a new religion...

"But the air is freshening. Let us go up to the Acropolis in order to watch from there the sun extinguishing its gold over Saronica..."

II. Theodota

When Critias stopped speaking, Socrates went to look for his sandals, which he only wore rarely and exceptionally. He put them on.

"Since you say that the beauty of Theodota is indescribable, it is necessary to go see it," he said. "Only the eyes can enlighten us with regard to what words cannot express.[10]

As he went out, escorted by his disciples, he took the route that passed through the Ceramicus.

"I would like to take the tanner and shoemaker Simon with us," he explained. "I hold him in high esteem. Abandoning himself to a monotonous métier, he nurtures just thoughts in the silence of his shop, which the even fall of the hammer n the leather accommodates to the laws of harmony. He has written a treatise on Amity and I believe him to be an excellent appreciator of beautiful things."

And after having saluted his friend, the armorer Pistias, who was repairing and adjusting an old Persian bow, the unusual length of which recalled the glorious days of Plataea or Salamis, Socrates approached Simon.

The shoemaker was sitting in front of his workshop, against the door of a low building that contained his shop. His beard was covering a red leather sandal ornamented by long laces, which he was holding between his hands.

"Winter is easing, Socrates," Simon said, smiling at his friend from a distance with an amiable expression. The day is mild and the air coming from Olympus has lost its bite."

"I've come to procure you a happy afternoon and to instruct you in your métier," said Socrates, drawing nearer.

"How will you do that, Socrates?"

---

[10] The name of Theodota of Elis was preserved by Xenophon as that of a courtesan frequented by Socrates, but nothing more is known about her.

"By Jupiter! Nothing is easier: by showing you a beautiful woman! Perhaps you've heard mention of Theodota who, recently arrived from Sicily, her homeland, is already inflaming Athens. We're going to see her. If you accompany us you'll obtain a double profit from it. As a philosopher and a shoemaker you pay tribute to beauty, as much because of your craft, which necessitates gracious forms, as the tendencies of your thoughts. Let go of that sandal you're holding in your hands like a cherished nursling, then, and come with us."

Meekly, Simon rose to his feet, took off his apron, and walked with them.

They went around the Acropolis, passing before the grotto of Pan.

"Since, according to all probability, we'll soon be judging a lovely woman, let us sharpen our eyes on a beautiful landscape," said Socrates, without stopping. "Nothing refines the taste better and renders the serenity of thought more perfect."

The sun was scarcely declining, and the daylight still retained a brilliant and pure youth. The air was limpid and appeared to be resonating like crystal under the vibration of the light. The mountains stood out clearly, and one might have thought that their line were drawing together in order to embrace blue Saronica more tightly.

There was, above all, a harmonious correspondence between the curves of the rocks, the slopes of the hills, and the meanders of the coves and bays. The landscape, disengaged from all vegetation, offered itself so perfectly in its divine nudity, that it could only be separated by the savant and rhythmic creations of man. The Parthenon on its rock, the smiling statues on the banks of the Ilissus and the sculpted fountains seemed akin to a natural florescence of Pentelic marble, a superb vegetation produced by the sun and the Attic soil. And all of it was animated by the hum of beehives, by the bleating of flocks wandering between the olive groves, and the clear laughter of young women drawing water for the Fountain of Nine Jets.

A joy of gods and children was mingled with the clarity of the day.

"Don't you think," said Socrates, "that Bacchus is confused with the son of Latona and that the fruit of the vine has yielded its virtue to the light? The air is as intoxicating today as old Samos wine, and fills the lungs with an orgiastic joy. As there is scarcely any vegetation in Attica, the new season is flourishing, impetuous and sacred, in the very hearts of men. But let us press on, in order to see Theodota sooner."

When they went into the courtesan's house, they found her posing for the painter Parrhasius, who wanted to lend her face and breasts to Venus, whom he was depicting appeasing the anger of Mars.

In order to resemble the goddess more closely, Theodota was wearing a diaphanous linen tunic that, while designing the lines of her body, made a charming mystery of her flesh and gave her skin the clarity and softness of a dawn over Hymetta. Only the breasts, in emerging from it, enclosed in their extended curves, all the joyous opulence of fecundity. That naked and perfect flesh was so radiant that it only allowed the severe beauty of the face to appear through a white aureole. Thus, the sight of Theodota enveloped the newcomers in the voluptuous and ample waves of a soft harmony.

Socrates, marveling, began to recite the Homeric hymn to Venus Anadyomene: "*The Hours with the golden thigh-bands welcomed with delight the one who gave birth among the gods to sweet desire. Covering her with immortal vestments, they placed on her head a resplendent diadem, attached flowers sculpted in precious metal to her ears, and ornamented her neck and breast with necklaces that they wore themselves when they mingled, in their father's palace, with the gracious choirs of divinities. Having completed her adornment thus, they took her among the Immortals, who saluted her and extended their hands to her, each desiring to take her for a spouse and draw her into his bed, so struck were they by the beauty of the Cytherean with violets in her hair.*"

And while Theodota smiled, very flattered, Socrates turned to Parrhasius and said to him:

"If it is true, as we agreed the other day, that painting does not only have the aim of imitating by means of colors, hollows and protrusions, light and darkness, softness and hardness, but also of expressing the passions and the movements of the soul, this is a marvelous model for you; for Theodota, such as I am contemplating her at this moment, is not limiting herself only to offering us the beauty of Venus; she also possesses the expression, and Laughter and Desires, admirably coupled, are nested in her body. You can consider yourself fortunate, Parrhasius. Apart from the figure respiring life and desire that Polygnotus painted on the wall of the Poecile, immortalizing the features of his lover Elpinice, I do not know any painting more expressive than the one you are in the process of finishing."

While Parrhasius picked up his brushes and lecyths and got ready to leave, Socrates addressed his companions.

"Do you think it necessary for us to thank Theodota for having allowed us to enjoy her beauty, or is it rather her who ought to be grateful for our admiration. I agree that she is gaining nothing from our commerce but eulogies, but we shall spread them far and wide, and she will surely profit from them. As for us, bitten in the heart by her perfection, we shall take away the desire to caress that at which we have only been able to gaze. In that fashion we shall be her slave and she our sovereign.

"By Jupiter!" replied Theodota, laughing, "is it necessary, then to render you thanks after having offered you the spectacle of my body?"

Already she was consulting her large ivory mirror. Her maidservants surrounded her, amicable and agile, presenting her with her garments, her jewelry and her golden clasps. Over her tunic she put on a crimson mantle bordered with white embroidery, and on her head she placed a circle of gold starred with hematite.

"You are rich, Theodota," Socrates said to her, humbly, seeing her ornament herself so superbly. "Do you own land?"

"None."

"Do you possess houses, then?"

"I don't even have a house of my own."

"She has slaves that work for her in the mines," Socrates said, with conviction, turning to his companions.

"I have no slaves, Socrates," Theodota replied, again.

"Where, then, do you find what you need in order to live so abundantly?"

"Friends, who come to me and wish me well, furnish what is necessary to me."

"By Juno, Theodota, you have something better than slaves and flocks! But how, then, do you attract that prey? Do you wait for the friends to come to you, or do you employ some artifice in order to attract them?"

"How do you expect me attract them by artifice, Socrates?"

"I thought that you would act in that as one does for any other game. Spiders employ ruses to catch flies, and hunters to catch hares."

"But what means can I use to hunt friends?" asked Theodota, coming to sit down next to Socrates, feline and laughing, on the low bed.

"Instead of the dogs that flush out hares, why should you not have someone who sniffs out appreciators of beauty, in order to lead them into your nets?"

"My nets? What nets do I have then, friend?"

"One alone, but the most inextricable: your body; and in the body, a soul that initiates you so effectively in the charms of your gaze, and educates you in the seduction of words, and teaches you to give a good welcome to the man who seeks you out, to send away the one you disdain, to visit a proven friend courteously and to be grateful for the cares that are rendered to you. For I cannot doubt that you inspire in your lovers as much benevolence as tenderness; your words certainly charm them no less than your gaze."

"By Jupiter!" said Theodota, looking at Socrates. "I am not conscious of any of those means."

"However, Theodota, you understand that it is not indifferent to act in harmony with the character of lovers, since it is not by force that one keeps them, but by the gentle attraction of pleasure and contentment."

"That's true," murmured the courtesan, thoughtfully.

"It's necessary, then, that you appear generous with them, giving them more than you receive, consenting, when they are in need, to share with them what you have and to seek to attach them to you solidly, rather than inspiring a caprice in them. And as the contrary of desire is satiety, it is necessary, too, that you know how to refuse yourself as well as to give yourself, sharpening appetites as well as fulfilling them, and above all, to accord your favors at the most propitious moment. Uncertainty stimulates lust and renders it exquisite, and the pleasure that one obtains with difficulty is the most precious. For that, Theodota, do not hesitate to make a free and voluntary gift of your presence and conversation."

"Well, Socrates," exclaimed Theodota, dazzled, catching hold of his mantle as he got up to leave, "would you like to help me hunt for friends?"

Smiling, he replied: "By Jupiter, I would if you can persuade me to do it."

"By what means can I do that?" asked Theodota, innocently.

"Seek and you will find, if you really have need of me."

"At least come to see me often!"

"Alas, I have other things to do, Theodota, and numerous clients who harass me day and night, some asking me for philters and others for charms and enchantments."

"What, Socrates?" said Theodota, increasingly amazed. "You know how to compose philters, then, like the women of Thessaly?"

"Naturally. Do you not know that Phaedo and Apollodorus never quit me, and that Cebes and Simias come from Thebes expressly to converse with me? I can only attract

97

them in that fashion, be sure of it, by means of philters, and above all with the aid of songbirds that I train to sing erotic verses."

Theodota looked Socrates in the eyes then, and the ugliness of the man seemed pleasant to her. Seriously, she said to him: "Since you don't want to give me a songbird to attract you to me, I'll come to your house, and I hope that you'll receive me."

"Certainly I will, if I do not have another person in my house who is even dearer to me," Socrates replied, gently detaching the courtesan's hand, which was clutching his mantle, and leaving immediately, following his companions.

The sun was setting. Young men clad in white tunics could be seen going toward the banks of the Cephise, followed by their slaves.

"The city is preparing for the Eleusinian mysteries," said Plato, "and it's becoming difficult to move through the streets."

"Let's head toward the gardens of Academus. There, it will be possible to discourse in tranquility," proposed the master.

"I'll return to my shop," said Simon. "Theodota is beautiful, but I wouldn't want to drink passion from her cup, fearful of going as far as drunkenness."

"You're wise, Simon, and prudent," Socrates replied. "Go, and may your sleep be light."

At the entrance to the gardens, Critias and Simias departed, leaving Socrates alone with Plato, who was still very young and had scarcely begun to frequent the master.

At first they walked in silence, but then the ephebe, who appeared to be obsessed by grave thoughts, turned toward Socrates and said: "I'm surprised by your conduct, master. You deliberately go to the home of a courtesan, and you even appear to take pleasure in it. Either I'm much mistaken, or that is in opposition to your irreproachable mores."

"Don't believe anything of the sort," replied the son of Sophroniscus, nonchalantly.

"You'll agree, however," the ephebe went on, "that courtesans are a source of frivolity and disorder, and that we ought to nourish toward them the disdain of Solon, who expelled them from the city."

"He was soon obliged to recall them, Plato. You appear to be forgetting that. But come and sit under this plane tree. The hour is mild and invites repose."

They had passed the venerable olive tree that was the second to grow in Attica and climbed a gentle slope. Socrates sat down with his disciple near a stone Hermes, on a little scarcely mossy hill, where scarce plane trees were nurtured.

The light was colored by vesperal tints. Hymettus seemed to be slowly being consumed by mystic violet flames. An ardent silvery gleam illuminated Salamis, while streaks of crimson cloud, scarcely formed, were wandering slowly, impregnating the Attic sky with an ineffable melancholy.

"Did you notice just now," Socrates began by saying, "the fine subject that Parrhasius took it into his head to paint? Venus, scarcely emerged from the water, appeasing the invincible Mars by the strength of her beauty alone. She dominates the one whom no one can subdue. The elements of discord, the impetuous anger, and the tumultuous spirits that animate the god of war are moderated and ordered by the mere appearance of Cypris. I beg to you see there a perfect symbol of the amorous force that, superior to wisdom and superior to virtue, leads the destinies of the world."

"Does something exist for Socrates that is superior to wisdom, then?"

"I've just told you that there is: beauty and the desire to which it gives birth. For beauty concentrates all gifts within it, as in a divine amphora. It inspires poets, inflames sages, incites men to virtue, engenders sacrifice, and suggests great thoughts and courageous actions. It is the dominatrix. Everything that we can try to find by dint of meditation, all the treasures painfully extracted by study, what we know and what we divine, are rendered tangible and concrete by the appearance of a beautiful woman, of a beautiful body.

"You can be sure, Plato, that the gods are only distinguished from humans by the greater perfection of their forms. And if humans existed as beautiful as the gods, we would accord them for their worship an absolute obedience. That is why our ancestors, in their wisdom, made of Cosmic Venus a goddess born of the sky, a primordial and mysterious divinity. And I repeat that I hold beauty to be the ultimate gift, the sole realization of the ideal on earth."

"But even admitting, Socrates, that beauty has the force that you attribute to it, why should courtesans pretend to it more than other women?"

"They are the sacred emblem of it, as you ought to confess, Plato. But tell me first, what government do you think worthy of free men?"

"I don't understand what connection..."

"Answer my question anyway."

"But by Jupiter, Socrates, it's republican government."

"You're right. Now, you'll grant me that republican government reposes on the equality of all and the uniform distribution of earthly goods, Athens has become the foremost city in Greece because she has been able to make the enjoyment of art, the attribution of justice and the agreeable and redoubtable responsibility of governance, privileges common to all her citizens. Now, since you admit, Plato, that beauty is the ultimate good, why should it remain, without injustice, the property of one person alone and not the indivisible property of all? Are you not revolted by the thought that a beautiful woman, who inspires poets and of whom sculptors make use in order to depict divinity, might remain jealousy locked up in the gynaeceum of a single man, who enjoys it to the detriment of others?

"Think, however, what a concurrence of fortunate circumstances, what a complicity of multiple hazards, the appearance of a beauty as perfect as that of Helen, Aspasia or Theodota presupposes. Nature seems to expend more effort in that than in the formation of a genius. Now, while we are all invited to hear a play by Sophocles and all have the right to enjoy a marble by Phidias or a fresco by Polygnotus, while the verses of Homer and the fables of Aesop are the joy and delight of the entire city, the beauty of Helen must remain the exclusive prerogative of Menelaus and that of Penelope the jealous property of Ulysses! Confess, Plato that that is an inconceivable restriction!"

"However, Socrates, I know grave reasons that oblige us to it."

"I know that," said Socrates. "It is at the price of that great iniquity that we have founded the family. The common enjoyment of beauty would, in fact, have provoked social difficulties the legislators would judge insurmountable. That is why they have instituted virtue and modesty. However, the world has never submitted entirely to the absurd yoke. The exclusive possession of beautiful women, on the contrary, has provoked struggles and devastations in all times, causing hatred and bloodshed, sowing discord and death.

"The beauty of Penelope cost the lives of a host of suitors, and that of Helen scythed down the flower of the elite youth of the Trojans and Greeks. My friend Herodotus, who visited many cities of the Greeks and barbarians, claims justly that a beautiful woman is at the origin of all the wars that have bloodied history. On the other hand, if one goes back to the primitive ages, one sees that men then savored freely and in common all the sublime joys of Venus.

"Moreover, certain nations, less presumptuous than that of the Greeks, still retain the memory of that distant custom. In Babylon, once a year, all the women without exception restore the ancient equality by offering themselves to whomever wants to take them. Thus once a year, out there, beauty becomes public again and appeases all desire.

"Do you not see, now, that it is thanks to courtesans that the order of nature is slightly reestablished? By their sacrifice, they permit other women to remain virtuous and men to support virtue. Prodigal with their beauty, in making it a common prerogative, they become our educators. They accord to all the usufruct of the perfection of forms, and in their sublime forbearance they slake the thirst of avid mouths in the mystic well of sensuality.

"Thus, the métier of courtesans ought to be considered as sacred and beneficent. It can truly serve as an emblem and symbol of Democracy. If Theodota bears the august name of *hetaera*, which means 'companion' and was once attributed to Venus, it is because she represents the goddess on earth and sows sensuality and amour. Each of her kisses is an emanation of the daughter of Uranus, the mother of the Muses.

"Think rather of the ills from which courtesans preserve us, and how we ought to be grateful to them for having chosen that métier. Beautiful as she is, Theodota could have drowned Athens in blood and provoked great rivalries if, like Penelope, she had given evidence of preferences and grim repugnance. But, far from displaying an inhuman virtue, she devotes her body to natural worship. Renewing in her bed every evening the sacrifice of Iphigenia, she saves the city and becomes the sacred fountain of pleasure.

"And certainly, you must understand now, Plato, why our ancestors confounded courtesans with priestesses in making them the allies and the commensals of the divinity."

"If I understand correctly, you are sustaining that courtesans are reestablishing the primitive worship that elevated Venus above all other gods, as the cosmic and universal power, the unique source of all life and all desire."

"That's correct. And you will find it just henceforth to honor courtesans and to wish that the most beautiful women choose that métier. On the other hand, it would be revolting if an ugly woman could pretend to it, for an ugly woman, in becoming a courtesan, would not only be failing in her humble duty to procreate, but simultaneously corrupting the taste of citizens by erecting her body as an altar and believing herself worthy of inspiring amour. Maternity is reserved to virtue; but as for pleasure and sensuality, they are the inappreciable fruits of perfect forms."

Suddenly, a curious question came to Plato's lips.

"Tell me, Socrates, what is amour? It inflames hearts and transforms beings, but no one seems to have fathomed its essence and scrutinized its mystery."

And Socrates replied: "Plato, that sentiment, which you easily inspire by your perfect face and body, cannot be translated into words. Rather seek to experience it. Amour is a natural initiation. It enters the breast like a mysterious arrow. Don't ask me such a question, then, and let me depart. The sun is setting and Xanthippe is waiting for me. Now, as you now, her anger is quick to ignite."

And without wanting to say any more, Socrates threw the flap of his mantle over his shoulder and drew away rapidly, leaving the young man in perplexity.

III. The Bed of Nicareta

The disciple remained under the moving shadow of the plane tree for a few moments longer.

What is this power of amour, then, which enchains people more powerfully than iron and wine, almost equaling in violence the divine virtue of lightning?

That is what the son of Ariston thought; and suddenly, he became anxious, for he recognized that it was not only his mind but his entire troubled being that was interested in that problem.

Plato looked around, and for the first time, he sensed with anguish that spring was triumphing throughout the area, that beings seemed to be awaiting their blossoming, and that nature entire was leading the enthusiastic dance of the Corybantes.

How can I fathom the essence of amour and initiate myself into its mysteries?

He got up and began to march at random, fully absorbed in his thoughts. He scarcely glanced at the women who were going to draw water from the only fountain near the Odeon, the slaves in tunics split down one side who were returning from mills crying burdens on their shoulders, and the ephebes with naked and agile legs who were emerging from the gymnasium clad in short mantles. He only raised his eyes from time to time toward the Attic sky, appeased by light clouds; and the amenable sun that was already touching the western hills above Eleusis poured a kind of gentle clarity into his mind.

Having chanced to engage upon the road that led to the Poecile he arrived in front of the temple of Mars. He was struck by the sight of the image of Minerva associated there with that of the impetuous god. The Attic legend that had given rise to that narrow linkage of the worship of two siblings came to his mind and appeared to him to be a response to the problem that was haunting him.

It was near Athens that the divine warrior, it was said, encountered his austere and immortal sister, who was flying through the luminous ether. His heart was inflamed by a sudden and impetuous desire for her. He then experienced in his body the intoxication of a Maenad, and all decency and all restraint abandoned him. He fell upon Minerva and enlaced her with such violence that, at the abrupt and fearful sidestep of the virgin, his hasty and ardent semen fell on the Attic soil, engendering Erycthoneus.

Plato was struck now by the recognition of the seal of universal desire that marked that legend. A wave of new thoughts invaded him.

Did amour consist of the violent attraction, the primordial appetite of the flesh, the profound need that drives humans to unite, to participate for a few moments in the sacred delirium of renewal?

As he gazed at the verdant hills, all attained by spring, the fields florid with asphodels, and the trees launching upwards young and straight, sucking up new sap, Plato sensed a kind of vague, unlimited and poignant disturbance penetrating his body.

He thought he was communing with nature, labored by desire. His spirit mingled with the spirits of all things. In the question that he had asked himself, it was the entire universe that now appeared to be taking an interest.

Nothing, he thought, can escape the blind need to hurl semen profoundly into the profound mold of generations, to enjoy and to create.

His youth, his long chastity and his ignorance of women now enfevered his thought, and rendered it sharp and vehement.

The best way to fathom amour would be to know sensuality.

105

Those words suddenly emerged in his mind, so precise and so clear that he thought someone had murmured them in his ear, or that his own daemon had dictated them to him.

To love, know desire!

And a great tenderness enveloped his soul as he approached the Poecile.

There, the silence seemed animated by the hum of insects, and the palpitation of their myriad iridescent wings.

The rare flowers were bursting forth all around, the richness of the new sap was melting the bark of the trees, and greener and more tender grass was enlacing the bases of the columns.

The inexhaustible thirst to possess and be extinguished, Plato thought, *is so imperious, so powerful, that the immortals themselves abandon themselves to it. The inflamed breath of desire reaches Olympus. Jupiter, the supreme god, is also the supreme lover, taking by turns the aspect of humans and birds, animals and natural forces, in order better to love and confound himself with the beloved. A rain of gold, a swan with a muscular neck, a bellowing bull, he exhausts the forms of enjoyment and participates in a thousand varied and delectable fashions in the universal and multiple desire.*

The legends of gods and heroes who, pierced by the mysterious spur, desired to the point of death, revived in the young man's thoughts.

Even the seven unparalleled men who are celebrated under the name of the seven sages could not escape the implacable law, he said to himself. *Did not the grave Periander forget the harmonies of the celestial spheres and the meditation of eternity, one day in Epidaurus when he saw the beautiful Melissa, more troubling in her light diaphanous tunic than if she were naked, distributing wine and smiles to her father's workmen?*

Desire now took on a symbolic force in the eyes of the adolescent. He saw it leading the universe, moving the stars, agitating the gods themselves and bringing together on a bed the hostile flesh of humans. And when he raised his eyes to the wall of the Poecile that sheltered him, the sight of the immense painting of the capture of Troy, which Polygnotus had traced there, gave a new force to his ideas; for in that grandiose and grave composition, in which one saw the final woes that the infidelity of the Tyndaride had provoked, it was once again desire that triumphed, ravaging equally the victors and the vanquished, uniting lust and death.

Near the cadavers of the Trojans, which Medusa, the daughter of Priam, was washing with lustral water, under the ruins of the devastated city, the most beautiful and the most exquisite figure was that of Cassandra, whom Ajax had just violated in the temple of Minerva. The prophetess had in her visage the illumination of pleasure, mingled with a grim and shameful irritation. Polygnotus, who excelled at magnifying and symbolizing the movements of passion, had imprinted such a great shiver into that indignant body, and such an intense and ardent vibration to that altered physiognomy, that one believed that one could see, beneath the young woman's garments, the lacerating wound that the passion of Ajax had made, and also the victorious frisson that had buckled her beneath the empire of the powerful embrace.

Why, then, would the amour of humans differ from universal amour, and why would it draw its source elsewhere than from carnal and imperious appetite? Would the ancestors have made amour into a frightful malady, a devastating force, if that passion resided anywhere other than in the senses and the appetites? It is the fury to embrace and possess that drives Phaedra to seize the body of Hippolytus between her arms and satisfy her ardor thereupon, and it is the impatient flame of the blood again that enfevers and burns Byblis for her brother, and which leads the incestuous Myrrha, fainting, to the paternal couch.

The sky was now covered by a tender weave of crimson clouds, and the silver of the sea was deadening in a great frisson of vesperal wind. And Plato saw in his mind's eye the mysterious powers of the world and mortal beings confounded under the same necessities. Believing that he had found what

107

he sought, he was rising to his feet in order to go when, near-by, in the nascent shadow, a voice called him by his name.

He turned round and saw an old man of noble physiognomy who was buckling meekly under the weight of the years. Plato went toward him swiftly, for he had recognized Philotas, the husband of his cousin Nicareta.

"Be welcome, Philotas," he said to him. "I know that thanks to the immortal Pericles, who once attracted into our harbor the wealth and products of all our allies, your commerce in Piraeus is flourishing. Is Nicareta well?"

"Your cousin's health is excellent, Plato," Philotas replied, mildly. "But accompany me on the road to the Pnyx. The evening is fine and, glad to see you, I also have something to tell you."

"Willingly, Philotas."

"Listen, young man," the old man went on, after having taken a few steps in silence. "Via your mother Perictione you are my wife's closest relative. And you are also one of our friends. I know your valor and our prudence and, although you have abandoned your father's métier, preferring to follow the sophists, I honor you and hold you in esteem. Nor am I scornful of your resolution to remain poor. Your words, when they are not too ironic or bizarre, respire a precision that satisfies me."

Plato made no reply, but gazed benevolently at his companion He was afflicted by the multiple wrinkles that insulted the face of that honest man, and the impression of a slightly limited rectitude that seemed to shrink him.

"I am therefore coming to you without dread," Philotas went on, "to invite you to fulfill a duty that the laws and the will of the ancestors render sacred and imperious, You know that your uncle, old Charmides, who was my friend and the companion of my first voyages to Egypt, wanted when he was dying to unite me with your cousin. The beauty and the grave modesty of Nicareta did not give me the strength to refuse or to consider my advanced age.

"You remember how splendid and joyful the wedding was! I have tried to render Nicareta happy and I have succeeded. I have furnished and equipped a sumptuous dwelling for her and when, holding the torch, you escorted us there with the other young relatives on the chariot drawn by mules, your cousin could have believed that she was entering the house of the rich Callias, so much did everything respire wealth.

"In accordance with the Athenian custom I had set up two beds in the nuptial chamber in order that the young woman would not be frightened and would not despair in only seeing one. But I must confess to you that I could not honor her bed, and that Nicareta still remains in her white virginal robe. My humiliation, however, has become known outside, for Nicareta is innocent and modest. She would never have dreamed of invoking the old law of Solon that obliged a husband to visit the conjugal couch three times a month.

"Unfortunately, she is an heiress, and ought to have children. That is why the family assembly and the members of the tribe have ordered me either to give my wife, in accordance with the ancient custom, the right to invite her nearest relative into the conjugal bed, or to separate myself from her entirely and to return her dowry. You can imagine my shame and my dolor, Plato! I cannot think for a moment of separating from Nicareta of my own free will. She doesn't want that either. And since you're her nearest relative, I've come to ask you whether you will come to share her bed and help us to have children.

"I'm not unaware that another, more self-interested than you, would refuse. For if you refuse and I have no children, Athenian law permits you to take possession by right of Nicareta's hand and fortune without my really being able to oppose it. But you wouldn't want, Plato, to give me so much chagrin, knowing that I love my wife tenderly and that she also, in her innocence, honors me like a father."

Philotas stopped, anxious, waiting Plato's reply. But the latter remained silent. However, that proposition, so ordinary, so much in conformity with Athenian custom, had caused him a movement of agreeable, almost joyful surprise, which he tried in vain to suppress, judging it contrary to the habitual gravity of his thought.

That evening, fully ripe for amour, he had collected the troubling seeds that spring was sowing in the air. His soul was sighing for the mysterious and unknown passion. And he believed now that it was Venus herself who, wanting to initiate him to sensuality, and sparing him a vulgar union, was offering him this young woman, this virgin who was appealing for his caresses. He had asked heaven and earth for a response regarding the nature of amour, and now Destiny was taking charge of introducing him into the sanctuary of sensuality, and presenting him with pleasure as a duty and an obligation.

Suppressing the tumult of his heart, imposing silence on his excessively keen desire, he said to the old man:

"You know, Philotas, that my life has thus far been in conformity with the traditions. I believe that the salvation of the city depends on it. As I am not yet married and am thus escaping the obligation to give children to the fatherland, I am accomplishing a double duty in ceding to the will of my cousin, and to yours. We have courtesans for our pleasures and wives for the imperious necessity of producing children. And if it is permissible for us to satisfy our own whims by paying hetaerae, Solon obliges us in his wisdom also to give the tender joy of efficacious cresses to our wives. Banish all anxiety from your thoughts. I would be incapable of nurturing any malevolent design upon the hand and fortune of Nicareta. Be sure, on the contrary, that I will strive to establish peace and contentment in your heart."

The old man approached and put his arms around the ephebe's neck as a sign of gratitude.

They were now headed, through the invading darkness, toward the tomb of the Amazon Antiope, where one emerged in order to go to Piraeus. There they mounted two donkeys and set forth along the Phalerian road, which led to Mounichia. When they arrived at Philotas' house, after an hour of travel, Nicareta appeared before them, in the soft light

110

of the torch illuminating the threshold. She darted a tender glance at her cousin with blushing.

She was not beautiful, and Plato knew that she was a little vulgar and limited, but he only saw her youth, her becoming smile and the promises hidden within it.

"Be welcome, Plato," said Nicareta. "For a long time we have desired to invite you to share Philotas' dinner, giving me the joy of serving you."

"My joy in seeing you is great, Nicareta," Plato replied. "Since your marriage, when, in accordance with Athenian custom, it was finally permissible for me to know you, my amity for you has remained strong. I always sought opportunities to encounter you."

Nicareta lowered her eyes and Plato remembered with tenderness the pleasant Athenian celebration where, alongside his uncle Charmides, he had brandished the hymeneal torch. Having arrived at Philotas' door, along with the other young people, he had simulated a struggle against the groom's parry, pretending to resist the forced abduction of the bride, in accordance with Athenian custom. It was at that moment that he had touched his cousin's body, holding her in his arms while the laughing Philotas attempted to draw her away, and the latter's elder brother, bearing the urn full of water from the Callirrhoe spring, awaited the new mistress of the house in order to purify her and initiate her into the cult of the tribe that she was entering.

All those memories flooded his mind and charmed him. It was with some disturbance that he sat down at the table. Breaking the bread and eating distractedly, he sensed a great pleasure in being served by his cousin, who poured wine for him and offered him the dishes.

She went out momentarily in order to bring the basket of fruits. Then Philotas turned to the young man.

"You will have to be careful of her modesty and her inexperience, Plato," he said to him. "Nicareta is ready to welcome you, since you are her relative, but she feels anxious and fearful, as before the unknown."

111

When the young woman returned, Philotas addressed her: "Plato consents to what we desire of him. He will not cross the threshold of our house to leave until morning. Obey him like a servant full of good will, and be grateful for the happiness that he will give you."

After the dinner, he conducted them to the obscure couch, and then withdrew into the men's apartment.

Plato experienced a moment of embarrassment, as if he were about to penetrate into the adyton where the mysteries are celebrated. The presence of that woman, whose soul and thought were unknown to him and who, after a few moments, would abandon herself to him, threw him into profound meditations. He saw himself on the threshold of the future, ready to make the hereditary gesture, the obscure and redoubtable act that perpetuates life via a frisson.

Then he took Nicareta by the hand, gently. Kissed her and said to her: "You consent, then friend that I enter the bed with you and that I enclose you in my arms like a husband?"

She was unable to respond and, agitated by fear, she extracted herself from his grip and took a few awkward steps toward the bed. Plato thought that she was rejecting him, and such was his own disarray that he stopped, fearful that the precipitate palpitations of his heart might make him totter. He recovered his courage quickly, however. Guided by the dim light that filtered through the window, he distinguished Nicareta, who was huddled in the bed, motionless, waiting for him. "You don't want me, then, Nicareta," he murmured to her with a mild reproach in his voice. "I have to depart humiliated, in spite of your husband's plea and in spite of my own desire?"

But he felt two arms that closed around his neck, and on leaning forward he discovered that the violence with which the female breast was heaving equaled his own. Nicareta seemed like a frightened bird. Enlaced with him, she now seemed avid for that embrace. It was Nature that was guiding her, and later, he recognized that blind instinct was guiding his own body, bringing it closer to the woman, and rendering his hands adroit.

In spite of the obscurity he distinguished clearly that Nicareta's first movement, under the caress, was one of recoil, and that the pleasure he sensed and that he gave was violent and tumultuous, participating in struggle, and a little in hatred: a pleasure that was akin to anguish and destruction. Meanwhile, sensuality inundated him, sharply, and he judged that only wine imprinted on men in orgiastic festivals, in the midst of dancing, a fury similar to that of kisses.

But when he finally detached himself from Nicareta's body, he found himself so fallen and saw her so bestial under the as-yet-unappeased spur of pleasure, so discordant with him in sensations, that a violent disgust gripped him, a sad disintoxication, a prostration of his entire being.

Animality, repressed for so many years by study and reflection, had triumphed momentarily over his body. The calm that Socrates praised so highly in him, the harmonious order of his being, was broken. Under the degrading empire of pleasure, obscure sentiments had emerged from the depths of his being, of which he had previously been unaware.

That woman now appeared to him as a stranger, likes a vanquished enemy. Her body no longer awakened any desire in him and he saw nothing but the mediocrity of her features, her nudity weighed down by sleep, which seemed to him to be sad and debasing. Gazing at her with a hostile attention, he noticed that her hips did not taper splendidly, in accordance with the lines of a slender amphora, and that near her navel there were slight creases that spoiled the luminous whiteness of her flesh.

I have nothing in common with this woman. Why am I in this bed?

Experiencing repugnance toward himself, ashamed on his previous delirium, Plato recognized that the pleasure was too close to its own disappointment. The fruit of sensuality was that of death. The amour that was praised as the organizer of the world, the supreme music, could only reside the demented movements, full of thirst and violence, of two bodies that seemed prey to the Furies.

And, unable to sleep or to tolerate Nicareta's slumber, he remained meditative and revolted until morning. Then he withdrew, almost furtively, at the moment when the Pleiades were disappearing.

The pure freshness of the dawn was an appeasement, and he returned to Athens at a rapid pace.

IV. The Secret of Sthenelais

Sexual intercourse is nothing but the animal gesture of amour, its fashion of depriving it of wings. It belongs to Venus Pandemos, while the veritable amour resides in the gaze of Venus Urania.

Thus thought Plato when he arrived home, rested and light, after the morning bath.

He had avoided all company and, alone at his window, he followed during the morning the play of the light on the summit of Hymettus at dawn, black and then gilded, and subsequently brightened by a rosy tint, and clad at midday in sparkling violet. While admiring that, Plato also lent his attention to the thoughts that were born in the depths of his consciousness.

Having been mingled in a bed with a woman, the scales had fallen from his eyes and the nature of pleasure appeared to him. The awakening of instinct had veiled the truth from him momentarily and had caused him to enter into the common illusion that bears people toward enjoyment as if it were the goal of life. But now, Plato knew that it was nothing but a fit of dementia, an impulsion of sovereign hunger, blinding men and dominating them.

As for amour, the divine flower of the soul, as the poets had praised it, one ought to place it outside desire, since its end was nothing but disappointment, and its aftertaste nothing but bitterness.

The proof, Plato said to himself, *that the flesh is foreign to amour is that the possession of Nicareta has increased instead of satisfying my thirst to know that sentiment. After having sampled intercourse, my curiosity, my ignorance of amour, remains the same.*

Shaken by contrary thoughts, Plato went out when the heat eased, wanting to wander and to think again. After having passed through the Agora he stopped outside Simon's shop and approached the shoemaker.

"Tell me, Simon," he said, distracted and smiling, "did Theodota's spur enter profoundly into your soul?"

The shoemaker raised his scintillating eyes, which illuminated his dull visage like a conflagration, and he replied: "The savant Meno came here yesterday, having need of a pair of sandals. He talked to me about astronomy and assured me that the sun, as Anaxagoras conjectures, is larger than the Peloponnese. The stars are, it appears, assemblies of molecules in ignition, and rotate in the sky following predictable curves. That revelation is still confounding my mind. While I hammer the leather of Amylceus I cannot deflect my meditations away from it. So, any other subject has become indifferent to me.

"Even so, I agree that Theodota is beautiful. I think her well-made in her body and possessing harmony. Unfortunately, she was enveloped in a tunic when we went in, so that we know nothing precise about her lines. The mind, creating in its fashion that which we do not know, gratuitously augments a woman's charms, her beauties and the enjoyments that might flow from her. We attribute imaginary perfections to Theodota, and if she has flaws we will never know them."

"You think accurately, Simon. But tell me, can you define the essence of amour for me? The problem has been occupying me in vain since yesterday, and nothing can suggest a satisfactory solution to me."

"Even if you're speaking this time without irony, of which one can never be sure with you, I can't give you any precise response. I only know amour indirectly, via those turtle-doves that you can see flying heavily over the roof of my hovel. They've been there for ten years. They're my family, and I can tell you that it's amour that leads and guides them. They're its prey and they only live to cover one another, motionlessly, to savor the quivering silence of intercourse, and then procreate and die. Such as I see amour, via those winged creatures, I have to declare to you that it appears to me to be a sublime mystery."

"But isn't it a simple desire that agitates your doves, Simon?"

"I'm not able to affirm or deny that, young man. Do you remember the verses of an ancient poetess who lived in the era when Sappho herself inflamed Ionia? *Nothing is as delicious as amour,* sang Neossis, *and no rapture is comparable to the one that it procures. But the man whom Venus does not designate, by according him her flame, is incapable of forming an idea of that joy, just as it is impossible for him to imagine enchanting roses before having scented their perfume and seeing their color.*"

"And what if amour only existed in the imagination of poets?" said Plato, thoughtfully.

"Then you would not be wise, you would not have that desire always to learn more, and nothing beautiful would exist," Simon replied. "But there you go. When you reach my age, you'll no longer be inclined to deny that which you don't know. Rather look at those turtle-doves. As it is spring, they're more beautiful. Their bodies become harmonious and their cooing and their flight, thanks to amour, discover the laws of a divine music."

And Simon lowered his head and began to strike with his hammer, attacking the leather as if he wanted to punish it for its resistance, and for Plato's.

The son of Ariston left the shop and headed slowly toward the Acropolis. Since human intelligence was not furnishing him with enlightenment, he wanted to meditate the problem that was preoccupying him under the calm gaze of the Immortals.

As he went past the temple of Demeter Chloe, which rose outside the enclosure, he saw Agoracritus, the beloved disciple of Phidias, who was slowly coming down the stairway carved into the rock. He stopped in order to look at him from a distance, so pleasing was the rhythmic stride of the artist, the measured movements of his body, and his face, illuminated by a masculine persuasion. There was a generous strength imprisoned in the sculptor's torso, and one might have thought that creative lightning traversed him, inflaming his body.

"You're leaving the Acropolis early, Agoracritus, said Plato, going to meet him. "Did you go up to see Ictinus, who is still retouching the colors of the Propylaea, or to admire the little temple of Victory, so pleasing to the gaze?"

"I'm glad to have met you," the sculptor replied, "And if you'd care to retrace your steps, we can walk together. I'm heading for my studio and I'm coming from the Parthenon. I went there in order to thank the Poliade,[11] who has deigned to acquiesce to my dearest wishes. You know Callinicus, the young ephebe that I love. He's as handsome as the Pentarces of whom Phidias has left the portrait in marble to the Eleans. Callinicus has just been victorious in the Megaran games. He took part in the kissing contest that the Megarans have founded in memory of a hero, and won the prize, for his kiss is very soft and melts on the lips. I'm proud of his victory."

"You love Callinicus, then?" asked Plato.

"I engrave his name on the hand of all my statues and I find his body so perfect that I attribute it to the gods whose images I sculpt. Callinicus' forms are worshiped by the Greeks in Apollo and Minerva, Venus and Jupiter. How can I not love him, since I recognize in him the reflection of divinity?"

"But is it admiration for the perfect beauty of the young man in question that you experience, Agoracritus, or amour? Answer me I beg you, for the interest I bring to that question is singular."

"But what is amour, Plato, except an adoration of beauty, the imperious joy that we experience in contemplating the most successful efforts of nature, the greatest perfection of human appearance?"

"Perhaps you're right," said the young man.

"That's why amour is worthy of veneration. It elevates humans by the effect of beauty, all the way to the regions

---

[11] i.e. the protective goddess of the city—Athene/Minerva.

118

where the Immortals dwell. Is a perfect body anything but the crystallization of a mysterious music, the material symbol of an impulse of prayer, the human revelation of the Divinity? I love Callinicus, and in saying that I love him I'm enunciating my desire to communicate with Beauty, to elevate myself as much as possible toward the perfect forms of the Olympians, to approach, by means of the exaltation that his body gives me, heroes and sages, in that amour is a harmonious impulse and the most religious action of human beings."

"But then, according to what you are saying, amour would entail in its essence a kind of superior orchestration, since it would be inspired by the harmony of forms and would be the product of a certain assemblage of lines. It enters into the category of bewitchments provoked by rhythm."

"Well put, Plato! Amour is music and it has its source, like the arts, in enthusiasm. To create a beautiful image or to possess it—that is the object of esthetics, that is amour. That's why, when I find myself before masterpieces in marble or in ivory, I experience a quiver of passion. And I see all the mysteries of creation and the enchantments of life through the perfection of a curve or in the occult movement of a beautiful line."

"I doubt, however, Agoracritus, that beauty can satisfy us fully. For I suspect that, for me, there are differences between beauty and amour. A beautiful body only inspires desires in me, without contenting them."

"We're talking about perfect beauty. Now, that frees us from passions and makes us forget desire. Desire—and you are skillful enough in philosophy to agree with this—is only, in sum, a sort of irresistible need, which impels us toward an ever greater perfection. But if the beauty is perfect, it contains all the satisfactions and only inspires the desire to contemplate, and not to possess."

And Plato, who was walking in silence beside the sculptor, thought that it might indeed be the case that the ideal amour, the superior amour whose definition he was searching, was a sort of elevated harmony, a supreme comprehension of finished forms, a sublime conversation with beauty.

I've sampled carnal sensuality, he said to himself, *but I found it inferior and I felt disappointed by its ashen taste. It gave me the memory of ties that link me to the beasts of the forest, to elementary beings. But beauty such as Agoracritus conceives it is specifically liberated from desire. His statues do indeed inspire a sweet meditation and, enticing us outside our carnal envelope, they enable us to soar in ideal regions.*

"Would you like to come to my studio?" the artist asked him when they had circled the hill and found themselves in the southern part of the city. "I'm finishing a Venus that the Rhamnusians have asked of me I'd like you to see it, since you're skillful in the appreciation of poetry and the arts. I've modeled it on a beautiful slave that Alcibiades brought from Sicily and whose name is Sthenelais.[12] She's a flute-player and her body has the gracility of the infant Apollo. One does not discover in her forms the harsh necessity that rounds out the limbs in order to give them the possibility of bearing children. But Sthenelais has something sharp and bitter in her beauty, a thrust of all her members toward the heights, and when she smiles she unveils so many mysteries by her smile that one might think that she is gazing at Olympus."

They were now entering the low studio that was at the foot of the rock. Plato saluted in passing Paeonius, a friend of Agoracritus, and the young Theocosmus, who also worked in marble and created fortunate figures. Then he stopped in front of a statue of Venus, who was placing one foot on a tortoise; it was the work of Phidias, and had been sculpted in Paros.

"Isn't it true, Plato, that one recognizes in this the goddess composed of the frisson of the foam?" asked Paeonius.

"Yes," the ephebe replied, "One can see the modesty and the passion dividing the Urania. Phidias was able to enclose

---

[12] The name Sthenelais appears in an anonymous fragment in the Greek Anthology as that of a high-priced courtesan "who sets cities aflame."

desires in her body, but assuaged by I know not what ideal tenderness."

"Come on, Plato," said Agoracritus, "And don't forget that we're here for the Rhamnusian.[13] A particular fever possesses me while I'm working on my statue. I believe that it will be my finest work and I shall thus be able to approach before dying the excellence of my master Phidias. In any case, I've never attacked the marble with so much surety and contentment. After work, on putting down the chisel, I feel more repose than when I picked it up in order to begin the day. So natural is my effort that it appears to have its source in the same imperious necessity that makes the grass grow and the flowers bloom."

And, passing through a long gallery, they entered the sculptor's private studio, in which the Venus stood that the Rhamnusians were later to call Nemesis, clad in dazzling colors, dominating the place with all the splendor of her beauty.

Plato remained plunged in a profound meditation for a few moments. The apparition of the goddess seemed to illuminate the depths of his own soul, and he felt inundated by repose and rapture. The daughter of Jupiter, holding a branch of an apple tree in her hand, appeared to him as if she had surged forth miraculously.

The marble was warm, respiring life. The feet and the legs rose up in a thrust of grace and strength, as if to support, not the loins, but a sacrificial altar. The breasts swelled in a

---

[13] It is relevant to this passage that much of Agoracritus' posthumous fame relates to a controversy regarding a statue known as the Rhamnusian Nemesis, a fragment of whose head is now in the British Museum. Pliny's account alleges that the sculptor, who was from Paros, initially conceived it as a statue of Venus, but when it lost a competition held in Athens to a statue by the Athenian sculptor Alcamenes he altered it slightly in order to change it into a Nemesis, selling it to the people of Rhamnus on the condition that it was never exhibited in Athens.

luminous wave, and there was, especially in the face, so much concentrated beauty that the young man experienced a slight intoxication, akin to the possibility of accomplishing super-human actions.

"Behold the source and the goal of amour," he said, in a low voice.

But at that moment, the sculptor went to the back of the studio and called: "Sthenelais! Sthenelais!"

Then, addressing Plato, who was still absorbed, caressing the statue with his eyes, he said: "After the work, you'll have the chance to see the model!"

A young woman came in, clad in a saffron-colored mantle with short sleeves, which left one shoulder uncovered as a sign of slavery. Her step was light. A layer of air seemed interposed between her feet and the ground, and invisible wings sustained her shoulders, annihilating the weight of the limbs.

Plato delighted in gazing at that being, whom Nature had enveloped with all her mysteries, and then the somber and mild face in which the beauty became tragic and proud. For Sthenelais' eyes were wide open, seemingly contemplating in the distance a beautiful and frightening head of Medusa. There was such a soft shadow on her eyelashes and the curve of her mouth, and the expression of her features was so changing and varied—like the forms of clouds, like the ripples of water—that when the young woman smiled in saluting the two men, Plato was gripped by it and reminded of the enigmatic faces of Sphinxes.

"Behold an incarnation of beauty that can conduct the spirit into the paths of joy and aid a man to support destiny with surety," said Agoracritus. "Does an enigma exist more profound than that gaze? And for all the questions relative to wisdom that you study with Socrates, could you find a book richer in information than the lines of Sthenelais' sides, descending toward the hips with the sinuosity of a spring?"

And Agoracritus approached the flute-player, gently removed the clasp that attacked her mantle, and allowed the cloth to cede, to fold and to fall to the ground. The nudity of the woman was radiant, pure and ordered, like a flash of wisdom. In accordance with Athenian custom, the young woman burned with the flame of her lamp the nascent hair of puberty, and her body was neat. The flexible and harmonious lines triumphed stainlessly.

Yes, to love is to break the chains that hold our soul captive, Plato thought. *And how can one break them except by contemplating a perfect beauty? I believe that I'm a creator in looking at this young woman, and I find myself full of life and happier, more winged, before this body, which, although perishable, bears the seal of infinite perfection! Agoracritus is right, and I find therein the definition of amour: it is our communion with the beauty of the universe.*

And, addressing Sthenelais, because he felt irresistibly drawn toward her, he said: "Young woman, you are fortunate, being a sanctuary in yourself and retaining divinity in your body. I believe that when your mouth opens, it will reveal a sublime secret to us. Perhaps it will enlighten us regarding the enigma of the eternal force that makes the spheres move in the heavens and also animates living beings. Confide to me the thought that is lending so pure a light to your mouth and your gaze at this moment. I promise you to meditate upon it to the point of conceiving an immortal work therein."

Steneelais looked at him for a few moments with motionless eyes, and then replied to him:

"I am thinking, young man, since I ought to speak to you sincerely, that I need two talents to buy my freedom, and that old lovers, the only ones who pay well, are becoming rare at present in Athens. I don't know the advantageous secrets of Medontis, who is from Abydos, a city knowledgeable in sensuality. In any case, the brothel in which Alcibiades makes me work is near Phalera, with the consequence that our clientele is all sailors and miserly Phoenicians."

Her voice was rough, a trifle hoarse, and had a dolorous effect in emerging from such lips.

In listening to that discordant sound, and understanding the meaning of the words. Plato sensed affliction, almost pain, as if a taut bow had been abruptly released within him.

At the words of that perfect being, he thought, *I experience what Achilles must have experienced when, by trickery, the cowardly Priamide cut the tendon of his heel, the only vulnerable part of his body.*

And in reply to Sthenelais, he said:

"So those are the thoughts that render your forehead so glorious, young woman. But why do you want to find the two talents? Is it by virtue of an innate sentiment of liberty? Would you like to devote yourself to some divinity, to practice amour henceforth as a divine art? Or do you desire to reveal your beauty in future as a special gift to sculptors and poets, in the sacred arbors of Eleusis, or during the festival of the Panathenaia?"

"I'm not speaking for you but for Agoracritus," the young woman said, irritated by not being understood. "What I want and what I would succeed in accomplishing, if Adrasteia were not rendered jealous thereby, is to open a brothel of my own and make others work as I have worked myself until now. I know a merchant of Delos, the same one who sold me. He has promised to procure me agreeable young women and boys at a good price. I'd quickly obtain the means of attracting a clientele, and I'd be sure of making a fortune."

"Fortunate Agoracritus!" said Plato, after a few moments of silence and discouragement. "You are more fortunate than Prometheus himself! You create perfect beings, but you seal their mouths with a divine silence. Everyone, on seeing your statues, can lend them his own thoughts, and suppose the language that appears to him to approach the sublime most closely. Your Venuses and Dianas are as beautiful as Sthenelais, but I decipher in their features the designs of Jupiter, and I believe that they are thinking nostalgically of the celestial meadows where they hunted and reposed beside radiant Apollo.

"Such meditations I also attributed to your Rhamnusian. However, she is only inflamed by the desire to enrich herself by opening a brothel, since you have made her faithfully in the image of Sthenelais and Sthenelais is only cultivating that unique thought. I salute you, dear sculptor. No, amour certainly does not reside in beauty and I was mistaken, as you are mistaken. When this young woman spoke, a spark finally sprang forth in the disarray of my mind; and I am certain now that beauty, like desire, belongs to the domain of the body, while amour can only be the prerogative of the immortal soul."

And, saluting the sculptor, Plato left the studio, returning to the daylight, without looking back once. His thought was struggling in darkness, searching for the truth.

V. On the Way to Aspasia's House

On the following day, which was consecrated to the festival of Prometheus, Plato met Socrates in the gardens near the temple of Hercules, known as the Cynosarges.

The master was standing still, his eyes riveted to the Venus by Alcamenes that rose up, beautiful and powerful, in the midst of olive groves.

Plato sat down beside him and respected his silence. He knew that at such moments, Socrates heard the voice of the spirit that resided within him. Plato even had it from Alcibiades that, during the battle of Potidaea, Socrates had gone for an entire day without speaking or taking nourishment, motionless in the middle of the camp, enraptured by his meditation. The interior life was so rich within him.

The disciple wondered curiously what problem was possessing the son of Sophroniscus at that moment.

Socrates finally raised his head, like that of a Faun drunk on nectar. And, designating with his finger an invisible insect that was singing, he turned to his disciple as if he were continuing a conversation already commenced and said:

"Do you not believe, Plato, that cicadas are desiccated poets, singers that passion has consumed? All of estival nature seems to exhale its heat through that little winged voice. One might think, in fact, that on the pleasant Attic soil, birds and insects have a human voice and that their songs respond to one another like the strophes of a chorus."

"I've been beside you for a long time, Socrates," Plato said. "In spite of my impatience to hear your voice, I could only respect your meditations."

"I was enraptured by the season that is ripening the grapes. In contemplating this marvelous image of Venus, and also aided by the visitation of the sun, which inflamed my mind, I thought I could glimpse the Empyrean and follow the Olympians. What majestic evolutions, participating in music,

126

must animate the interior of the heavens when chariots conduct the Immortals to their divine banquets. Souls also mingle with the gods because they too are immortal. Liberated from their carnal envelopes, they navigate, albeit more painfully, following the celestial furrows. And it appears to me clearly, at this moment, that the essence of the divine is the beautiful, the true and the good. Souls will only be able to identify divinity and contemplate it in the Empyrean if they have loved beautiful truths on earth and have nourished themselves on intelligence, science and goodness.

"Thus, I'm convinced, Plato, that after death, the friends of wisdom, of beauty and the Muses, will rise to Bliss, cross the Empyrean and be incorporated in the celestial harmony, while those who have not striven to perceive the divine in life, and who have gorged themselves on the impure aliment of vice, will feel their wings weighed down after death and will fall back to earth in order to inhabit the bodies of vile animals. And I would have liked to be a poet, like you, Plato, in order to translate by means of rhythm that vision of the heavens and their hierarchies, all of the iridescence of light, wings and wisdom that dazzles me."

Socrates raised his eyes again, listening to the hectic song of the cicada, and then said:

"In turning my eyes just now, I saw the imposing tomb of Nisus that rises over there behind the Lyceum. You remember the legend of that unfortunate prince. He had the promise of the Immortals of remaining invincible so long as his beautiful golden hair remained intact on his head. He scorned the Cretans who besieged him, and remained victorious. But his daughter, wounded by amour for Minos, the handsome enemy, cut her father's hair by night and provoked his death and the doom of the city. Such is the violence of the arrows of Eros!

"That tragic legend made me think about our conversation the other day. You've come to look for me, and I'm sure that you must have discovered the secrets of amour. Speak! I'm attentive now, chasing away my thoughts in order to fill myself with your own science."

"You're mocking me in vain, Socrates! The problem is too great, and surpasses me. I've come without shame to admit my disappointments and ask you for the thread of Ariadne in order to get out of the labyrinth."

"Have you found nothing thus far, then, son of Ariston?"

When Plato had recounted his adventures, the night he had spent with Nicareta, and the apparition of Sthenelais, Socrates patted him on the shoulder, smiling.

"Don't be discouraged, excellent child. If you have already been led to propose the soul as the seat of amour, the progress is satisfactory. You ought to congratulate yourself for it. However, I advise you to proceed with prudence, for the road is full of mirages. Now you're disposed to reject pleasure and beauty entirely and to see them as insults to amour. Refrain from doing that. They are, on the contrary, two powerful wings on which passion relies in its ascent.

"Above all, don't forget that amour is a sentiment so tightly woven with the elements of life that one finds it at the root of all great and fecund things. It is the abundant source that vivifies bodies and souls, the instigator of bold actions, beautiful thoughts and profound sensualities. Spread nobly in the body it is called beauty, impatient to pour forth its fruits in the future it is named desire, and when it rises nobly in the mind, vivifying with its seeds not the womb but the intelligence, we call it wisdom."

Socrates paused momentarily, avidly turning his face toward the breath of the sea breeze that was coming from Phalera, rippling the trees. Then he continued:

"You adventures with Nicareta and Sthenelais will help you to find the origin of amour hidden in the secret accord of souls. Without that accord, beauty remains inefficacious and sensuality only produces disappointment. If, on the contrary, the radiance of beauty and voluptuous grace descend to crown and, so to speak, complete spiritual affinities, then they can lead a man all the way to the bosom of the Eternals."

And as Plato pressed him to continue speaking, Socrates said: "Evening is arriving, and I must go to Aspasia's house to watch the celebratory torch relay commemorating the Promethean conquest from her terrace. I think that you could come with me. Aspasia enriches her beauty with new harmonies every day. The death of Pericles touched her without casting her down, and she continues to crown everything with the flowers of her thought. I consider frequenting her as a benefit of the gods. Don't hesitate, then, and come with me."

"I would like that very much, Socrates, if you think that, not knowing Aspasia, I can go to her house without inconvenience."

"Don't worry about that. Just hurry up, for fear that we might be late."

Night was falling and the mountains were clad in cloaks of somber purple. There were still red gleams above Aegina, but clouds were invading the horizon, rendering the night black.

They went along a deserted and winding street on which Pericles' modest house was located, in which Aspasia still lived.

"Every time I come this way," Socrates said, "I remember a trivial event, which seems memorable to me because it is linked to the grandeur of Athens. While still young I was going along this same street, on the evening after the stormy session in the Agora during which Pericles obtained from the Athenians the money necessary to build the Parthenon. It had been necessary for him to beg, almost to weep. Then, seeing that it was all in vain, he threatened that if the people of Athens refused the expense, he would punish them by building the temple with his own money. It was by means of such efforts that he ended up convincing the turbulent crowd. We had watched the session with Anaxagoras and we were walking this way in order to spend the evening with Aspasia, as usual.

"Suddenly, as we arrived in this deserted street, we heard coarse vociferations and we distinguished a man of tall stature who was walking preceded by a slave carrying a torch. Another individual was following behind him, addressing insults to him: 'Thief! You don't want to respond when I list your crimes,' he shouted. 'You've sold five thousand Athenians by auction, and now you want to snatch the last obol from the treasury of Delos! The world has never seen a corrupter like you, just as it has never seen a head resembling a squash like yours. But just because you find fine words and stupid people to believe them, it doesn't mean that you won't end up throwing yourself in the Cocytus anyway.'

"Meanwhile, the abused individual walked on, imperturbably, at a measured pace, avoiding the ditches and remaining as calm as if his ears did not hear the insults. 'But it's Pericles!' Anaxagoras said to me, recognizing him and hastening his steps in order to catch up with him.

"'Are you going to build more temples to impiety, stealing with Phidias, who procures women for you in his studio,' the insulter continued, 'or are you going to bring the Furies down on us by following the advice of Anaxagoras, the contempter of the gods?'

"'What's happening, then, Pericles?' asked Anaxagoras, when we drew level with Pericles, who was continuing tranquilly on his way.

"'It's nothing,' Pericles replied, saluting us amicably. 'This citizen has pursued me from the Agora, haranguing me in the fashion that you've heard, but we're at my house now. We have no more need of light.' And, turning to his slave, he said: 'Go now and illuminate this vociferating citizen, in order that he doesn't fall into some ditch on his way home. I'd regret it eternally if, because of his dementia, he took a false step and broke a leg.'

"And while the man stood, as if petrified, behind the slave, who was waiting for him, torch in hand, Pericles went into Aspasia's house with us.

"But we're there ourselves, Plato! Take care to contemplate that inimitable woman attentively, and try to nourish yourself on her words and profit from them."

VI. The Torch Relay

When Socrates came in with his young friend the wine was already being passed, and the guests were beginning to extend themselves more limply on the low couches.

Next to Aspasia was Sophocles, and then the young Agathon, Alcibiades and Aristophanes.

"If I'm late," Socrates said, as he entered, "You'll certainly forgive me, Aspasia, since I've bought a companion avid for learning, and who will gather within himself the good seeds of your wisdom, and enable them to fructify. He'll be a disciple much less dense and mediocre than I was when you taught me rhetoric. I promise you that he won't disappoint you like me, but will do honor to your lessons."

Aspasia received the handsome adolescent with amicable words and then, having looked at Socrates with a smile, she turned toward the other guests and said to them: "Look at this man! He's redoubtable for his wisdom, and Nature was prudent in creating him as ugly as a Silenus."

"He always reminds me," Alcibiades put in, laughing, "of those old deformed Satyrs that the sculptors fashion hollow, like boxes. When you open them, you find hidden therein the radiant image of an Olympian deity. Such is the sublime and harmonious soul of Socrates in his poorly compassed and thickset body."

"Can you see him smiling under his snub nose?" Aspasia went on. "I'll wager that the vicious man has been preparing some embarrassing question in the street."

"Every day I observe your wisdom, Aspasia," Socrates replied, "but in calling me vicious now you've surpassed yourself in clairvoyance. Only yesterday I was with me friends near the Pnyx when Zopyrus, the celebrated physiognomist went past. He didn't know me, but he stopped close by and stared at me in surprise. 'Why,' he exclaimed, 'I've never seen a face more imprinted with evil instincts, more steeped in vice, than this man's!' And while my friends laughed, I blushed, full of confusion, recognizing how right Zopytus was. I was, in fact, a treasure-trove of vices, a den of evil passions. If I have vanquished my instincts somewhat, it is only by dint of assiduous determination and constant effort..."

Socrates was about to continue, but Alcibiades intervened again. "Cease this performance, Socrates," he said, "and don't hope to fool us or draw us into the nets of your irony. It would be easier to convince us that you're stupid than to make us see you as a rascal. We know you to be judicious, generous and insupportable. The evidence is abundant. I only have to furnish Aspasia with the most recent for her to be able to judge.

"You'll all recall that last year, my chariots won the prize in the Olympic races. Perhaps I was more swollen with pride by that than wisdom and dignity permitted. In any case, my friends flattered me by running to me and heaping me with honors and felicitations. Only Socrates didn't condescend to do that. He was among the last to come to my house, toward evening. Instead of asking the porter to be brought to me, he asked to be shown the way to the stables. There he praised n a loud voice the horses that, he declared, had won the victory by their merit. He distributed cakes to them that he had brought with him, and then, without seeking to converse with me or to salute me, he left.

"Don't you agree that I'm right, and that the man is insupportable? What do you say, Sophocles? You've known Socrates for a long time. Don't you share my opinion?"

At that moment, however, a young slave from Crete, with sparkling eyes, who was pouring the wine, had reached Sophocles in order to refill his glass. The poet, moved by the beauty of the cup-bearer and having a soul always inclined toward amour, did not hear Alcibiades' question. On the contrary, turning to the ephebe, he said: "Would you like me to drink with a double pleasure the Thasos that you have just poured me, child?"

"I would indeed," said the Cretan, in a velvety voice, moving the bowl closer.

"Then present me the cup slowly," said the poet, "and let me savor the wine for a long time."

And as he saw all eyes turned toward them, the intimidated ephebe, who was conscious of his beauty and the effect that it had produced on the old man, blushed and became hesitant in his movements.

Sophocles, who was still gazing at him, found that the modesty went well with his features and perfected heir beauty. Without taking his eyes off him, he exclaimed: How right old Phrynicus was when he said in a verse: 'The flames of amour shine in his crimson cheeks.'"

But the poet Agathon, in order to animate the conversation and excite the old master, replied to him:

"In poetry, Sophocles, you are the master of us all. I concur with that! It seems to me, however, that Phrynicus did not strike accurately in giving his crimson cheeks to his adolescent; for, in sum, I think the color crimson is ugly and garish. If a painter had applied it to the cheeks of a young man we'd have found the portrait poor. That's why I believe that it's necessary not to compare what is beautiful with what is not."

Sophocles laughed then, and replied to Agathon with slight irony:

"In that case, excellent man, you won't approve any more of Simonides, who said, to the approval of all Greece, moreover: 'The virgin pronounced those words with her rosy mouth,' nor Homer when he gave 'golden hair' to Apollo. The painter does in fact give him black hair, for with gold in his hair you would certainly have found the painting very poor, with reason. In the same way you would disapprove of whoever said of Aurora that she has 'rosy fingers.' If anyone covered her fingers with the color of a rose, he would have tinted hands, but not beautiful ones."

That response was appreciated, and Sophocles turned to the pretty youth, who, still holding the full cup, was trying to remove a little wisp of straw that had fallen from the bowl along with the wine.

Smiling, Sophocles invited him to blow lightly on the cup. "Blow adroitly," he told him, "And above all, blow at very close range. The straw will fly away."

And as the young cup-bearer bent over innocently in order to follow the advice and blow into the cup, his cheek approached the poet's. Then Sophocles took hold of him, laughing, and, holding his head in his hands, deposited a swift kiss on his lips.

Turning toward the others then, he said: "You can see that I'm as fertile in artifices as the divine Ulysses. It's only in war that I lack all invention."

"Like your heroine you were born for love and not for hatred," Aspasia said to him, laughing. "But I ought to warn the young people that in amour, you seem to be very fickle and capricious."

"People are even recounting," the wily Aristophanes insinuated, "a humorous adventure that happened to you, it appears, the other day. Should we give any credit to it, Sophocles?"

"I don't know what you mean, Aristophanes," replied the old man, distractedly. Having forgotten the present, he was lost in his meditations.

"Tel us what you know anyway, Aristophanes," said Agathon, curious and pricking up his ears.

"You're all going to say that I have a venomous tongue, and Sophocles will hold it against me; but I'm nothing but an echo and only repeating. So, I'm assured that our glorious friend, transported by the flames of amour, followed a youth the other day whom he judged handsome. He followed him as far as the tender grass that grows around the Cynosarges. There they lay down together, and, as the child's mantle was small and narrow, they covered themselves with Sophocles' sumptuous cloak. But when the cruel moment of separation arrived, the youth went away with the poet's rich cloak and left him his own."

"It's Euripides again who's spreading that lie!" exclaimed the irritated poet.

"Yes, I must confess that it's Euripides."

"I knew it. That malevolent anecdote had already been repeated to me. Here's the very epigram that I sent to him in response. You can judge whether the lines are beautiful: 'Euripides, it was the sun and not a handsome youth who, testing me with his heat, stripped me of my cloak. But you, wretch, it's Boreas who chills you in the arms of other people's wives. You must not be very thoughtful to occupy yourself in all your remarks about the amours of others, while you have in your own home the very person who steals their clothes.'"

When Sophocles fell silent, Aspasia turned to Socrates and said: "You've scarcely spoken, Socrates, and yet, as I said, you appear to have a question or an enigma to pose. Am I right or am I in error?"

"Can you ever be mistaken, Aspasia? You don't believe incorrectly that I have a question to pose. That question will please Sophocles; it is, in fact, a matter of the tender and redoubtable passion that attracts and bring beings together. Young Plato, whom I took the liberty of bringing here, confounded me the other day by asking me innocently what the essence of amour was. I did not want to spout in reply the hollow and vague phrases that run around on that subject. But, on the other hand, I was obliged to recognize that I had nothing personal to say about it. Both finding ourselves thus embarrassed, we thought of having recourse to your science, Aspasia. You, who teach eloquence and poetry, and whom Pericles himself recognized to be wise, can assist us to triumph over that problem."

"Socrates," Aspasia replied, without smiling, and fixing Plato with a serious gaze, "your question is thorny. Defining amour appears to me to be as difficult as defining the form of a wave or the colors of a sunset. But it is necessary to have courage in extreme circumstances. Since we all love ideas and science, it would be cowardly to retreat before the problem in question. In any case, I won't permit us to separate before honoring the son of Venus and contenting Socrates. Let us set aside the wine, put down our crowns and each say in turn what we think about the properties and nature of Amour. It is for you, Ion, to begin.

"I consider Amour," said Ion, after a few moments of silence, "to be the most ancient of the gods, the primordial, original and venerable source of everything. I believe amour to be beneficent. It incites to action. It is, in sum, the ferment and the salt of the earth. The mysterious fire, stolen from Jupiter by Prometheus and which animated clay, must have been a spark of amour. And it is also amour that inspires the appetite of heroism. Among the glorious statues that populate the Acropolis, there is not one that I venerate as much as that of Laena, the lover of Aristogeton, who preferred to bite her tongue in two and spit it out rather than fail in her sentiment by denouncing under torture the man she loved.[14] We see thus that amour stimulates all our moral strength. Like an internal sun it brings to their full florescence the good seeds contained in the human soul."

Sophocles said in his turn:

"I commenced the meal by citing verses. I believe the best thing would be to continue. I shall therefore recite you a superb ode on Amour. I was part of an old tragedy. Simple, it appeared to me to be more inflamed than what Simonides and Sappho herself have said on the subject:

---

[14] The original text renders this courtesan's name as Lacaina, which must be a misprint, perhaps resulting from a failure to read the author's handwriting correctly. She was the lover of Aristogeton, who attempted to overthrow the tyranny of Hippias and Hipparchus in the 6th century B.C.; he was captured and she was arrested and tortured in the hope of forcing her to reveal the names of the other conspirators, but she died without saying a word; the Athenians erected a statue of a lioness without a tongue at the gate of the Acropolis to symbolize her courage, which some later commentators interpreted as an assertion that she had bitten off her own tongue.

"*Amour is the invincible force, the insensate rage, the unrestrained delirium, dolor and tears. All existence is submissive to that god. The fish and the species that live in the water do not escape his reach, and the beings that live on the surface of the earth experience his arrows. With his divine wings he visits the birds, the beasts of the forest, humans, and the gods themselves in their celestial abode.*"

And Agathon said:

"Oh, Sophocles, after such verses, what could one address more melodious in honor of the son of Aphrodite, except perhaps the sublime chorus of your *Antigone*? But I shall refrain from citing that to Athenians. All have it on their lips. In following the excellent things that have been said about the omnipotence of Amour, I should like to exalt in my turn his tenderness. Thanks to him we know humanity.

"The first beings, whom fear and the need to gorge themselves rendered hostile and ferocious, felt their hearts soften under the visitation of Amour. Their lips were no longer extended to bite but to kiss. Thus it is to the virtue of Amour that we owe the first bonds of relationship and the great pact of the family, spreading over the implacable warriors the appeasing breath of fraternity. Like the soft harmony of the flute of Amphion, which joined stones together and elevated also, the pacifying power of Amour cemented societies. Gradually, uniting us in mildness, rendering human beings apt to communicate with one another, Amour purged us of our primal impurities and gave us a common consciousness. That is why I honor him, above all, as the great polisher of human mores, the divine civilizer."

"All that is very well," said the young Aristophanes, but I see it rather as the eulogy of amour than its definition. For me, this is what I understand and what I repeat regarding the origin of that sentiment.

"Know, then, that in very ancient times there were three sorts of beings on the earth. In addition to males and females there were also androgynes that united the two sexes simultaneously. Both male and female, the androgynes were free and did not know passion. That rendered their courage powerful and their strength invincible. In consequence they attempted the most reckless things and ended up making war on the divinities of Olympus, as did Ephialtes and Otus whose story is told by Homer.

"Jupiter wanted to punish the androgynes and, reluctant to destroy them completely, he rendered them weak and miserable by splitting them in two, leaving them only a single sex and throwing them mutilated and incomplete on to the surface of the earth. Since then, the distraught androgynes have wandered, but every time they rediscover their other half, they feel violently impelled to unite with it, to reconstitute the ancient ensemble, to complete themselves. Thus, Amour is the force that drives us to join together, in order to realize our ancient integrity and rediscover our glorious and perfect primitive form."

"And you, Alcibiades, what do you have to tell us about amour?" asked Aspasia, smiling. "You are young, Amour haunted you too soon and you commenced to empty the cup of pleasures and sensations so gluttonously that one might think that you already about to drain it."

"My ideal, thus far," Alcibiades replied, "has been to satisfy my senses, to enrich myself with the universal sensuality. I know the beauties of all the lands of the world. The supple Athens, the crazy Corinth, and Abydos, whose women are so knowledgeable in the redoubtable science of caresses, have aided me to fathom pleasure, and also distant Egypt and the impure Babylon, and the strange land of spasms and lust that is Phoenicia. I was thus able to assimilate all the expressions and sensations of the flesh and I believe that in that way my wisdom also was increased. For true pleasure renders grave. It approaches us to death and communicates to us the knowledge of profound and tragic things. It is a terrible initiation. And I could, Aspasia, respond to your request by defining amour as an intimate perfection of knowledge, a communion with the soul of the world."

Everyone applauded Alcibiades, and Aspasia who had praised him, gave the floor to Socrates.

"I do not know the essence of amour," the latter said, "but I can repeat what Plato and I were saying. We have fallen into accord in that amour does not consist exclusively either of desire, as some are tempted to believe, or beauty. Its significance is more profound and its seat must be placed in the soul. Alcibiades appears to me to have touched upon its veritable character in telling us that it is an intimate perfection of knowledge. In that, amour participates in desire and beauty, since it enables us to know which souls are the most perfect and unites us with them in ineffable pleasure. Progressing toward perfection, a ladder that takes us very high, accomplishing our goal and our destiny, such is amour. That is why our ancestors attributed wings to the god. It elevates humans, enables them to participate in immortal mysteries..."

Aspasia was about to speak in her turn and Plato was looking at her with avid eyes, but as she allowed her eyes to stray beyond the open terrace, she perceived a vivid flame furrowing the nocturnal serenity.

"That's the torch relay commencing," she said. "What a pity we can't follow it at close range."

At her invitation, everyone went on to the terrace in order to contemplate the mystic celebration. A religious frisson elevated their breasts.

Over the obscure extent of the plain they saw the light crossing areas, drawing away, vacillating, appearing to die out, and then emerging again, flamboyant. Passing from hand to hand, always gaining ground, it became more distant but always present.

"That is the true symbol of your sublime amour, Socrates," said Aspasia, indicating the errant flame. "That torch gives me the perfect signification of amour, which is the hectic desire of creation. Don't you feel a frisson at the aspect of that ardent course, during which the ephebes are passing the torch from hand to hand, like the life that we pass from flesh to flesh at the whim and to the rhythm of amour? A sublime image, in truth, of the only divine thing in which we participate.

"For while everything perishes and fades, as the centuries succeed one another, while the body dies and the animating intelligence yields and vanishes, amour persists, continuing its work, touching us momentarily in order to render us creators, then going toward other beings. Thus, each of us is transfigured for an instant with the aid of passion, elevated as far as the gods, holding the sacred flame of all life. Then it is handed on to another. And while we disappear, the divine spark is eternal, hurling our seed beyond worlds and continuing to weave the future, to prepare the ends..."

All eyes were how turned toward the woman. Transfigured by the flame of her enthusiasm, she appeared new to her friends, as if they were seeing her for the first time.

She was simply wearing a linen tunic. Her hair, ornamented by a golden ring, spread out around her head in numerous meanders. She was beautiful, but her beauty was dominated by the radiance of an intellectual clarity, a flame of genius that transformed her features and made her entire visage into a pure and bright mirror, in which one could follow the soul weaving harmonious thoughts.

When she stopped speaking, a breath of grandeur inflated their lungs. They all respired the fever that is emitted by elite cities during great days, when humans take a step forward in the knowledge of their destiny.

Plato, who was invincibly penetrated by the philter that Aspasia's visage was pouring forth, suddenly experienced a strange tenderness. While the woman was talking, he discovered secret affinities that linked her soul with his own. He believed that the roots of his existence and her existence were adjacent, overlapping, intersecting in the unfathomable abysses of destiny. And Aspasia appeared to him to realize in her person the perfect accord between the extreme beauty of lines and the extreme nobility of the soul.

And as a disturbance of a sublime order, an unknown joy, visited him, he finally understood that the woman in question, who was at the summit of grace and knowledge, awakened in his soul a new and sacred sentiment, and initiated him solely by its presence into the ineffable mysteries for which he had so far sought the solution in vain.

The ephebe was sure henceforth of knowing amour.

As for Aspasia, who was standing there, her gaze lost among the stars, beautiful and almost frightening, such was the profound harmony that presided over the lines and the movements of her body, she sensed a circle of anxiety grip her, and knew the obsession of an immaterial and invisible contact.. She therefore turned her head and encountered Plato's gaze posed upon her, motional, desirous, amorous and dominating.

She understood, and a strange flood of tenderness invaded her, giving her consciousness of a divine force, of an infinite power.

Meanwhile, the torch relay having concluded, the guests withdrew. When Socrates' turn came, Aspasia put her hand on his shoulder gently.

Stay for a few moments more, with your disciple, son of Sophroniscus," she said. "The night is clear and fine."

And she sat down next to the young man.

"Is amour not the revelation of the universe in a miracle?" said Plato, feeling as if he had been transfigured by an increasing tenderness of the emotion that he was experiencing.

It was Socrates who replied.

"You're right, Plato. And now that, being alone, we can speak without offending the ears of men, I will reveal to you that Amour is the sole veritable god, the solitary guest of Olympus. For the world is nothing but inert matter, and it is the breath of passion that animates the Totality. It takes on by turns the aspect of flame, the fluidity of water and the vivacity of intelligence, and by means of its faithful servants, Beauty and Desire, it succeeds in moving everything, in mingling with everything, in eternalizing everything. It is not only the plants, the birds, the beasts and humans, but also the earth itself, the planetary bodies and the infinite universe that are ordered and

141

animated by amour. What we call force, intelligence and exaltation, that which is the science of the heart and the science of numbers, the matter of mechanics and the matter of psychology, are all submissive to amour. The ancestors were correct to make Eros the most ancient of the gods, the animator of chaos. We can still call him the opener of Destiny."

He fell silent. Then, suddenly saddened by feeling old and in darkness, he inspected the mysterious horizon with his gaze. And he saw a white aureole emerging in the Occident and which, struggling with the darkness, illuminated the sacred rock on which the Parthenon shone.

"It's late, Aspasia," he said, finally. "I have to go. But the night is clear and pure. It will be beneficial and precious for Plato to remain by your side. You can initiate him further in matters of amour.

"My desire would even be that you become for him what a priestess of Mantinea named Diotima was for me. I knew her when I was young. I will not tell you about the beauty of that woman, nor her wisdom. I remember her like the apparitions of the Eternals that the initiates see in the Eleusian Mysteries and of which it is not permissible to speak. By means of her speech and by means of her gaze, Diotia gave me in a moment, as if in a fulgurant flash, consciousness of the world and knowledge of passion.

"It was wisdom that linked us. Gradually, in speaking to me, she appeared to me to be the sister of my soul, like a reflection of myself, a more harmonious receptacle of my own thoughts. Our meditations, in the bosom of nature, near sources, in the sacred rustle of forests, opened to me the splendid routes that lead to the ideal. Diotima talked to me about the Egyptian science that she possessed, having once lived in Memphis, and all the Ionian wisdom with which she was familiar.

"It was by a sort of intuition and not by cold reflection that she advanced in knowledge; and often she made me understand not only the substance of things but their occult force, and after that which is the object of thought, she unveiled to me that which divine science is.

"One day, when we were talking about the ideal, and obscurities appeared to arrest and trouble our understanding, Diotima drew me to her and hugged me. And that gentle approach, that tender contact, was for us an advancement toward clarity, a perfection of understanding, a supreme mystical refinement in which our thoughts touched more intimately, in which the language we were speaking became more expressive, more profound and seemingly alive.

"After that, we talked and we caressed, exhausting human knowledge as much as it was possible for us to do. From initiation to initiation, we rose as far as the contemplation of pure wisdom, of pure science, and of the pure verity that is God."

And, rising to his feet, Socrates added, looking at Aspasia: "Be for Plato what Diotima was for me, and my disciple will subsequently be able to reveal the supreme mysteries to the wonderstruck understanding of men."

He fell silent.

And, leaving Plato with Aspasia, he went away, meditating matters of passion, and those of eternity.

VII. The Celestial Abode

"By the expression on your face I recognize that you are agitating in perplexity," Socrates said the following day and they were going down the hill of the Pnyx slowly.

"Great problems are, indeed, haunting me," Plato replied, "surging forth in my mind one after another, and I feel as if I am lost in their meanders."

"Let us make our way together through the detours of those problems, then," said the master. "It's possible that in both making use of our eyes and rubbing our ideas together we might arrive at glimpsing some clarity, a enlightenment, in the same way that putting two pieces of wood in contact can cause a spark to spring forth."

"And perhaps," Plato completed, "while juggling with words, we will both end up receiving a vision of life, and even of reality."

They sat down next to a field of asphodels with tender, slightly funeral hues.

Plato's face was grave. The ephebe seemed suddenly to have entered into virility, as if the knowledge of amour, extracting him from his tender years, had suddenly ripened him and placed him in the very heart of life.

"This is what is happening to me, Socrates," he said. "I was initiated to amour in proximity with the rhythm and the music that emerge from the soul of Aspasia. And by virtue of having known the glare of tender passion, I feel as if I were lost in a new ignorance. The world has enlarged before me, and by that very fact, the problems of the world have multiplied. Glimpsing other, unexpected difficulties, I feel troubled more than ever by the enigma that is the universe, by the enigma that is life."

"The state in which you find yourself, very dear one, appears to me to be excellent," replied Socrates, smiling. "I have experienced it myself many times. The road of wisdom is thus made. At every height that one reaches, one immediately perceives an even higher summit, surrounded by darkness, which it is a matter of attaining. For that reason, life is a perpetual effort of knowledge, and old age itself is an apprenticeship."

"To know! That is the ardent desire that possesses me. Having penetrated amour, I feel thirsty also to reveal the goal of life, the why of things."

"That is already a result acquired, and a precious result," Socrates approved. "The thirst that is devouring you is, moreover, necessary. If, in fact, you do not learn the why of things and the goal of life, you will not be able to determine the place and the importance of amour, of that marvelous sentiment to which you have been initiated, for one only truly knows something when one has perceived its relationship with the whole. You have felt amour and its mystery, but amour will continue to propose new enigmas to you so long as you have not determined the fashion in which it serves the divine design, and the harmony that it contributes to the universal concert."

"Yes, after amour, and as a complement to the science of amour, it will be necessary to know the goal of life, to go by means of thought into the depth of things," Plato agreed.

"Or, to put it better," Socrates corrected, "after the love of a woman, the love of creatures, one ought to pass on to the love of wisdom, to *philosophy*, to employ the sublime word created by Pythagoras. We shall succeed in that. For you are, I see, an intrepid lover, Plato. I too am tenacious and passionately amorous. Now, it is by means of enthusiasm, by the divine folly appropriate to the amorous, that we integrate nature entire, that we become the center of the world, entering into possession of all the ideas and all the substances that we love."

They got up and took a few steps in the direction of the temple of Jupiter, crossing the Ilissus.

"The idea that haunts me the most," the disciple went on, after a pause, "is an idea, or rather than illusion, that suddenly visited me yesterday, next to Aspasia, at the moment when my lips quit hers. It suddenly seemed to me, at that moment, that I was seeing again hours already known. I remembered having felt before the same rapture that the kiss of the beloved procured for me, of having stared before into the same beautiful face of Aspasia, of having exchanged before the same fraternal words that linked me to the Milesian so tenderly and so passionately. Yes, it seemed to me that I was not savoring those supreme moments for the first time. However, I searched in my past and my memory in vain; nowhere did I found the real foundation of any such remembrance."

"And what if it was not a memory of your past, Plato?"

And as the disciple looked at him, amazed, already divining and sensing himself fill up with an extreme emotion, Socrates said: "Yes, what if, by a miracle of amour, you found yourself capable of remembering, not your past life or another life, but the divine country from which you are momentarily exiled, the etheric abode from which souls come, and where it is not perishable appearances that reside but the essences of things?"

"According to your words, Socrates, amour would then be a miracle of recognition."

"Yes, it would be the sublime testimony and revelation of our celestial origins, the spark that illuminates temporarily the ignorant darkness of perishable life and shows us the eternal unity from which we come."

"The darkness of life!" repeated Plato, pensively.

"Is it not plausible, in fact, that amour, in closing our eyes, which deceive us incessantly, in causing silence in our fallacious senses, permits us a mystical vision of the unknown from which we come? Because, Plato, the terrestrial human being, the human being of flesh, ought to be imagined as a prisoner enclosed in a cave that only receives light from one side. Enchained there and unable to turn his head, he cannot see the illuminating fire projected behind him by the cave entrance. He is, on the contrary, incessantly distracted by the phantoms designed on the back wall of his prison. In fact, between the captive human and the eternal fire that shine outside the cave, there is a steep slope along which chimeras incessantly pass, of which the shadows projected in front of the human being constitute everything that he calls reality."

"And one can never emerge from the cave, behind the true light, fathom the reality of what one sees?"

"Not during this life, Plato, except by means of fugitive flashes of remembrance obtained with the aid of amour. Thus, we can now define the place of amour in the ensemble of things. It is the bridge—or, rather, the ladder—that links the inferior world of appearances, in which humans are enchained in this life, with the world of substances, the eternal world, from which they come. Every time a man feels extracted from himself by passion or the beautiful, he remembers what he has already contemplated before being introduced into terrestrial life. Then he feels winged, he soars, and enthusiasm transfigures him; he forgets his oyster-shell, the body that is like a burden and a punishment. The memory returns to him of the time when his soul was part of the happy choirs of Immortals and when, going beyond the sky, he was able to contemplate the Ideas."

"The Ideas?"

"Yes, the Ideas, the only real verities: the Ideas, the eternal models of things, of which we only see the tarnished and vague reflections down here. Beauty, Justice, Reason, and everything that we try vainly to realize in this life, we have glimpsed up there, in an ideal and perennial completion."

"So this life," said Plato, dazzled, "is only the specter of another, perfect, ideal existence, the approximation of a higher reality that is found elsewhere. As for Philosophy and Art, they are only celestial nostalgias, vague reminiscences of what we once knew, and which we shall rediscover again one day if we are worthy of reintegration in our eternal fatherland."

"Well said, Plato, and, as usual, you have anticipated my own words. Philosophy, art, piety and enthusiasm are only means of ascension, wings that extract us momentarily and incompletely from terrestrial exile, attempting to bring us closer to liberty.

"Thanks to those wings we can soar above the unstable and imperfect world in which the phantoms of things agitate, and contemplate, or at least recall, the divine and joyous realm of the Ideas, the realm of the eternals, where nothing changes, where nothing happens, where nothing perishes, but where everything is complete, radiant and eternal."

It was midday.

A bird intoxicated by light started singing in an olive tree. And the two lovers of wisdom, lost in that light song, divining obscurely that, by means of a magical operation, they were in the process of opening celestial paths of liberation for humankind, remained motionless and silent for a long time, prolonging the conversation in thought, reunited in a burst of harmony by the august peace of things, and sensing the flight of Time without fear.

VIII. Three Shades

The next day, Plato emerged from Aspasia's house in the white twilight before the dawn.

He had mingled his body with the woman's body. Through the carnal envelope, by virtue of a complete confusion of impulses and desires, he had believed that he was in communication with the soul of the beloved, and he had sensed all that the concordance of intelligences can add to carnal affinities, how a thought transfigures bodies, and how a purifying flame of human sympathy burns what remains of the animal in the embrace.

And as Aspasia, in the moment of sensuality, her eyes closed and weary, had show him her face in a relaxation that left more apparent the little that the years had introduced there of alteration and damage, Plato experienced now, as well as the intoxication of pleasure, a kind of melancholy tenderness, a sympathetic emotion inspired by the idea of death.

Emerging from those intense hours, during which the senses and the soul had participated in a kind of great feast, Plato was seized by an imperious avidity to create, to stamp his seal on nature entire, to embrace the infinity of thought by means of his intelligence.

Socrates is right, he thought. *Amour ought to incite us to link a greater amity with wisdom, in order to progress in the integration of the universe*.

The young man climbed the rising path by which chariots entered the Acropolis.

In matinal lightness, the city was still asleep. The frontons and the iridescent columns were scarcely designed. Plato sat down at the foot of the Propylaea, watching the accomplishment of the mystery of the sunrise, reflected in the distance on the ripples of the Saronic.

The sea, the sky and the nascent light, stirring in the grandeur and beauty that they revealed, incited him to consider more intensely the task that was to orientate and elevate his existence: to explain the world, to give a meaning to life, to enlighten humans not with regard to their relationships with one another, like Solon, but with regard to their relationship with the ensemble.

The figures of the great precursors who, in the isles of Ionia and the lands of Sicily or great Greece, had already tried to provide a response to the redoubtable and august problems of the universe, appeared before Plato.

Three of them had dominated his mind intensely, and still did.

Plunged in great thoughts, ready to open new and sublime routes to knowledge. Plato evoked those august initiators.

First he saw, great among the great. Heraclitus, the descendant of kings, the great Ephesian who had retired from society, scorning glory and the purple, and only quit his retreat on the mountain in order to go and deposit his offering in the temple of Diana: a royal present, the true sign of his great lineage, his book, in which he had enclosed the flower of his meditations of genius.

Then Plato thought of the living Apollo, the sage of Samos, the divine Pythagoras, the depositary of all the light of Asia, the inheritor of the revealed wisdom of sanctuaries, who, finding himself in communication with the harmonious spirit of things, read with ease the intimate arcana of nature.

Finally, Plato saw the disciple of Xenophanes, Parmenides of Elea, the man who, going further and beyond appearances, wanted to pierce the essences, discover the unity, and cut the divine knot.

Plato reviewed mentally the revelations that those three geniuses had brought to humans, the three responses that they had given to the enigma that the eternal Sphinx proposes to the living.

"Nothing is, since nothing remains," said the grim Ephesian. "Everything flows like water, everything is devoured as if by fire, incessantly transformed, passing and already passed, agonizing and already dead. No one crosses the same river twice, and even for the man crossing it the first time it no longer exists, since it changes during the crossing. Everything is in eternal motion, and nothing, at any moment, is the same as it was in the preceding moment, or will be in the next moment.

"A perpetual flux, an incessant death: that is life; that is the fugitive spectacle—or, rather, the vain phantom—of the universe. Do not trust your senses, then, and do not stop at forms or substances. There are no fixed forms or permanent substances, but an eternal and mutable current, the current of annihilation, which precipitates incessantly in the bleak bed of the river of death."

Thus spoke Heraclitus.

"What do things matter?" replied the Samian. "They are nothing but the servants of the eternal harmony that rules the Cosmos. The universe is order. And forgetting nature, you have only to open your intimate ear to the music that orchestrates the spheres, orders chaos, and regulates space and time in accordance with divine laws. It is there that it is necessary to seek the universal soul of things, which is itself merely the reflection of a superior world from which everything comes and to which everything returns.

"Thus, although forms pass, the harmony of the relationships that regulate them remains indestructible, escaping death, constituting a mystical knot, a divine number, which emerges from the universe like a mysterious murmur. Close your eyes, therefore, which can only see matter, and then, in the darkness and the silence, a supernatural light will shone upon you, a celestial melody will charm you, and you will perceive something of the world's beyond, a reflection of the superior order, and Olympian glow, the true anticipation of immortality."

Thus spoke Pythagoras.

And the Elean said:

"I am burning with a desire for eternity. Beyond this variety, which dazzles my eyes when I contemplate the changing spectacle of the world, beyond the relationships and the harmony of things, I want to find the divine reality. That is the research of my unique, eternal, uncreated God, into which I am launching myself. From that, everything emanates, it alone is real, only it exists.

"The absolute, such is my goal, such is my task. And it is by means of the absolute that I shall pass through the scale of beings. How can a human being be worthy of humanity except by wanting to discover that immutable center, distanced from the perpetual mutation of things, the eternal harbor where everything is calm, formless, colorless and changeless? God is my thought; it is God that will also be my permanent reverie."

Thus spoke Parmenides.

And Plato, sitting on the stone, tried to reconcile those sublime responses, which surged from the human mind at grips with the eternal enigma.

And while the intellectual enlightenments brought to the world by his predecessors traversed his mind, the great enlightenment of the sunrise also triumphed before his eyes. A flamboyant sword sprang from Pentelicus, reddening the earth, casting a vast frisson over the sea, putting an aureole of glory over the isle of Aegina, above which the sapphirine sky was paling. To the left, toward Sunium, the water seemed enameled by a florescence of mystical violets, while to the right, the Bay of Salamis, the sanctuary of the deliverance of Greece and the humiliation of the Mede, still retained its vestiges of shadow. But soon, the water there caught fire as well; a flood of gold steamed over the hills. Hymetta took on the color of dazzling hyacinths. One might have thought that a sudden fire was setting Attica ablaze, magnificently.

Everything was joy now, everything quivering with life. It was as if the slaves that were going in the direction of Piraeus to turn the mills, and the flute-players returning from orgies, were all clad in a marvelous royal mantle by the splendid dawn.

To put the same clarity and the same joy into human thought; to enable a ray of that solar light to penetrate into suffering hearts, to give human beings Hope and Beauty as divine assistants, to make the ideal spring forth like a divine auroral spring—such will be my work.

Everything that Socrates had said the day before—his theory of remembrance, and his brilliant descriptions evoking a superior world in which the divine prototype was found of everything humans see down here—was organized in Plato's mind, forming a harmonious cortege.

I shall place on Olympus, not the abode of the gods, but the ideal fatherland of humankind, he thought. *I shall remind my brethren of their celestial origins, convince them that their essence, although weighed down by the body, is a divine plant that finds itself momentarily distanced from its roots. And I shall give human beings as sublime instruments, capable of bringing them closer to the heavens from which they come and to which they will return, the beautiful, the good and virtue. To ennoble the earth, to purify the world, to inaugurate a grandiose effort toward perfection that will draw humans away from their miserable origins and divinize them: that will be the goal of my philosophy.*

And Plato saw that amour would be the center of his doctrine: amour, the mysterious spark clarifying origins and preparing ends.

Plato went back down then, joyful and light, as if borne by winged spirits. He was conscious that, a divine workman, he was about to commence sculpting a monument as great and as durable as the one that Phidias had erected on the hill of Minerva.

IX. Love and Death

Spring was returning, and one afternoon in May, Socrates went into Plato's house.

"Put on your chlamys and follow me," said the master. "Our friend Simon died last night, and it is appropriate, in accordance with the custom, that we go to salute his body before he disappears from the surface of the earth."

The disciple got dressed in haste, and followed Socrates,

They both headed for the narrow streets neighboring the Ceramicus.

"I saw him only yesterday," said Plato. "He was standing outside his shop smiling at the little children who were going from door to door singing the praises the spring, in accordance with the custom in Rhodes. How can he no longer exist?"

"He was passing, he has passed," Socrates replied. "But I'm glad to know that he was smiling at children yesterday."

"That formed a gracious image: the old man, very thin, and the little ones surrounding him, singing and gamboling, with their thousand combined movements, which made them resemble a beehive. Simon gave them a honeyed cake, and they shared it out avidly, arguing, while praising the return of the beautiful season. Do you know the song in question, Socrates, so frank and so unpolished?"

"Yes; it's as frank and unpolished as the people who invented it," said Socrates. "I sang it myself when I was very young, from door to door, with comrades:

"*She has come back, she is here again, the swallow, and with her the spring, the fine days. She is white underneath, as always, and black on top. Will you give us a fig from your lovely garden, or a ewe and wine, or a basket full of flour and cheese?*

"*Shall we have something, or must we go? It would be good if your hand opened to give; otherwise, we won't budge. Or we'll take the door and the threshold and go into the depths of your house to abduct your little wife. She is small, easy to cry away, your little wife! Go on, don't be difficult! Bring something, give us at least a piece of wood. But open your door to the swallow. Can't you see that we're children!"*

Socrates and Plato went into Simon's house, from which rhythmic and tearful soft cries emerged, lamenting the deceased.

Next to the humble bed on which Simon had rested from his cares, his labor and his eternal thought, the veil had been placed with which his face had been decently covered during the mysterious struggle of agony. The body lay there, clad in white, they feet turned toward the entrance, as was customary, with the eyes and mouth piously closed. Green garlands and wreaths of asphodel had been placed all round, as well as a bottle of perfume.

Friends came to salute the remains while awaiting the burial, which, as usual, would take place at dawn, before the first rays of the sun.

"He had a difficult life but he was hopeful," said Socrates, pausing before the cadaver. "Poor but proud, he did not want to accept monetary aid from his friend Pericles. And in his dialogues, he only had tanners speak, wanting thus to honor his métier and ennoble it. I'm told that before his death he thanked heaven for having permitted him to be born a man rather than a beast, and a Greek rather than a barbarian."

Socrates and his disciple left the mortuary house after they had been sprinkled with water from a cypress branch in order to purify them. They hated almost instinctively toward the countryside and went out of the Thriasian Gate, the departure-point of the procession of the Panathenaia. Three roads opened before them there. They hesitated between the avenue of the Academy, shaded by pines and olive trees, which the Dionysian processions followed, and the Eleusinian Way.

Finally, Socrates set off along the latter.

"Let's go visit the steadfast places where Simon will reside permanently tomorrow," he said.

Tombs were aligned alongside the three rural routes, haunted by legend, which served as was places of celebration and ritual, and also amorous liaison, for there, near the tombs, courtesans came to line up in the evening, offering themselves to passers-by who had previously inscribed there the name of the one they desired and the price that they were able to pay.

On the most ancient tombs, vases decorated with scenes of lamentation and farewell were rusting, while on the more recent ones marble steles sculpted in bas-relief rose up between monuments to soldiers who had died for the fatherland. And everywhere, the figures of sphinxes, sirens and lions loomed up, funerary guardians.

Socrates gazed in a melancholy fashion at the scenes of supreme reunion ornamenting tombs, in which the deceased was representing sitting down, and then lying down, while his relatives surrounded him and saluted him standing up, since they still had to strive, to agitate and to struggle on the hard road of life. The master paused particularly before a bas-relief of a young woman, whom a humble disciple of Phidias had represented, choosing without melancholy or joy her favorite jewels from a casket held out to her by a slave.

"They're not sad and they're not cheerful, the dead," said Plato, thoughtfully.

"Why would they be?" relied Socrates. "The artists have depicted them, rightly, tranquil and concentrated. They have only spread melancholy over the faces of those surrounding them and who are still ignorant of what the dead already know."

"Where might Simon be at this moment?" Plato asked then, without expecting a response.

"Perhaps in nothingness—in which case, why worry about it? Or perhaps with the others, the great, the elect, in the society of Pericles, Themistocles, Sappho, Homer and Pythagoras, conversing with those who are definitively good, definitively wise, and definitively happy."

"How did he disappear so suddenly?"

"He died by accident. Impassioned by the sky, he fell into a ditch when he went out, for he was only looking at the stars. And before dying he stammered that he was grateful to Jupiter for having brought him nearer to the heavens, since his eyes, obscured by age, could no longer see the stars from so far away."

Plato stopped, in order to follow with his gaze two women clad in long peploi, one very old, the other much younger, who were depositing cakes and clay dolls on the tomb of a little girl, in order to maintain a kind of illusion of life there.

"Even so, one doesn't want to die entirely," he murmured. "One clings on to life desperately, ardently."

Socrates proposed that they sit down for a few moments near the torrent of Eridans, which channeled the waters of Mount Lycabettus.

The sun was declining toward the horizon, dragging mantles of amethyst and ocher. The surrounding mountains lit up with its sumptuous agony.

Socrates remained there, savoring the emotion of spring, which was tempered and appeased by the calm end of the day.

Then, as Plato, plunged in thought, repeated "Even so, one doesn't want to die entirely," the master said to him softly: "The other day, I didn't report to you precisely what Diotima of Mantinea taught me with regard to the object of amour.

Plato turned avidly to hear what Socrates was saying.

"Yes," the latter continued, "I didn't report her words to you exactly. They summarize marvelously all that we have already thought and repeated. If I want to quote them to you here, at his moment, it's because, according to Diotima, the ultimate objective of amour is to aid Simon, and every man, and every being, not to die entirely."

"Was Diotima a priestess?" Plato asked.

Socrates turned a surprised gaze upon his disciple.

"She was more than that," he replied. "She was an initiator."

And Socrates evoked the woman who had revealed the supreme mysteries to him.

"The Mantinean was young, on the threshold of life," he said. "All the generous forces stirred in her body, but disciplined, quieted and, ordered. Her full face, her arms and her torso, having the sinuous forms of striking Egyptian marbles, offered a beauty that was not effeminate and limited, but complete and compassed, in which the strength and grace of a third sex, participating in the male and the female, were combined. She spoke softly, not seeking to hold forth or debate with others, but to communicate, with the result that even her conversation was amour."

Then, after a pause in which he appeared to correspond mentally with the initiator, Socrates continued:

"Diotima had explained to me many times that it is thanks to amour that we become permanent and constitutive elements of all that is beautiful and all that is good on earth. Uniting ourselves with another being that appeals to us by its strength, virtues or excellence, we aspire to endure with it eternally.

"Finally, one day, Diotima said to me: 'Have you noticed, Socrates, how all of nature folds up and concentrates itself, suffering and calling out, under the desire to engender? A sort of malady agitates animals when the hour of coupling sounds for them. At such moments, any privation becomes easy for them, and they are capable of fighting or dying in order to realize their desire. If animals that do not reason go as far as sacrifice and immolation, it is because amour is superior to life and superior to wellbeing. And how could it be otherwise, since amour is eternal life and immortality?

"'Yes, Socrates,' Diotima went on, 'it seems evident that in loving we vanquish death; for we have other means of preserving ourselves from it than that of substituting by the birth of a young being for the old being that we are or will become. In any case, we act thus incessantly, and every human gesture is, to tell the truth, an act of amour and an aspiration to immortality.

"Remember, in fact, that from birth until death, an individual who retains his so-called identity and continuity, is, in reality, constantly changing, dying without respite. He is not the same from one moment to the next. His hair and his flesh, his bones and his blood, are being worn away and renewed in their elements, and even his thoughts, desires, pleasures and pains change and die. Fortunately, his consciousness is also transformed as his ideas, his aspirations and his joys change. Otherwise, a human life would be comparable in its anguish to an endless agony, and a man would become incapable of recognizing himself while the days succeed one another.

"'And it is also to remedy that continuous instantaneous death that he gives birth amorously to memories, which are like the witnesses of his life and which escort the future, attach him to the past and enable yesterday to survive into tomorrow and mingle with it. A friend who disappears, an image that is effaced and a pleasure that comes to an end, leave traces within us that maintain and eternalize that friend, that image and that pleasure.

"'Thus mortal beings are conserved, perishing in reality and already dead, having none of the immutability, the reality, proper to the gods, but trying to continue themselves by means of reminiscences and to ward off death by means of amour.

"'That is why, in every animal, in every living being, amour has a supreme importance. Self-perpetuation is the primordial preoccupation for everyone. Many sacrifice themselves for glory or renown, which are also forms of immortality, braving dangers, scorning suffering and accepting a more rapid disappearance in order to leave a memory for future races. If Alcestis accepted to die instead of Admetus, if Achilles sought death in order to avenge Patroclus, and if Codrus went toward it in saving his fatherland, it was in order that they could continue to remain alive among us. People will sacrifice anything for that glorious or virtuous immortality, in the same way that they will do anything to save their carnal posterity, their children, their works.

159

"'For amour, Socrates, is multiple,' Diotima added. 'There are men who can only procreate with the aid of their semen; they turn to women and fecundate bodies in order to live again in their children; but others are fecund in the mind, and their amour takes other forms: that of wisdom or that of justice. They too, sensing the divine need to procreate, perpetuating what is excellent within them. They go hither and yon, seeking the beauty in which they can deposit their spiritual semen—for they are never able to procreate in ugliness. Driven by their ardor to produce, they attach themselves to beautiful bodies, and if, in a beautiful body they encounter a beautiful, generous and well-born soul, they do not quit it again. They try to instruct it, they pour into it everything they have of the best.

"'By means of a perpetual generation of beautiful discourse, beautiful thoughts and beautiful works they satisfy their desire for immortality. And the children they produce are more perfect than the carnal ones. Homer and Herodotus have left us, in consequence, their sublime poems, a true and eternal posterity, inseminated by their genius, which remains immortal for us. And it is also by an operation of amour that Lycurgus and Solon gave birth to their institutions.

"'Yes, such are the works of amour,' continued Diotima, 'works of all kinds. And if one desired to go further, to hollow out the mystery more deeply, one could specify the ascendant march of immortality that is thus accomplished through amour. The perfect lover, we could say, seeks out beautiful bodies in his youth—or, rather a body that is the receptacle of all perfections. He engenders perfect sentiments and perfect thoughts therein. Then he perceives that the beauty that is contained in the body in question is sister to the beauty that is found in all other bodies. Henceforth he will seek, not a particular perfection, but perfection in general, made of all those distributed in nature.

"'Then the veritable lover rids himself of the paltry weakness of concentrating his passion on a single individual, and strives, through the beauty of bodies, to divine a more precious beauty: that of souls. And in order to reveal in beautiful souls higher ideas and aspirations, he will be led to meditate upon human occupations, on the sciences and the arts. Gradually, he will acquire a broader conception of the beautiful and, liberated definitively from any idea of limiting himself in one body and one individual, he will swim in the ocean of all beauties. Accumulating treasure incessantly, he will give birth to creations of genius that will perpetuate him immaterially and divinely and preserve him from death.'"

Socrates paused momentarily, caressed by the supreme appeasement of the evening. Then, as his disciple was looking at him avidly, he continued.

"Diotima said to me then: 'The Lover who, from one beauty to another, elevates himself to the supreme initiation, will suddenly perceive a marvelous beauty, the goal and crown of all his previous efforts: an eternal, uncreated, imperishable, infinite beauty exempt from diminution or increase; a beauty that does not change with the milieu and the time, and does not exist in one place or another. That beauty has nothing sensible about it. It does not attract particularly, as the face and the hands attract, and does not reside either in a discourse or in a science, since it cannot be attached to anything material. That eternal beauty exists by itself, without the support of any object, but it participates in everything that is beautiful, without anything capturing it or modifying it.'

"Finally, the Mantinean concluded her discourse thus: 'Dear Socrates, when, from one body to another, uniting all the formal beauties in a unique type of beauty, and from once science to another, concentrating all human knowledge in a single beauty of thought, one arrives at the contemplation of absolute Beauty, one already feels as if visited by a sentiment of immortality. One has the consciousness of being victorious over death, communicating with the divine. Try to imagine, Socrates, what the joy might be of savoring such a Beauty, since the limited and imperfect beauty of a human body, a feminine body, already troubles us to the point of being ready to neglect eating and drinking in order to spend our life gazing at it. To render oneself conscious of perfect Beauty, to live in the sublime in contemplating it, thus becoming immortal, not in our flesh by engendering a child but in our essence, by means of the consciousness of the divine existence of the beautiful that animates us: that is the ideal of amour, the supreme victory of the human being over Death.'"

They stood up in order to return to Athens at the first approaches of dusk.

They passed through the Ceramicus again, where all sadness was fading away under the double mantle of the earth and darkness.

"I find, in fact, in the words of Diotima, assembled and organized, everything that I had divined and everything that we have previously said about amour," Plato exclaimed, marching beside his master.

Socrates stopped and pointed at the road that was extended toward Eleusis through the tombs, and which the procession followed.

"Look, Plato," he said, "there are only two deities that can aid us to triumph over the tomb; they are Ceres and Amour. The former reveals to us that nothing finishes for the soul, the latter that everything is perpetuated by the rapprochement and the fecundation of beings and substances."

"Thus one can escape death," murmured Plato.

"Do you not know that, and are you not sure of it? So love, Plato, think, excite others to think, give birth to beautiful ideas, combine everything that you find beautiful and good and enclose in your discourse, in your works, everything that you have accumulated by means of meditation and emotion. If you succeed in putting your personal seal on it—I mean your semen—Plato will not die; for Plato will be identified with eternal Beauty, with the eternal Idea, the support and pivot of all things.

"Yes, think hard, dear friend, on what I have said. If Plato succeeds in offering to those who succeed him a mirror reflecting the true Beauty, the true Amour, Plato will live among them eternally. More than that, it will not be them but

Plato who will be the only living being. Everyone else will be condemned and consecrated to thinking via him, to existing via him. Future philosophers will be Plato, while believing themselves to be themselves; founders of religions will be Plato. Plato will become human thought, the very Soul of the universe, and effacing Plato will be the equivalent of effacing the beautiful and the good, everything that ennobles human-kind, everything that enables humans truly to live."

"Now, the words of Diotima that you repeated to me just now are fully explained for me," the disciple murmured. "If, progressing from one beauty to another, from one idea to another, one identifies oneself with the force of amour, with the ensemble, one lasts as long as beauty, as long as the idea."

"That's right. One becomes the Substance, one is the To-tality. If he succeeds in personifying the perfect lover, Plato will be, in the future world, everything that it is worth the trouble of calling a world."

They both felt the frisson of the sublime that visited them every time that their mortal understanding brushed in its flight the divine Mystery.

A kind of uncreated light, sprung from within themselves, inundated them while they walked through the darkness toward the Acropolis.

And from then on, Plato knew that he possessed amour.

NAÏS IN THE MIRROR

I

Men say that I am beautiful and prove it by always haunting my house. When they look at me, their faces reflect their desire and vehement images alter their pupils. My mirror also smiles at me benevolently. It shows me limbs so supple that one might think that the bones themselves were pliable, flexing at the whim of movements, and a cleavage so glorious and proud that Apelles might have been inspired by it to depict Venus Anadyomene.

My name is Naïs, like my mother, who was also a courtesan.[15] She conceived me during the memorable night when the great king Alexander, who was her lover, burned the city of Persepolis.[16] At the banquet that had preceded that orgy, my mother had the imprudence to drink the wine of Heraea, which grants women fecundity. But as, on quitting Philip's son at dawn, she went to join a Thracian oxherd whom she loved in secret, she was never able to say which of them was my father, the king or the peasant. In any case, I scarcely care.

My mother abandoned me when I was still prepubescent and tender. She died shortly thereafter. My childhood was difficult, first in Corinth and then in Athens, where, having no

---

[15] Alcidamas of Elaea, a pupil of Gorgias, is reported by Athenaeus to have composed an *Encomium* to a courtesan named Naïs who lived in the fourth century B.C.; she has presumably been appropriated as the mother of the narrator of the present story.
[16] Alexander the Great captured and looted the Persian capital, Persepolis, and burned its palace, in 330 B.C.

experience in the profession and knowing my body to be still spindly and ignorant, I lent myself to the amour of the aged barber Gymnochete, who had a shop near the Ceramicus. He was talkative, but not without a certain charm. He sold mirrors of his own invention and also earned some money raising trained magpies and talking crows, and amusing the populace with a kind of concert that he obtained from his razors by skillfully striking them against one another. For two years he kneaded my body with his reckless caresses, but nature had failed so extensively in him that after his death, Mnesicles, the son of the dye-merchant, was surprised still to encounter and break the feeble seal of my innocence.

It was him who initiated me in sensuality. I acquired such a taste for it that afterwards I changed lovers several times and earned enough money to buy a house and permit myself three beautiful slave-girls. I received in my house Demetrius of Phalerum, the governor of the city, and the poet Menander. One evening, Diogenes the Cynic, who had known the glorious bed of Laïs, came to extinguish one of his last ardors in my arms.

I am amicable and pleasant; that is why all women resent me. I believe they call me Danaïde, meaning by that that I am never sated, and Sheep-shearer, because I ruin young men. But I accept those nicknames suggested by jealousy and see them as the affirmation of my empire over men.

In any case, every courtesan has her insulting nickname. One is called Clepsydra because she measures the pleasure of her lovers according to the solar watch and divides the fortunate minutes between them with a cold exactitude. Another is named Crow for her vices and another Proscenium because of the false and artificial beauty of her breasts. I even know an old one who is known as Abyss, and that is the worst of insults for a courtesan.

For myself, I flatter myself with being faultless with regard to my body and in adoring pleasure and beauty sincerely. It is true that I tint my cheeks with acanthus. Sometimes I even spread yellow powder in my hair. But I do not elevate my height by lining my sandals with cork, and I am scornful of padded hips and false breasts, a supreme and heroic remedy against dangling and swollen bellies. Nor do I judge it necessary to tilt my head over my shoulder in order to seem dainty, nor to paint my eyebrows or brighten my skin with ceruse.

The days go by and Venus favors me. Someone is always knocking on my door and my bed is incessantly animated. I am, above all, proud of living in the most beautiful city in the world, in the midst of a population of statues, where Aspasia and Theodotus, Alcibiades and Harpalus loved and enjoyed life, causing the world to marvel.

It is true that Demetrius Poliorcetes has recently taken possession of our city of Athens, whose citizens have lowered themselves to the extent of divinizing him, confounding his cult with that of Pallas. They do not even recoil before the ultimate sacrileges, and in order to flatter Demetrius more they have given him the Parthenon as a dwelling.[17] At least that conqueror favors pleasure. Thanks to him, frolics succeed feasts on the sacred rock. Demetrius treats courtesans like a king and gives them magnificent presents. When I see him go past, with his tinted hair, his powdered face and his cloak laden with gold embroideries, I cannot help admiring him.

Athens is not free, but we have not ceased to amuse ourselves. The flutes and lyres have never resounded so numerously or more cheerfully in the city; wine and amour have never been more triumphant; nor has the Attic air ever been

---

[17] Demetrius Poliorcetes—i.e., "the Besieger"—(337-283 B.C.) eventually became King of Macedonia from 294-288 B.C. In his days of military glory he expelled Demetrius of Phalerium from Athens in 307 B.C.; he was subsequently deified, and took up residence, in the winter of 304-3 B.C., in the temple of the Parthenon, where, according to Plutarch, his conduct was scandalous, although that reputation seems to have been obtained more by his homosexual depredations than the gifts he is recorded as having given to courtesans, including one named Lamia.

lighter, more inflamed by the spirit of joy. Considering our eternal delight and our love of debate, one would willingly attribute to us the nature of the cricket, whose excellence is in singing.

Yesterday, in passing before the Pnyx, I saw the sacred procession of Delphi, which, changing the ritual, went to request obsequiously from Demetrius the orders that were once received from the mouth of the goddess. That offended me a little. But the same day, in a fit of prodigality, the generous son of Antigone tithed the crops of Attica in order to pay for my friend Lamia's perfumes.

I therefore have reason to say that I live in a happy city, and at a moment of agreeable folly. Then too, the source of my contentment is that my lovers love me and I adore my profession.

The other day, in the home of Glycera,[18] the poet Cratinus tried to insult us by sustaining that courtesans were similar to bath-attendants who are obliged to wash the good and the bad in the same basin, without distinction. Then I stood up and closed his mouth by reciting the verses that the great Pindar once consecrated to us, and which make our profession illustrious:

"O young women who receive all strangers and give them hospitality, it is you who burn in your hands the pure tears of incense in honor of Venus. And after you have rendered the mother of amour obliging and propitious by your secret prayers, you also procure us delightful moments, and you permit us to pick on soft beds the fruits that are the most agreeable to our pressing needs."

---

[18] Glycera, meaning "the sweet one," was a popular soubriquet of courtesans, but this one is the most famous; originally the mistress of Alexander's friend Harpalus, who died some time before the present story begins, she was subsequently the mistress of the poet and dramatist Menander (c.341-c.290 B.C.).

II

Six days ago my lover Athenagoras abandoned me and no longer wants to cross the threshold of my house. He is rich, but it is his beauty that I regret. It has often happened that I have wanted to retain him in my bed in the morning, after the joyful endeavors of the night. By that sign, I know how much he pleases me. During our long liaison I sensed the irresistible hunger easing within me, the necessity that once drove me to leave my house every evening in search of the surprise of an unexperienced caress, kisses springing from a passionate mouth, and a sensuality more generous, more gripping or more tragic.

I have, however, always prized the sole attraction of our profession, which is the liberty to lavish ourselves splendidly upon everyone, like the sunlight. We have the privilege of being able to try the warmth of all enlacements, to offer our body to all kisses, and always to hollow out, to fathom and to scrutinize the carnal mystery. And since it is evident that, as priestesses of Venus, we owe ourselves to the multiple games of the goddess, I believe that loving a single man jealously would be, for us, a kind of default and forfeiture, tantamount to renouncing our perfection, abdicating our liberty and diminishing our attractions.

Exclusive passion is a monstrosity and the equivalent, in a courtesan, of a sacrilege. Men, in any case, are equally monotonous in their amour, and do not seem worthy of the passionate distinctions that we make between them. Priapus veils their eyes and understanding so forcefully at the moment of pleasure that they can scarcely think about us. I have observed that all of them act in amour as if they had tasted the leaves of the hippomane, which are said to communicate madness.[19] At

---

[19] *Hippomane* is the name given by Linnaeus to a genus of plants that includes the highly toxic manchineel tree, but that genus is native to the Americas and Naïs could not know of its existence. The term had previously been used by Pliny in his

the moment of caresses, a sort of necessity spurs them and forces them to seek and solicit and rapid and blind satisfaction of their needs. They never linger in voluptuousness, and rarely perceive the profound essence of pleasure, which is subtle, all slowness, and is only revealed after a patient initiation. They only have in mind an obstinate idea of intrusion and larceny, like young mules who would like to penetrate a field. Their desire is all the more promptly exhausted the more tenacious it seems.

Women, by contrast, vary and renew themselves, always altered by perfection. Complaisant seekers of long exultations, they enable sensuality to unravel, meditating and diversifying their enjoyment, and seem to possess the source of wisdom and the source of pleasure in the same part of the body. Male amour is like an obtuse mole staggering in darkness; that of the female, by contrast, evokes the image of tender odorous corollas that, being soft and ticklish, love to be crumpled, shaken and raided by the rummaging bumble-bees that gorge themselves therein on honey and perfumes. Like the eyes of certain insects that are composed of a thousand facets, female sensibility is infinite and diverse, and only reflects, multiplies and confounds, incessantly and eternally, the charming incarnations of sensuality.

And I repeat, attachment to a single man appears to me to be a disgrace, a scourge similar to ignorance or poverty, and, in any case, an insult to the goddess who wants us to obtain joy from all the parts of our body, by all means and with all beings, trying to accord ourselves, by coupling carnally, not to one man but to humanity, in order to be able to grasp and penetrate the forms and resources of universal desire.

I therefore defend myself against any accusation of loving Athenagoras. No, I scarcely love him. The proof is that the other day, when Pannychis, armed with an evil smile, came to

---

Natural History and many other Classical authors including Aristotle and Virgil, but the range of its reference in those sources is unclear.

tell me that he had seen my lover in the company of my rival Melitta, I did not feel pierced by jealousy, and did not conceive even the shadow of a chagrin.

Pannychis was, however, telling the truth. Yesterday, in the home of Glycera, I was able to assure myself of the infidelity of Athenagoras, if not his lack of amour. Throughout the dinner I saw him full of attentions for Melitta. He gave her many caresses, albeit without ever taking his eyes off me. I even thought that I divined that, if he was dying of amour for Melitta, it was in order to annoy me and awaken my jealousy.

Sitting next to her, he had passed her a quince into which he had bitten, and then, at the end of the dinner, he placed on her head a crown of flowers that had already faded on his own bosom, but which had not touched me. In order to be disagreeable to me, Melitta also indulged in a thousand coquetries, swooning with laughter and squeezing my lover's knees furtively.

At one moment, Athenagoras having accidentally spilled a little lecythe of wine on his tunic, she leaned over and immodestly, brazenly, brushed his breast with her lips. It was then that, filed with disgust, I got up and went to sit down far away from them, next to young Stagonium, the auletride, who has in recent days cheered up my solitude and shared my bed. That girl believes me to be afflicted by the unjust and inexplicable conduct of Athenagoras, and in order to console me, lavishes the most tender caresses upon me. She is young, without usage or experience; if I love her it is because of the slenderness of her body, for her pointed and dainty hips, and also for her breath, tentative and gentle, the breath of a child, still a trifle sour, with a savor of fruit. We enjoy ourselves together amicably, and as I am fearful, we always go to sleep enlaced.

In consequence, I am giving no thought to fathoming the resentment and the caprices of Athenagoras, who appears to me to have a twisted and deformed understanding. If I regret him slightly, it is, in sum, only for his limpid and fresh youth, for his joyful insouciance, which is contagious and which charms me.

III

By Jupiter, how impulsive and obtuse men are, and how idle and slack their intelligence seems!

I got up late this morning and abandoned myself to the cares of Herpyllis, who excels at anointing and powdering the body, and who steeps my fingernails delicately in benzoin reddened with paederota powder. Stagonium, my lovely friend, was there, and I was gazing at her with pleasure.

Suddenly, someone knocked on the door rudely. The visitor was Athenagoras. He came in, wrathful and taciturn, and sat down on the bed without wishing us good day. I waited for a moment, but as he continued to remain silent, I also made a semblance of ignoring him and, unfastening and dispersing my hair, I leaned over in order that Herpyllis could attach a cluster of pearls and slender gold chains to it.

Time passed thus, weaving the silence and fomenting a storm.

Then, when Herpyllis went out and Athenagoras recognized my firm determination not to be the first to speak, he suddenly demanded, in a broken and cavernous voice: "Who is your new lover?"

"Melitta," I replied, laughing mischievously.

"Don't hope to deceive me with your smile and your lies," he said. "I'm not one of these men who, delivered until an advanced age to the hands of sophists, have no experience of matters of amour."

"Are you not rather ashamed of offending Naïs, who is more faithful to you than Penelope was to Ulysses?" Stagonium said to him then, fearful of a quarrel, her pretty eyes already swollen by tears.

But I made my little friend shut up and, addressing myself to the young man, said to him: "Do you have need of hellebore then, Athenagoras, or is it Melitta's amour that has rendered you stupid and brazen? For truly, it would have been necessary to blush and hesitate before daring to come here and speak to me in that fashion. You're forgetting the insults you thought of addressing to me by showing yourself enchained to Melitta's lap, like Hercules to the charms of Omphale. It's you alone who are ingrate and unfaithful.

"Certainly, you have only come to make these ridiculous reproaches to me in order to disculpate yourself and disguise your inconstancy and abandonment. You want to make the world believe that it is me who is releasing you. You're acting wisely. Otherwise, no one would be able to understand how you could push bad taste so far as to prefer a ruin to me! For, after all, you know that people call her the Trap, and the Tomb, and that she had the beauty by which you seem so smitten in the days of Nestor. Your grandfather is still alive; ask him to give you news of Melitta. He must certainly have shared her bed, like all of Greece, when she was young. But tell me: have you ever seen her in the light, your new mistress? Have you ever looked at her back?"

And, as Athenagoras was about to reply: "I'm sure that she wouldn't undress in front of you, even if you gave her ten minas,[20] for her back is striped like that of an onager, and the veins in her legs extend like the blackened rigging of a vessel that has been at sea too long. When you've had the opportunity to see that treasure at close range, instead of any other caress, give her hair a flick. You'll see then that the crown of her head is crumbling like the venerable walls of Troy, and that nothing persists in haunting her temples but a few hairs like those of a young white ewe. How can you not experience scruples, how can you not feel a frightful remorse, while indulging in familiarities, like a new Oedipus, with that woman, who might have been your mother?"

And I said other analogous things to him, for I was genuinely angry. I saw that he was nonplussed, and it was out of

---

[20] A mina was a Greek unit of weight; with reference to silver it referred to a hundred drachmae.

pity that I stopped. He did not want to appear vanquished, however, and tried to respond.

"If I frequent Melitta, who is not as old as you say, I have my reasons. But explain to me rather, why you have not informed me, as honesty demands, before belonging to another man. I would have preferred that rude frankness rather than see you making mock of me and lulling me with your perfidious words."

"I have no desire to respond to you, nor do I care to comprehend what you want to insinuate," I told him, "for, after all, if I took a new lover it would only be natural and ordinary, being a courtesan. But I tell you truthfully that I have not entered into relations with anyone and that you are showing yourself ingrate in sustaining the contrary. You know that I prefer you to all others. I do not demand large sums of money from you and I do not urge you to steal from your father. Have I ever refused my body to the slightest of your caprices? Let us explain ourselves to one another more clearly, then, and confess first why you are heaping me with so many stupidities. I recognize that you are still nourishing some affection for me, since you have come here expressly to insult me. That is why I advise you to speak without disguise. Is it, by chance, that someone has calumniated me in your presence, leading you to believe false accusations?"

"That viper Melitta must have launched her venom," said Stagonium.

"No, it's not Melitta, it's my own eyes that accuse Naïs!" cried Athenagoras. "She cannot deny her crime, since I witnessed it myself."

"He's surely mad," I said, addressing my friend.

"Only remember the festival of Adonis," Athenagoras went on, "and you will be rapidly confounded. I had announced to you in advance that it would not be possible for me to come and join you that night. In fact, my father was keeping me locked in the house. Having been informed of our amours, he feared the expenses. He had given orders to the porter not to let me out. I was therefore getting bored in my room, never ceasing to think of you, wicked woman! It in the middle of the night, however, hearing the plaintive and voluptuous cries of courtesans going to the festival, I could no longer support your absence and, opening the window, I leapt boldly into the courtyard, at the risk of killing myself.

"From there, I ran along the exterior enclosure and then slipped outside by climbing over the wall. Running all the way here was a matter of moments for me. I found the door of the terrace open, and, as everyone in the house was asleep, I succeeded in reaching your room without making any noise. I felt myself shiver as I went past the bath where I had seen your lactescent and capricious nudity triumph so many times and I approached your bed furtively. But then..."

"Then, great Jupiter...?" I cried, very curious.

"Then, I heard the rhythmic respiration of two sleeping persons, and my blood froze. I took a few more steps, I put out my hand, and alongside your head with the wavy tresses, I touched another head with close-cropped hair, and a very young face, since it still had no beard. If I had had a sword, in my wrath, I would certainly have run the two of you through..."

Athenagoras could not continue his narration, for Stagonium and I were suddenly seized by mad laughter, which made him stop, nonplussed, open-mouthed with surprise.

"Why are you laughing? Do you believe...?"

"But it was me who was asleep beside her," said Stagonium. "You mistook me for a man, then?"

"It's not true—you're lying!" cried Athenagoras.

"But yes, it was Stagonium, who kept me company all those nights. Is that the cause of your anger and abandonment then? Why didn't you say something sooner?"

"You can't deceive me so easily, Naïs! The person who was lying beside you did not have Stagonium's abundant golden fleece of hair."

"By Jupiter! Don't reply to him, don't tell him anything," the auletride begged me then, clutching my robe.

Bur, without paying any heed to her, and without replying immediately to Athenagoras, I put my hands around my friend's head and I pulled off the wig that she had worn since the fits of a hot fever that had caused her to lose her natural hair.

"There, Athenagoras, there's your rival! You can beg her pardon and not demand that she be subjected to the torture of raves, the cruel punishment of adulterers. Be tranquil! I've kept your bed pure of all soiling."

Thus I succeeded in softening and taming Athenagoras. Gradually, he recognized the truth of what we were saying and experienced so much joy in consequence that he started kissing Stagonium and calling her "little brother."

Ought I to confess, however, that while still benevolent toward him, I felt myself less amorous in his regard?

He was impatient to embrace me, and because of his very ardor and haste, he disappointed me in my desires and my expectation. Furthermore, his head was scented with saffron, a perfume that always makes me nauseous Those were only small annoyances for which I did not bear him any grudge, but, on the other hand, what can one do when one is not smitten with a man and one does not sense one's body stirring with emotion and one's arms eager and alert at the idea of enlacing him?

I must, however, admit, to my own confusion, that on leaving my bed that morning, Athenagoras declared to me that he had never previously experienced so intensely the bitter and rapturous joys. He was right. I had lavished on him, yesterday, the most expert caresses; but he had not understood that it was because of lukewarm enthusiasm and poverty of desire. I was not impatient, as taut as a bowstring, as is usual when I find myself with him. In vain I waited for my senses to arrive at delight. Desire did not abolish consciousness within me, and the amorous furies did not come running to agitate me with their violent transports. Calm and docile, I only thought of satisfying my lover. I followed coldly the advice that old Laïs had once given me in Corinth, while exercising my body and initiating me into the profession, after having cut my hair one day, with silver scissors, near the altar of Venus.

IV

Athenagoras is leaving tomorrow for Naucrates, where his affairs will retain him for a long year.

He is leaving me four silver minas because he loves me and he does not want me to deceive him during his absence. We went to Eleusis, in accordance with the common usage, and I swore fidelity to him above the sacred well called Callichoron, but I do not know whether the goddess will want me to keep my oath.

Today, in order to make long adieux, we spent the day in the plain of Dionysus at the foot of Mount Pentelicus, where Athenagoras' father possesses vast gardens. We went there on two mild white donkeys, following the current of the river Cephise and going past the column of the nymph Amaryssia.

It was a beautiful morning, entirely traversed by the vehemence of spring. The sun solicited the earth keenly, and the countryside exhaled an ardent spirit.

Scarcely had we arrived on the edge of the plain than Athenagoras, intoxicated by the flame of the renewal that was flowing in him, as in the trees and the grass, sent away the slave who was leading the donkeys, seized me in his arms and began running like a madman toward the plane trees.

An impetuous abductor, he held me violently, and procured me the delicious alarms that Hippodamia must have experienced when she was abducted by the centaurs.

I understood that he wanted to reach the broad shady ravine, propitious to amours. At first I made a semblance of struggling against him and wanting to extract myself from his grip. As I did not succeed in that, I inclined my head and began to blow softly on the nape of his neck and run my pointed and dry tongue along the hollow ticklish path that separates the shoulder-blades. Pierced by ardent desires, however, he scarcely seemed to sense my teasing, and ran, leaping hedges and brushing the iridescent softness of hyacinths and narcissi.

Finally, when he reached the most obscure part of the garden, where the plane trees inclined toward the spring and compose a moist opacity with their foliage, he bent his knee and, like a courier, he deposited me in the green grass, still shiny with morning dew. However, he did not liberate me entirely. He still kept my hands imprisoned, squeezing them gently between his own. Our gazes sought one another, met and touched, and his eyes were bathed by a troubling and tender humidity, advertising desire.

"Why are your eyes staring at me as if they wanted to pierce me?" I asked him, slyly.

"I'm not looking at you, I'm looking at your grace, and I'm also gazing, wonderstruck, at the soft violence with which your breasts are repelling the peplos that covers them."

He said that, and the, with a feverish hand, he removed my strophion and unfastened my girdle, only leaving me with the delicate and supple crocotos that flowed like a sheet of water all the way to my feet.

Then my flesh became mysteriously transparent through the light fabric, and the tunic seemed to be a mirror in which my body was reflected.

"Your beautiful lines animate amorous covetousness, my love," Athenagoras exclaimed. "You are as taut as the dryness of the earth opening avidly to the dew."

In fact, I was weak with desire, and that mad run, during which I experienced the sweet and intoxicating sensation of being a prey and belonging to a master, had aroused and alarmed me.

That is why, instead of replying, I squeezed the fingers that were still knotted around mine for a long time. Then, applying the palms of my hands, closely to his, I lifted them up gently, breathing in the odor of the flesh.

Then he drew me to him, and, without yielding, with the strange smile that I have in sensuality, I held myself against him rigidly, in such a way that our lips met abruptly and our cool, sharp teeth collided.

I sought then to unfasten his lips, swollen by the tension of desire, and gently communicated my breath to him, perfumed with helenium.

And what shall I say now about the end of our day, except that the earth was varied and splendid in its vegetation, the flowers blooming, and the sky affable and limpid. We felt a delicious innocence weigh upon our hearts. The pleasure, equal to death, that abolished all anxiety had renewed and restored serenity to our souls.

The gardens were immense. There, pomegranate trees were sagging under the weight of their split and bloody fruits; here, apple trees were prospering, so bushy that one might have thought that we were in an orchard consecrated to the Nymphs.

I remember that we wandered in a long pathway shaded by pepper trees and invaded by vine ceps. The vine was the frolicsome and capricious queen of the place. No audacity arrested or intimidated her. Extended, eccentric and lascivious, she climbed everywhere, suspending her grape-clusters like an offering to the branches of the trees, or, even more recklessly, crowned the high summits with her unfurling branches. At the bottom of that vale snaked an arm of the river Cephise, and we resolved to eat there very agreeably, while dipping our bare feet in the coolness of the running water.

We contented ourselves with a few new figs, picked by our slave, a little goat's cheese and ripe olives. And imagine our surprise and joy when, after the meal, when we were thirsty, we saw two wooden cups, following the current of the stream and coming toward us, bobbing like little Phoenician ships. It was Herpyllis who had thought of sending us Samos wine without troubling us with her presence. She had taken the precaution of diluting the wine with warm water, calculating the cooling that the journey ought to produce. And in fact, the noble beverage reached us at a just and agreeable temperate.

179

We both drank from the same cup, careful to place the lips at the place where others had posed, in such a way that we kissed many times via the wine. Afterwards, Athenagoras went to pick apples and playfully put them between my breasts, alternately biting and squeezing the carnal fruits and those of the trees.

But our approaches, innocent until then, were suddenly enfevered by ardor and somber desire, at the moment when we leaned distractedly over the stream and saw our coupled image flowing, dark and fluid, at the whim of the waves. We knew then that we were ephemera, wretched and perishable, unconscious playthings of a mysterious destiny. Then fear, the sentiment of death and the image in the water, as fleeting and fluid as life, united us almost involuntarily in a hectic and brief caress, full of joy and distress. Thus sadness came to add itself to that day, already prodigal in so many sensualities.

When we thought about returning, pressed by the violet light that announced the advent of night, Athenagoras said to me: "Do you not think, Naïs, that we have savored today the sweetest moment of life? For myself, nature has never been so graciously welcoming, and voluptuousness has never filled me with so many enchanting gifts."

"You're right. I too experienced the same joy. But let's not talk about it, for fear that Adrasteia, the jealous goddess, might hear our reckless words. It's necessary to receive happiness with prudence and modesty, in order that the gods are not offended by it."

"I've heard Epicurus say," Athenagoras continued, "that it's a custom among the Scythians to open their quiver before going to bed every night, and to throw a white pellet into it if they judge that they have spent a happy day, or a black one if they estimate the contrary. When they die, the relatives surrounding them have only to count the contents of the quiver and, if the white pellets outnumber the black ones, they call the man who has died happy. But I think that in acting thus they are behaving dully, like true Scythians. For, in sum, Naïs, don't you think that one day like the one I've just spent with you, is sufficient on its own to compensate and counterbalance entire years of misfortune?"

I did not reply to my friend, feeling that I was assailed and conquered by the softness of the surrounding things. The splendor and the crimson of the setting sun penetrated all the way to my soul, which buckled in a delicious weakness.

In my perpetual mobility, I then experienced a vague chagrin, a fugitive distress in knowing that Athenagoras was about to depart, and thinking about uncertain returns, the risk of shipwreck, the danger of pirates, the omnipresence of death that lies in wait over all things and unfailingly ends up attaining them and swallowing them...

V

Today I went along the chariot route that descends from the height of the Acropolis to Pireaeus. I went to the port to wave farewell from a distance to Athenagoras, whom I could not accompany overtly because of the presence of his father.

Herpyllis and another slave went with me. We were mounted on three donkeys led by a single drover, and as it was the day of the public assembly we were shoved and pawed by the people who were crowding the road. The wretched Philetas, the old athlete, a naturally malevolent man, even tried to take advantage of that flood of people to insult me. Perhaps he thought he was dealing with one of those fearful dicteriades who only go out at night and give themselves meanly for the price of a few dates or a measure of wine.

He arrived, fat and thickset, coming from Phalera, when he was obliged to stop because of our donkeys, which were blocking the path. Instead of standing aside or being patient he burst into vociferations and abused our donkey-drover.

"Know," he cried, "that if you don't bestir yourself and hurry along your paltry donkeys and the she-asses that are riding them, I'll lay your entire company on the ground and walk over them."

The donkey-drover seemed nonplussed, but I, unmoved by such braggadocio, intervened in the argument without delay, addressed myself to the old graybeard and shouted: "It's a long time ago that you forgot how to lay a woman down, wretched Cecrops! I doubt very much that you're capable of such an exploit."

The crowd started to laugh at those words, and our lamentable braggart judged it prudent to make himself scarce, muttering vague insults. As for us, we passed on through a rumor of triumph and approval.

I had promised Athenagoras to place myself near the tomb of Themistocles, facing the Bay of Salamina, in order that I could be the last to salute him, as the departing ship skirted the coast.

The sea was calm. In the distance, the isle of Aegina was visible, crowned by the acroteria of the temple of Minerva. An even mist, rosy and tender, married the sky to the sea, while light clouds, scarcely fringed with crimson, announced the approach of sunset. Finally, I saw the Egyptian ship set forth with the aid of oars, the sails still undulating slackly in the feeble wind. But it passed by quite a long way from the coast and I could scarcely make out Athenagoras sitting in the prow and agitating the flap of his cloak with my intention.

As the sun declined, the water suddenly seems to be strewn with faded violets, and the ship, which was heading westwards, seemed to be going toward an apotheosis. The waves played around its flanks like Panope and Galatea, girdling it with foam.

For a moment, I experienced the desire to be on that curved wood myself, venturing toward strange lands, but it was sufficient for me to dart a single glance at the Acropolis to recognize the sentiment of the homeland vivacious and imperious within me. There is no hope that I could find such a splendid city as Athens anywhere else, entirely clad in glory, all sculpted in marble: Athens, where the men are intoxicated by thought and voluptuousness is a privilege common to the mind and the body. My city, my dear city, is the source of all the essential beauties, the lighthouse of the world, and one cannot take a step therein without encountering an ornate intelligence or a great memory.

In thinking about Athens I turned my head and piously caressed with my gaze the monument near to which I was standing, erected to perpetuate the memory of the conqueror of the Persians, the greatest among the Greeks. The land of the Magnesians jealously retains the ashes of Themistocles, but his real tomb is here, near the Salamina that recalls the proudest pomp of his glorious life and before the Saronica that saw his victory, every wave of which awakens the remembrance of his triumphs.

As I reentered the city, however, I felt sad, because I lacked Athenagoras and Stagonium was at the festival of Megara. I wandered therefore, somewhat randomly, through the deserted Ceramicus, and then went listlessly into the quart of Scyros where I live.

For a few minutes I had understood that a man was following me, but I was entirely absorbed by the thought of Athenagoras. As I went past Melitta's house, I saw her sitting outside her door and making engaging signs, fruitlessly, to the young sophist Agathon, who was crossing the street.

"Melitta guarded the grape jealously when it was gilded and appetizing," I said to the sophist, ironically, as I caught up with him. "Now that it's dried up, she doesn't hesitate to lavish the pips on all comers."

"She's mistaken, in any case, in addressing herself to me," he replied. "Even young and fresh I'd still have disdained her. I'm wearied and disappointed by amour."

He was leaning on his staff and speaking to me indifferently.

"What! You claim to be blind henceforth to the charms of the goddess?" I asked the young man, very surprised.

"What do you expect, Beauty?" he said. "Courtesans give nothing but chagrins and only engage expenses. If one approaches the bed of a young woman, one is obliged to share one's fate eternally, unless one wants to become a perjurer, not to mention the distaste of the obligatory caresses that a husband gives to his wife. There remains adultery, but I don't want to climb up to windows by night, giving myself to the larcenies of amour. I prefer, therefore, to follow the example of Diogenes, who sang the nuptial song to himself alone."

I only replied with a scornful glance, and I continued on my way.

As I was about to cross the threshold of my house, the unknown man who persisted patiently in following me became bolder and approached me.

"Good day."

"Good day to you also."

"What's your name?"

"What's yours? You'll know mine later if I want to give it to you."

"You seem to be in a hurry."

"So do you."

"Is someone expecting you in your house?"

I hesitated or a moment, recalling Athenagoras, and then I said, proudly: "The man who loves me is always expecting me."

"Proud woman! I'll give you anything you demand as the price of the least of your favors."

"Would you like a single kiss in exchange for a mina?" I proposed, arrogantly. "I can't give you a longer caress this evening." I knew that he would never accord such a large sum for such a brief sensuality.

But he approached, trembling and joyful, and he held out his lips and the silver. I saw then that I was dealing with a passionate individual at the emergence from childhood. I took pity on him. Offering him my lips, therefore, I drew his mouth, which no down offended, toward me. clasped my hands on the nape of his neck, and leaned toward him like a thirsty hind inclining over a spring.

"Your kiss has the scent of nectar and am intoxicated by amour merely for having touched your lips," he stammered. And he circled my tunic with his arms, like a supplicant.

Then I took pity on his young desire, his tender novelty. I did not want to imagine him lying in a cold and solitary bed. That is why I permitted him to pass over the threshold of my house.

VI

I am happy, without alarm, and yet full of anxiety. That is because I can foresee the exhaustion of the quarry of my desires. The other day, while the depilatress was polishing my body, I examined myself in the mirror of Paphos, seeking my skin in vain for the slightest wintry imperfection, the smallest sign of frost and withering, any suspicion of a wrinkle.

What frightens and disquiets me is perhaps the excess of happiness, the accomplishment of all my wishes. Yesterday, the supreme day, surely the most glorious of my life, I savored all the intoxications of victory and even drank the cup of triumph.

What a keen amusement, what a frank delight, and how unforgettable that night will remain for me! On the Acropolis, at the Parthenon, in the violated sanctuary of the Protectress, Demetrius Poliorcetes gave a banquet. The Athenians, who had ceded to him the temple of Phidias, where the Virgin alone had her dwelling, also paid the expenses of his table. In addition to the habitual commensals of Demetrius, we were ten courtesans, the ornament of the city: Lamia, the tyrant's mistress; Glycera, who accompanied her lover Menander the actor; Laena, the lover of the great Epicurus; and then Mnais, Stenelais, Plangon, Ioessa, Myrtale, Parthenis and me. Demetrius had also invited the cynic Crates, with his disciple, the young Hipparchia, a strange couple who live conjugally in the public square, before everyone's eyes, for amour is, in their eyes, merely a legitimate and innocent natural function.[21]

---

[21] The Cynic philosopher Crates of Thebes (c.365-c.285 B.C.) married Hipparchia of Maroneia, who lived with him in poverty on the streets of Athens.

Athens will retain the memory of that banquet for a long time.

Crowns of rare and various had been placed on our heads. Lamia had one of roses of Emathia, those that the nymphs offered to Ion in the vicinity of Pisa. They have sixty petals. Glycera's lot was a crown of very singular lilies known as "the joy of Venus" because of their indecently arboreal pistil. Stenelais was crowned with roses of Tenedos known as "white eyebrows" and Plangon with ambroisia, a tender floret that, it is said, was born on the head of a statue of Alexander. And there were also crowns of asphodels, cosmosandales, wild mint and spring anemones.[22] As for me, I was offered one woven with the violets that Proserpine rendered darker than all other flowers, and which exhale and insistent and sweet spirit.

Of the variety of perfumes I renounce giving an exact idea. As soon as we went in we were enveloped by a flood of nard of Tarsus and saffron. And after the first course the doors opened of their own accord unexpectedly and a flock of doves, saturated and steaming with even rarer essences, flew into the hall and sprinkled us with rose of Capua, magalion of Ephesus and panathenaica.

The service was so well extended and the dishes succeeded one another with such perfection that, toward the end, Demetrius summoned his cooks. There was Agis of Rhodes, who only knows how to fry fish, but fries them inimitably, Nereus of Chios, who deigns to prepare conger eel, Cuthinus, who has the modest specialty of lentil purées, and the glorious Cariade, nicknamed "the transformer of the pig."

We had awarded them a silver crown; they were worthy of it. Among their masterpieces I still remember a dish composed of the bellies of piglets that had been aborted to render their flesh more delicate. We were also served white swans

---

[22] The flowers ambroisia and cosmosandales are mentioned in Athenaeas' *The Deipnosophists; or, The Banquet of the Learned*, from which numerous other details of Demetrius' feast and some subsequent references are appropriated.

macerated for forty-eight hours in warm water in order that their color would not change, suckling pigs garnished with pheasants, and peacocks that still preserved their splendid plumage.

After the appeasement of hunger we engaged in conversation. It was fluent and full of enthusiasm. I retain, however, a disordered and confused memory of it, so much did all those eloquent guests sustain, as was their habit, contrary opinions, cursing and extolling amour by turns, spreading sarcasm over courtesans or deifying them, pronouncing alternately for ataraxia and passion, for the just and the unjust, for the Academy and the Portico. I only collected rare disconnected fragments, strayed by hazard to my ears, which only gave a pale image of all that effervescence of wit, all that vain but agreeable human birdsong. Thus, I recall that at one moment, the glorious Menander decided to speak in the midst of a general respectful silence.

He had curly hair mingled with gold strips, which was elegantly draped over his mantle. The staff with which he sustains his majestic stride was reposed by his side. He spoke to us about destiny and chance in charming words, pronounced through the veil of a soft and studied melancholy.

"There is no philosophy of happiness," he affirmed. "I consider as the happiest of men the one who, having contemplated placidly the august and essential things of the world—the sun that shines, the stars, water, clouds and fire—returns quickly whence he came; it is futile that he live any longer, since he can see nothing better henceforth. The most enviable good, in my eyes, is a beautiful death visiting a young body."

And as everyone remained silent, he went on: "If you wish to know who we are, look, in passing through the Ceramicus, at the tombs that border the road. There are the bones and the vain dust of kings, of the powerful, of sages—in sum, all of those who rejoiced in fortune, greatness, renown and beauty. But see that time had taken everything away from them, and that all of them are presently confined in a narrow subterranean dwelling."

"The things you are telling us lack gaiety," objected young Stilpo, my neighbor at the table, then, readjusting a stray lock of his hair. "Let us therefore drain our cups, let us seek the superfluous in dissipations and delights, and sate ourselves with enjoyments. Long live uproar, as your uncle said, O Menander! Nothing is more eminent than the belly. The belly is your father and your mother. Glory and privileges, virtue and good mores, are merely vain baubles, the dreams of lunatics. The only real and solid thing that you will have possessed, definitively, is what you have eaten and drunk. The rest I only count as dust and illusory shadow."

"Yes," replied the parasite Criso, in the midst of general laughter, briskly swallowing a locust. "The mouthful that one holds between the teeth is the only positive thing, and, I even dare say, the sovereign good. When I see that my dinner is assured, I'm joyful; and when, on the contrary, I'm belabored by blows in the guise of amusement, I become sad. That, for me, is good and evil. I will always praise to his face the man who permits me to fill my paunch. If any of the guests dares to contradict me, I shall make it my task to taunt him and turned him to ridicule. Then, gorged on meat and wine I shall withdraw and, as I have no domestic to light my route, I shall crawl all the way in darkness and advance craftily, ever fearful of encountering the watchman making his round, who would not fail to belabor my back with blows..."

He stammered. Vivid tints reddened the cheeks of all the guests, announcing imminent drunkenness. For some time the cupbearers had been bringing pure wine.

Slaves distributed silver headbands as a precaution, and we wrapped them round our heads above the temples in order to prevent an excess of drunkenness, which might trouble our brains excessively.

Women from Rhodes who played the guitar entered the hall. From a distance they appeared to me to be naked, but he men, very sagacious in that matter, assured us that they were wearing discreet veils, molded to the body in the form of a sheath. Then we saw auletrides advancing, dressed as nymphs, pretending to be pursued by satyrs.

For a few seconds, I felt slightly dazed, and I was gazing distractedly at a mime who imitated by turns a pleading woman and a drunken old man when I felt the brush of a kiss tickle the nape of my neck.

It was my neighbor Stilpo, the young Epicurean. Placed beside me on the same bed, while biting my earlobe gently, he whispered: "Dear Naïs, you are the peace of the body, the ecstasy of the soul and the culmination of sensuality..."

But I pushed him away gently, saying: "You're sounding beautiful but futile things in my ears, my friend. I've resolved to refuse myself amour for tonight."

I said that to him because I could see Demetrius peering at me complaisantly, and, on the other hand, I sensed the gaze of Polemon, the rich and elegant philosopher who has the reputation of scorning women, fixed obstinately upon me.[23]

Stilpo was about to persist, but at that moment the cupbearers brought ewers in the form of tritons, and we washed our hands before passing on to the second tables.

Slaves entered a moment later carrying vessels shiny with grease, on which there were the rarest entremets and the finest delicacies: cheese mixed with multigrain flour, chickpeas grilled in butter, and virgin honeycombs. A gourd of lotus wine was then unsealed and Lamia, the tyrant's mistress, filled a large golden cup with it.

"Friends," she said, standing up, "the divine Demetrius invites us to drink. Let us drink to his health, and drain the cup without measure. There no peril in it unless you are overtaken by the pleasant adventure of the rude Arcadians who once sent an ambassador to King Antigonus. Having never tasted Thracian wine before, they soon lost their heads and pushed audac-

---

[23] A philosopher named Polemon was head of the Academy from c.314 B.C. to c.270 B.C., and was succeeded by Crates; none of his writings survive, but he is mentioned in *The Deipnosophists*.

ity so far as to lay hands on the royal concubines, within the sight of everyone."

"In any case," said Demetrius, laughing, "don't be inhibited for so little. Everything is permitted here and everything is at the disposition of the guests, including the women. But since the wine is still according us a few moments of sagacity and one wearies of always discussing philosophy, I want to propose a new amusement to you. Assembled here are all the beauties of Greece, and we can, for that reason, repose our eyes on enchanting bodies. Nevertheless, these sirens that surround us are mortal. They can, therefore, only partially appropriate the charms of Venus, and each one is distinguished above all by the accomplished perfection of a single part of her body: one for her mouth, another for her waist, another for the sculpted treasures of her breasts.

"I therefore propose to offer, after preliminary examination, three golden crowns to the three most outstanding beauties. We shall award the first crown to the one that displays the most perfect breasts. We shall award the second to the one who possesses the most perfect hips. As for the third and most honorable crown, it will be given to the one who appears to us to excel in the difficult science of the kiss. By acting in that way, I believe that the essential attractions of womanhood will be united and exhausted.

"The breasts are the recipient of caresses, that which we contemplate as the eternal landscape while we float in the ardent infinity of sensuality. On the other hand, the hips summarize line and movement, painting and statuary. They are the vase of the flower, that which inspires and satisfies amour. Their divine curves, more perfect than those of the most beautiful mountains and the happiest valleys, trace naturally and in an occult fashion—in going from the armpit to the ankle, launching forth and easing down, rebounding and swelling—all the fatal signs of desire. It is the hips that create the amorous woman and consecrate her to the fervor of caresses.

"And what can one say of the kiss, the spark that ignites sudden conflagrations, the ardent breath that grants simultaneously burning and freshness, the tongue of amorous, mute and maddening, which expresses itself quite naturally and possesses the instinct of sagacity? It is the kiss that commences, realizes and completes all voluptuousness. There is laughter in it, the frisson, and there is also anguish and vertigo, and there is also sovereign bliss in a kiss. The mere contact of the lips thus runs the entire gamut of pleasure and substitutes for all the other joys. Lip upon lip, humans equal the gods."

We applauded those words, and vices thickened by wine rose up to demand the competition.

Then Macedonian trumpets announced the end of the meal, and at the same time, the white curtains of the sanctuary were drawn back, to reveal the Amour of Phidias, the Bacchus of Praxiteles and the Pan of Lysippus, and a great many other statues, as well as several celebrated paintings, cleverly lighted by a multitude of golden lamps.

Lamia, Hymnis and Ioessa stood up to dispute the first prize, which did not interest me. I could not take part in it and therefore did not pay any attention to it. For myself, I like Hymnis' breasts, which are soft and proud, like two roe deer fawns. I would have given the prize to my friend, but the opinion of the men was quite different. In order to flatter Demetrius they gave the crown to his mistress, Lamia.

When the second contest was proclaimed, everyone's eyes turned toward me. I stood up, pushed by secret springs, feeling suddenly emboldened, sure of myself. In a single moment I was transfigured, dominating the wine, mastering fatigue, and also challenging all the surrounding covetousness.

O Venus! I thought, addressing a silent prayer to the goddess, *let me be victorious in this struggle and I shall consecrate to you my silver mirror, still moist with my warmth.*

I knew that only Stenelais would dare to compete with me, firstly because of our intimacy, and also because she has a perfect body.

I let her go forward first. She unfastened her belt and kicked off her sandals, but conserved a tunic of violet gauze, believing that her flesh would trouble the men more through the diaphanous shadows of the fabric. First she curved her arms like the handles of amphorae, tilted her head toward her left shoulder, and began to dance, swaying her hips rhythmically, flexing her torso and arching her back. Her entire body flowed and undulated like the water of a spring. It was truly beautiful. Gradually, the emotion of the flesh rose invasively, and Stenelais appeared to awaken vehemently to passion.

And it was in the midst of a long murmur of admiration that I succeeded her.

I was conscious that chance was on her side and in the absence of a superhuman skill and a great sensual splendor, victory would escape me.

Then, with a rapid gesture, I undid my golden clasps and allowed my unfastened tunic to fall. Then, completely naked and natural, I turned my back to the spectators, graciously and mischievously, and as Apollodorus said later, made my hips laugh, so successful was I in making a violent and staccato movement by which all the flesh appeared to take fright and rebound as if suddenly enamored.

Then, without delay, turning to face the men and snatching one of the burning torches suspended from the columns, I approached it to my body and I illuminated with a trail of flame the most secret lines of my clean young flesh. A moment of quivering silence followed, and I read so much sensual inclination in all the gazes that a sort of disturbance took hold of me, and I know not what sudden timidity, some abrupt awakening of modesty. It is to that that I owe the victory, for my forehead was natural covered with red, and a decent flexion of the entire body concealed my nudity. At the same time, undoing my hair with a natural movement, I made myself a mask and a mantle by allowing it to stream and spread around me.

"By Jupiter, Lysippus," said Demetrius, "do you not think that she is more gracious and more modest than the Cassandra that Polygnotus painted as she emerged confused from the arms of Ajax, son of Oileus?"

Then I heard the sound of applause, and then the king came to kneel before me and, advancing his head, he brushed my breast respectfully with his lips. I believed that I had collected my entire triumph, and could not suspect that Venus would deign to favor me further.

For the prize of the kiss we were all invited to enter the lists.

The king chose Epicurus as arbiter because of his great wisdom and his sharp and impenetrable soul.

Each of us , therefore, had to go to him and kiss him on the mouth.

Stenelais, who was the first to take her turn, was the most admirable. She had learned her art from the sacred hierodules of the temple of Dendera in Egypt. She approached Epicurus, and instead of leaning over for the kiss she extended her hands to him, drew him toward her and, capturing him with the aid of her gaze, she studied him for a moment, attentive, anxious and almost tragic. Then she darted a kiss at him, as rapid as a flash: a bitter and piercing kiss.

Then it was the turn of Laena, Epicurus' lover, who, without kissing him, took his hand amicably and said to him: "Remember the long kisses of our bed."

Among the others, the men esteemed, I believed, Ioessa, who closed her eyes dazedly and instead of kissing appeared to drink Epicurus' lips avidly, and also Myrtale, whose tumescent mouth was like the bud of a poppy. She kissed in a swoon and a state of tender weakness.

All of them, however, had shown a profound understanding of sensuality. I approached in my turn without any illusion and without thinking of succeeding. I strove, instead, to be simple, and I remembered the kisses with which my Phoenician nurse had flattered and pampered me, gluttonous, effervescent and multiple kisses.

Forgetting all artifice, therefore, I leaned over and kissed Epicurus on the corner on the mouth. And after a first full kiss I gave him several others, rapid and reiterated, which the spectators scarcely saw because I repeated them without moving my lips by means of rapid touches of my teeth.

I felt Epicurus shiver, but I did not believe that it signified victory, until he turned to me at the end of the competition and said to me smiling:

"It was certain, and we ought to have divined it, that, possessed of the most beautiful body, you would also offer the sweetest liaison of the lips. In all the other kisses I recognized a skillful caress, sensuality consciously provoked, while in yours the avid and orgiastic force that moves the world burst forth and triumphed: primordial desire, the organizer of the universe, the same fecundating virtue that animates the sun and draws rising saps."

It was my apotheosis. They all ran and united their arms in order to carry me in triumph. In truth, they all wanted to stroke me, to touch me, at least to experience the contact of my flesh, since they could not clasp me in their arms at greater length.

I had never sensed the bestial concupiscence of men more exuberantly, more nakedly and, more acutely. I savored the vehemence of the groping hands, the tactile impatience of fingers that tried to impregnate themselves with female nudity, as if it were a matter of the perfume of a flowerer. And the empire of desire was such that Demetrius, his eyes shining and his gestures feverish, spilled over my breasts, as if by accident, an amphora of red wine of Anthilia, and then followed me into the opisthodomos, where I went to wipe myself. And without caring that it was dark there, that he could not see my beauty, he possessed me on the bronze chest in which the treasure of the goddess had once been contained.

The wine was running in floods again when we returned to the banquet. Certain redoubtable plants were even mixed therein, which exited and exacerbated desire. And I can scarcely remember with any order the rest of the evening. I vaguely remember having participating in an orgy and having seen bodies lying asleep, cups overturned and trickling, and couples...

At one moment, as Apollodorus lifted me in his arms, I perceived the somber Crates, steeping Hipparchia's breasts in wine and then kissing them, pensive and concentrated, as if he were accomplishing an ineffable ritual.

I went home at dawn, utterly exhausted by fatigue.

VII

Socrates claimed, it is said, that Amour was born from the furtive caress that Poverty obtained from the god Plutus. Personally, I think that it was rather Jealousy that engendered Amour. In any case, Jealousy aliments and sustains human ardors abundantly. Many a time, her sharp spur aids us to obtain and retain our lovers.

I remember a rich dye-merchant who sacrificed the entire cargo of his ship for me, and whom I kept on a string for eight full months. It was insinuated that I had cast a spell on him, but the only philter that I employed to lead his reason astray—I swear it by Adrasteia—was infidelity. When I saw his inclination becoming lukewarm, I arranged for him to find my door ajar, as if by chance, and to hear my sighs confounded with the moaning effusions of another man. Then he yearned to resume his chain, and desire flooded him again, young and ardent. Warmed by other kisses, I appeared to him to be embellished, not to say irresistible.

The same adventure is happening to me now with the young poet Posidippus.[24] I had no motive to refuse to welcome him, since he is rich and likeable. But on the day when he took it into his head to come and declare himself, I was waiting for my faithful Cottavus, a reliable client who always pays me three minas and possesses imprescriptible rights over my body. For having been thus rejected by virtue of hazard and temporary necessity, Posidippus has been sighing after my

---

[24] The author might have in mind the epigrammatic poet Posidippus of Pella (c.310-c.240 B.C.), although the character cannot be him, given the datable events featured in the story..

favors every since, and follows my footsteps in a servile manner. The other day he sent me a spring crown with this gracious epigram:

"I am sending you this crown, which I have woven with my own hands with the most beautiful flowers. It includes a rosebud, a lily, a dewy anemone, a warm and living narcissus, and a secret violet. Thus crowned, cease your proud rigor toward me. You are blossoming now like these flowers, but do not forget that, in their example, you will fade."

It even appears—at least, the parasite Cratias assures me of it—that Posidippus was so smitten with me that he wanted to come with his friends one night in order to abduct me.

However, he has Plangon for a mistress, and Plangon is a vivacious and desirable young woman. She is from amorous Delos, so highly reputed for its beautiful women, but Posidippus is disdaining her. Enfevered by my resistance, he is allowing himself to languish and etiolate. For my part, I am amusing myself by spurring his amour, disappointing his appetites. Such maneuvers will certainly complete his infatuation and put him at my mercy.

Today again, when going early in the morning to the rocks of Phalera in order to bathe, I saw him waiting on the shore. He was holding a rod, pretending to fish, but the glances that he cast at the road, his disturbance on seeing me approach and his tender confusion told me the truth. It was not Neptune but the son of Venus who held him prisoner.

Far from fleeing, I headed negligently toward the rock where he was sitting. There, without looking at him, I took off my garments and got ready to go into the sea.

First I took off my sciadion and my crimson sandals, and then my emerald-colored robe in fabric from Cos. When I unfastened my hair and it covered me nothing remained over my body but a light tunic. But I did not separate myself from that yet; I lingered over unfastening the attachments one by one, in order that the stripes and erosions that the belt leaves on the skin would have time to fade.

The will of Boreas was otherwise, however, for before I could perceive it, an impetuous gust inflated my tunic, lifted it up like the hand of a lubricious old man, and exposed my legs and my bosom to the daylight. And I contemplated all the beauty of my body, reflected in the desirous eyes of Posidippus. That vision had inflamed him. He seemed bewitched by it, as if he had been admitted to sound with his gaze the goddess' own girdle.

Then I rid myself of that final veil. In full confidence, for I knew that the light of dawn was always favorable to my charms, I went to met him and I said: "I beg you, young man, by the Nereids and Neptune, to watch my clothes while I'm in the water."

He did not reply, dazzled and nonplussed, staring at me incessantly, but not daring to touch me.

Then, without appearing to pay any further heed to him, I advanced toward the sea, walking slowly, in order give him the leisure to gaze at my firm buttocks. Once in the water, I marched to assault the waves, making a white foam all around me by clapping my hands, and in that fashion, I seemed to be mounted in a snowy and tumultuous turbulence. Playing confidently with the sea, bounding and then falling backwards, I sometimes allowed my flank to show, prudently, sometimes the tip of my foot and sometimes the mysterious shadows where a black dove appeared to be feeding. When I finally wearied the waves by my frolicking I emerged, shivering, my body glistening with a thousand droplets, which reflected the silver morning variously.

This time, it was Posidippus who approached me timidly.

"While you were in the water," he told me "I composed a brief epigram. I want to recite it to you, since it belongs to you and befits you. 'Cytherea, having seen you naked, cried: O Olympians, how is it then that without the semen of Ouranos, the bay of Phalera has caused a new Venus to spring forth from its fecund waves?'"

As he saw that I was smiling with amenity and that I was not nurturing any ill will toward him, he was abruptly emboldened, and, dreading that I might cover myself, he dared to touch me, to wrap his arms around my knees, and even tried to kiss me on the hip. But I thrust him way angrily, for the imprudent fellow was about to imprint his mouth on the exact corner of the flesh where I am most amorous and most sensitive.

"You're as impetuous as Priapus, young man," I said to him. "You think that everyone shares your impatience. Give me my tunic and calm down."

"O Naïs, can you not see that I am burning, and that I have a desire to steal your clothes, as Amour once did to the Graces, in order that I would always see you naked?"

My silence and my insouciant manner augmented his desire. Soon, he knew no restraint. Raising wild hands, he rushed at me passionately and tried to knock me down. I sensed that he was filled and overflowing with sensual ardor, and that subtle fire was altering his blood. Had it not been for the refreshing effect of the sea I would scarcely have had the strength to resist him. Lightened as I was, however, and pacified by the bath, I amused myself by teasing and inflaming him with my disdain. When he finally resigned himself to sitting down in disorder near his fishing-rod and his pitiful nets, I dressed myself diligently and got ready to depart.

"You don't want to give me at least a hope, cruel Naïs?" he exclaimed.

I drew away without responding.

"You're implacable. You're not even saluting me."

"Your maladroit manners don't merit any salutation," I replied, mockingly. "But as you've addressed a flattering epigram to me, I'll teach you in my turn a song from Thessaly that is perfectly adapted to your condition: 'What a vigorous and well-honed weapon you have taken from your arsenal, O Priapus. Veil yourself, ready for the wedding. Come on! Come on! Calm down, moderate your desires and hide them under the chlamys! In any case, you do not live on a deserted mountain but in the vicinity of Attica and the sacred city of Minerva.'"

He tried to launch himself forward again, but I ran away.

VIII

For three days, I did not see my admirer, the young and impetuous Posidippus. I believed in the possibility of his amorous cure, but I only believed it slightly and weakly. In fact, it was nothing of the sort, for one afternoon, while I was trying indolently to prolong my slumber, the door opened and his mistress Plangon, who lives not far away, came in, her face distraught and her eyes tearful. We scarcely had any relationship. I remember having encountered her at the temple one day when I went there to offer my saffron veil, my girdle and green crowns of ivy after the first night I spend awake in the arms of Mnesicles.

"O Naïs," Plangon said to me, throwing herself at my knees and advancing her hands in supplication, "forgive me for intruding here without knowing you, but we have never disputed a lover, and whenever I saw you, either at Eleusis or at the festivals of Bacchus, I admitted aloud your beauty and praised your skin, which is white without artifice."

"I know you too, Plangon, and you please me. But tell me the cause of your disarray and your disturbance."

"Posidippus, my lover, whom I took when young from the hands of the philosopher Aristaenetus, no longer wants to see me, and weeps in my bed, desiring you."

"How do you know that?"

"O Naïs, can we be mistaken in these matters when Amour is our guide? For I have loved that child for three years, and I love him with the disinterest of a virgin, forgetful of the calculations so necessary in our profession. I only asked him for money at the commencement of our relationship, and now I believe that I belong to him by right and owe him even the air that I breathe. For his part, he appeared to be attached to me like the lamb to the mother that suckles it. But a month ago, my attention was attracted by the thinning of his body and his decline.

"At first I thought he was ill and later, struck by his coldness, I had recourse to witches, thinking that he could no longer burn flames of Venus. Whereas once we were always coupled in our bed like two turtle-doves, now he spends cold nights beside me. In vain I pressed the quivering weight of my body against him, or, imploring, huddled against his breast. Finally, yesterday, as he remained taciturn and in lamentation, letting a sob escape from time to time, I begged him so insistently to tell me the reason for his desolation that he ended up yielding and confessing to me.

"He loves you, Naïs, he has loved you since he saw you near the Parthenon, on the Acropolis. He sighs after your charms, and your image is planted in his heart, from which it can no longer be removed. While he was telling me his woes, I observed such distress and such a mortal affliction in his features that I understood how powerfully passion had subjugated him. I had neither the strength to complain nor the courage to be irritated. My jealousy gave way to pity. Without thinking any longer of hating you, I thought, on the contrary, of coming here to implore you in favor of Posidippus. I fear that he might attempt to kill himself! As he was once a disciple of Hegesias he might think of quitting this life voluntarily and reposing in the annihilation."

"And you, Plangon—what would become of you if I granted your prayers?"

"I abandon him to you, provided that he lives and that I no longer see the devouring fire, the scourge of the goddess, laboring and undermining his body. His sleep is agitated. At banquets, crowned with ivy or narcissus, he remains bowed down by dolor, his eyes glittering, his complexion feverish, and his lips contracted."

"But what if I didn't consent to welcome him, if I didn't want to?"

"Oh, you won't do that, Naïs! In any case, you'd be afraid of offending Amour, who punishes the cruel. Have you forgotten how Meles was precipitated from the citadel because of his insensible heart? It's said, also, that in Sicily the statue of the Venus of the Baths fell and crushed a courtesan who had led her lover to death by her coldness and her disdain."

I was silent for a few moments, pensive and indecisive, admiring Mount Hymettus through the open door, which reviled amethysts for transparency and hue. The sun, touching it obliquely, adorned it and granted it life, like Pygmalion, who once caused it to pass supernaturally into Galatea. Then I turned my gaze toward Plangon and I contemplated the mute prayers that were softening her features tenderly. I knew then that I found myself, for the first time, in the presence of an omnipotent passion and my being was filled with religious terror and commiseration.

"Do you know where Posidippus' house is?" I asked, suddenly

"How could I not know? It's situated near the enclosure of Diana, on the road that leads to the Areopagus."

"Did you intend to go and find him there today?"

"What would be the point? In my disarray, I didn't even tell him that I was going to try to bend your will."

"That's good! That's very good! Will you help me to get dressed?"

I kissed her on the cheek and, proud and joyful, nurturing a bizarre resolution, I dressed swiftly, and obliged Plangon to put a thick veil over her face. I covered my own with equal care, in such a way that no one could distinguish our features and recognize us.

Dusk was falling. The crescent moon was sailing nimbly, like a hollow ship, over the limpid sheet of the sky. The softness of the Phalerian breeze lulled everything, and the immaterial violets that ornamented and tinted Attica in the west were already fading. We went out and started walking, as silent and as decent as two Arrhephore virgins. We climbed the road that runs along the Propylaea and passed close to the Enneacrounos, in front of the venerable grotto in which Apollo hid in order violently to ravish the virgin flower of Creusa, daughter of Erechtheus. From there we followed the slope that leads to the Areopagus, and, in passing along it, stopped in proximity to the vessel that serves for the pomp of the Panathenaia. That is almost the countryside, the limits of the city. The Academy and the enclosure consecrated to Diana already have an agrarian aspect, with their florid vegetation and their olive groves.

"Do you think that Posidippus will pass this way?" I asked Plangon.

I spoke to her with tenderness and amenity, for, although our acquaintance was only a few hours old, I felt seized in her regard with a benevolent and sisterly sympathy.

"At least he passes regularly, at nightfall, returning from the Agora or the Poecile."

In fact, after a short wait, we saw the young man coming toward us in the lividity of the twilight. I whispered a few rapid words in Plangon's ear, and then we covered ourselves carefully again and advanced, speaking to one another excitedly, as if we were engaged in a long argument.

"A fortunate hazard puts you in our path, young man," I said, when we drew level with Posidippus. "You'll become our mediator in the quarrel that separates us. We are sisters, and both equally beautiful, with the result that we cannot decide which of us possesses the preeminence in charm and attractiveness. If you promise to judge us and to award the apple impartially, we're ready in exchange to remain with you all night."

As I pronounced these eccentric words, I took possession of his arm. For her part, Plangon put her arm around his neck. Thus, Posidippus found himself narrowly held and wedged between our bodies.

"Leave me alone, foolish young women," he said to us, laughing. "My eyes are not disposed to judge your beauty and, although it might seem strange to you, I decline the favor that you are willing to grant me."

"And why do you scorn us thus, presumptuous fellow?"

"Because I can make nothing of your amour. My heart is a prisoner and, if I wanted to soothe my dolors by collecting kisses, a faithful friend is always at her door awaiting my arrival. So cease teasing me like this and find a better and more cheerful companion for your frolics."

"Do you think, darling, that we will let you flee our arms without a ransom? Rather you shall perish under our fingernails, suffering the fate of Euripides, who, like you, bore no reverence to women, and died maltreated by the women of Thessaly."

"But I have not said that I'm insensible to amour!" he objected.

"Then come with us. We hold you by right of conquest and will not permit you to play with us and escape."

"What do you want of me, in sum?"

"You already know our pretentions. You shall open your door to us and realize the hopes that we conceived on seeing you arrive."

"At least let me see your faces, appreciate them and see whether it is worth the trouble of taking you."

"The moment has not yet come, but have confidence. Our aspect will be agreeable to you, and as for our games, only think of having the fervor of Hercules when he satisfied the fifty daughters of Thestius in a single night."

And, laughing and pushing him, we drew him along and went into his house together. Once there, though, he did not want to be patient any longer. After a playful but ardent struggle he snatched away our veils.

What his astonishment and joy was then, I shall not try to describe. When he had sated his sight and his spirits were appeased, I said to him:

"Dear Posidippus, know that I am yielding less to your own amour than that which Plangon has for you. It is to her that you owe having me in your house tonight. That is why I want you to think more of her happiness than mine. Receive us like two inseparable twin sisters. We will both love you, and you will have the illusion that our lips only form a unique source of kisses." And, turning toward Plangon: "Isn't it so, Plangon, that you consent to share him with me?"

She did not reply, but folded up and let herself fall into my arms. Posidippus' kisses confounded us...

Then, I understood how barbaric and vain a passion jealousy is, and how amour, healthily understood, can, on the contrary, fertilize amity and render it more humane.

At dawn, Posidippus closed his eyes and slept like a weary child. And I left, glad about having made two people happy.

Toward the middle of the day, Posidippus sent me three mina. Plangon added to that a small mirror in silver and onyx, depicting the goddess of amour sitting on two turtle-doves. Posidippus' wax tablets contained an epigram that I transcribe here, having found it harmonious:

"Naïs has kissed me gently, and Plangon while biting me. Then, it was Naïs who became aggressive and Plangon who showed herself as tender as a timid dove. And as their two bodies were similarly perfect, I scarcely knew whether I was embracing the graces of Naïs or those of Plangon. I therefore married the blonde tresses and the black tresses under my kiss, the ebony eyes and those of amethyst, I matched the breasts of my lovers and I clasped their double beauty in a single embrace, desiring, if it were possible, to penetrate the depths of their hearts. Why did the dawn come, why did the matinal cock announce so rapidly the arrival of the jealous spouse of Tithonus? It would have been easier to separate the tortuous enlacement of vines than to disentangle me from their mingled arms. I think of nothing but enjoying again their twin embraces, and I shall never consent again to possess one sole mistress, for where would I find so many charms united in a single woman?"

IX

The other evening, while walking alone in the moonlight, I formed insensate desires and my fluttering imagination went from one to another.

The sky lavished its voluptuous caresses of light, and the earth seemed to offer itself to them, swooning and submissive.

One might have thought that the temples of the Acropolis, their colors already faded, and the white Lycabette, and the soft Mount Hymettus, were not in the order of real things, but rather belonged to the light and chimerical countries that one ought to perceive in the Valley of Shadows.

I did not want to go home alone that evening but I could not resign myself to welcoming an ordinary lover. Men touched my peplos but I allowed them to continue on their way. I had not even thought of passing through the Ceramicus to see whether my name was inscribed alongside an advantageous offer. I appealed with all my prayers for the advent of a brilliant poet who would desire me and exalt me harmoniously, or even some supernatural and capricious lover, like Jupiter, who might penetrate his elect by taking on the appearance of a shower of gold or shading them sensually with a swan's wing.

My lunatic reveries led my complaisantly as far as the marvelous amours of Pasiphae and the white bull. I evoked the passionate queen at the moment when, urged by her ardor, she entered for the first time the golden cow sculpted expressly by Daedalus. She certainly leaned joyfully, I thought, on the fresh metal of its impatient limbs. She must even have molded herself to it narrowly, and I thought I could see her, curious and attentive, her breasts heaving with anxiety against the inflexible walls of the voluptuous prison...

I was wandering thus, entertaining chimerical thoughts, submissive to the charm of the lunar magic, when, as I passed close to the Enneacrounous fountain, I saw the house of Barathra singularly illuminated, and I heard light and numerous bursts of laughter coming from his garden. I experienced the desire then to go and salute the benevolent old woman who served as my mother in my difficult years. I admire her more than any of my other friends, for I believe that she has an excellent understanding of the resources of our profession.

She was nicknamed Precipice, and that malevolent soubriquet allows the divination of the great captivation that scarcely left Barathra any friends except for other Athenian courtesans. That is easily understandable, in any case, when one sees her eyes, which conserve a communicative warmth even today, her hair, naturally black in spite of the years, and the nobility of her stance, which made someone say the other day to Clepsydra that only Demetrius Poliorcetes and Barathra, outside of a royal lineage, possess such a majestic attitude.

I owe a great deal to that friend. It was her who initiated me into the profession, while revealing to me the reefs of youth and obliging me to retain the cleanliness of the body that attracts lovers and the mildness of manners that retains them. Before knowing her, I can say that I was scarcely formed, and that I did not know how to comport myself decently either at table or in bed. It was her who taught me to eat sparingly, not to precipitate myself upon the dishes, to appear to be savoring my lover's eyes rather than the wine, and always to show myself sated and sober, without stuffing too much food into my mouth and inflating my cheeks like a flute-player. I also owe to her the tact and the cunning of the profession and the little secrets of the alcove that enable us to retain lovers. Finally, it is her who advised me to display my hips innocently, to deploy my nostrils as if I were always lying in wait for amour, and to maintain an artificial virginal firmness in my body, in order to permit my lovers the most flattering illusions.

May Venus aid me to follow Barathra's example to the end. After having followed a long sensual career without amour and without entanglements with the law, she still earns money by making her slaves work. Retired from the profession but not from the business, she now procures auletrides from Lydia for the banquets of the rich.

On going in that evening I found her with the parasite Thrasys, a once-opulent citizen who ruined himself for her. He still remains her faithful friend. If she has squeezed his fortune out of him, at least she still accords him her favors gratuitously by way of interest, so punctilious and upright is she.

"Welcome, little Naïs," Barathra said to me, getting up and welcoming me graciously. "I follow your ever-increasing renown with interest. You are, moreover, worthy of the best destiny. Like Naïs, your mother, you ought to share the bed of a king. Unfortunately, the monarchs of today have lost strength and taste, and one would even search in vain for an Alcibiades or a Harpalus. Only Poliorcetes appears worthy of royalty, but he is wallowing with old Lamia. She has doubtless bewitched him in order to hold him prisoner with her lapsed beauty."

"She does indeed conserve a sovereign ascendancy over him," I replied

"Yes, my darling, but let us hope that it won't be for long. I don't hold it against her that she's rich and favored by a king—those strokes of luck scarcely touch me, having been the lover of Demosthenes and received the first amorous fruits of Menander and Philemon, our greatest poets. If I detest her it's because she has vulgar manners, the opprobrium of which falls back on us all."

"She has shown the depths of her ordinary nature again recently," said the parasite. "You know that Demetrius spent ten talents buying ellanion for his mistress. Well, it appears that Lamia does not appreciate that rare perfume and welcomed it poorly. It's not her fault. She's getting old without being able to overcome vulgarity. To gratify her with ellanion was as absurd as offering the tragedies of Euripides to the estimation of a Scythian. Nevertheless, Demetrius was offended by that lack of taste and shamed Lamia publicly for it in the middle of a banquet..."

"What a humiliation for us all!" exclaimed Barathra, scandalized. "In my day, such insults would not have been permitted, even to a king. But since you're warmed up, Thrasys, tell us again about the recent adventures of Gnathenion, who took advantage of the absence of her lover Andronicus to deceive him with a boilermaker. You don't know, Naïs, how amusing this man is in his narrations."

"Recount, Thrasys," I said in my turn. "If the story pleases me I'll ask Barathra to grant you a kiss."

"Why won't you give me your lips?"

"Because I think it's the same with kisses as with wines; one prefers those to which one is already habituated."

Then Thrasys, who has a round mouth and a well-planted tongue, became inexhaustible in malicious gossip. His stories only amused me temporarily, however. When he finally left, and I was alone with Barathra, I could not hide my pensive disposition, my corporeal disorder and the foolish doors that were traversing me.

"You're going astray, my girl," she told me. "Desires are taking too strong a hold within you. That's bad luck for a courtesan who has such an amorous constitution. I shiver at the thought that you might progress from weaknesses to go as far as attaching yourself to a man. For myself, I've never felt these obsessions, which you've mentioned to me before and which you say you're still experiencing. On reflection, I can only think of one decent remedy, one palliative for your illness, and that's not to remain alone any longer. Solitude excites. Why don't you find a friend who can distract you?"

"I have Stagonium."

"You chose her hastily," Barathra replied, shaking her head. "Stagonium is still young and weak in comprehension. Her natural vivacity, little inclined to delicacy, can scarcely suit you. But I'll do something for you. You don't know my auletrides. At the moment, they're amusing a Phoenician ship-owner, Arabon, in the garden, who is disposing of the money of an entire cargo of Tyrian purple. Come and see them. I believe that you'll have an agreeable surprise.

Taking me by the hand, she led me into the gardens. I thought I had been transported into a place reserved for Hamadryads, and stood there dazzled, so brilliant and gracious was the spectacle offered to my eyes.

The moonlight was amorously spread over everything. Through that bright veil I saw seven young women who were lying here and there in corporeal ease and perfect nonchalance. They were variously grouped in the lawn, and their beauties seemed as many strange living flowers blossoming under the lunar enchantment. One, leaning over an enormous lily, appeared to be mirroring herself therein, revealing an alabaster breast with tenderly colored nipples like rosebuds. Another was unfastening her girdle, allowing her hips to protrude, while a third, completely naked, was swaying gently like a reed caressed by the breeze. The whiteness of her body was so immaculate, so vivid, that it was as if it were aureoled by a vaporous and phosphorescent light. Finally, two Lydians with silky hair were dancing, twirling and then falling back on to the flower-bed, imprisoning clumps of violet and saffron between their legs.

Shadow and light disputed those moving bodies, and their harmonious competition exalted the mystery of delicate skin tones, transfiguring those mortal forms by means of I know not what ideal touch.

While reposing the eyes, that garden of aloes delighted the senses by its odorous emanations. As if warmed by the proximity of human life, the flowers emitted heady spirits, and the scent of marjoram, the fragrant caress of irises accorded in troubling concert with the secret perfume of desirous flesh.

I enjoyed the spectacle for a few moments, carefully avoiding looking at the obese Phoenician. The wine had plunged him into a drooling and slack bliss. Lying on Persian cushions, he was staring dazedly and admiringly at the distribution of the groups.

"Coronis!" my friend called, eventually, in a soft voice.

One of the Lydian dancers turned round on hearing her name and ran to her mistress. She had a neatly compassed figures and showed a great deal of presence. Had it not been for the whiteness of her skin one might have thought her a bronze statue, so smooth and polished did her limbs seem, with a masculine texture. The dance had imprinted a slight redness on her face, and her blonde hair, falling in compact masses, oppressed her shoulders with an opulent burden.

"You see here Naïs, who is my friend," said her mistress. "She is sad and her body is burning without respite or appeasement. Would you like to be her companion and amuse her with your wit and the stories you tell so well? She is as good as you see that she is beautiful."

Coronis approached me and put her hand on my shoulder affectionately. She said: "Be welcome, friend. I don't know why you're sad, but I'll do my best to distract your mind from ennui and to pacify your flesh, for you please me."

So saying, she kissed me, and I, who know kisses, found hers soft and caressant.

Barathra permitted me to take her home with me, and Coronis charmed me all evening, so loving and curious was her soul and so agile, inventive and unexpected her mind..

She talked to me about her childhood, the vast meadows of her homeland, and then her awakening to amour. A muleteer had abducted her when she was in her first youth. He had initiated her into the dolor of love. Then her mother had sold her to an inhabitant of Alexandria, and there she had learned the insolent games of Asiatics. She sang tender Ionian cantilenas for my amusement; she knew several of them. There were some that appeared to me to be very beautiful. A naïve song of Ibicus delighted me in particular. I learned it in my turn, in order to record it on a sheet of papyrus:

"It is in spring that the quince trees watered by the Two Rivers resume their vigor in the gardens of virgins. Then the vines also give birth to flowers and are garnished by lush grapes. But the passion that possesses me does not know the movement of the seasons, for it never knows repose, and like divine lightning, it burns with an inexhaustible fire. Precipitated upon me by the hand of his mother Venus, Eros himself would be alarmed by my devouring fever. He continues, however, pitilessly, to hold me in his cruel iron grip."

For a long time we chatted about the most various things. Then we delivered ourselves to games that carried us through until dawn.

But how could I enumerate Coronis' qualities? After having charmed me with her stories, after having cheered me up by the folly and originality of her speech, she ended up amazing me and almost frightening me by her metamorphoses. For she had the gift of changing like water illuminated by the tints of the setting sun, and being mutable and undulating.

Incessantly offering me the emotion of the unexpected, she made me think of the imitators who are invited to banquets and mimic in turn the masks of fashionable actors, celebrated courtesans, old philosophers, victorious generals and tortured criminals. In the same way, in a matter of hours, Coronis changed before me her attitude, her expressions, her age and her métier. At one moment, as I was becoming drowsy, she feigned a male voice, counterfeited masculine gestures and appeared to change sex. My illusion was so great that I believed that my lover Athenagoras had returned from Naucrates.

I could not extract her secrets from Coronis and discover how she succeeded in changing the order of things and natural laws so strangely.

She only told me in the morning that she had as a lover the tanner Kerdon. I know him. Kerdon possesses completely the art of tanning, which is, to tell the truth, an art that is akin to sculpture. He knows how to work the most delicate leathers and manipulate the softest. An artist in his creations, he has an immense science and invention and succeeds, like Phidias, in communicating a masculine smoothness to all the lines of his works...

Henceforth, when I am melancholy or unsatisfied with life, I shall summon Coronis, for her resources are immense, and in her company I can extract a great distraction against ennui.

X

I went up the Acropolis at the hour when the cicadas were falling silent. Demetrius had sent word that he wanted to see me. He had recently returned from Patras, where the famous Cratesipolis, the widow of Alexander, the son of Polyperchon, had charmed him with her tender beauty and kept him enslaved for long months.[25] He only thought about her. Obliged to return to Athens, he could not accustom himself to the torments of that separation and spent his days morose and lackluster.

"I have summoned you, Naïs, in order for you to give me a kiss similar to the one you put in the corner of Epicurus' mouth during our last night of feasting. The morning dew is pearling on your lips and their caress is supple and amiable. I therefore desire one of your kisses, but I also want to ask you for another favor."

"Speak, O King."

"First look at this golden bowl. It is very ancient and the great Theodorus sculpted it. I obtained it among the booty after my victory over Seleucus."

"It appears admirable to me."

"Now look at this painting by Protogenes, It represents Ialyssus, the sun of the Sun, and the nymph Rhoda. The Rhodans begged me expressly to save it from the pillage. Tell me now, Naïs, which is your preference? Is it the painting or the bowl that attracts you more?"

"Both are splendid, Demetrius, but I appreciate the cup more."

"Well, Naïs, I will give you the bowl if you will only help me confound the philosopher Polemon. Do you know him?"

"I encountered him here during the feast that you gave us."

"He is dear to me, I esteem him and I like him, but I cannot support his arrogant and rigid virtue. More continent than Epicurus, more chaste than Plato, he seems to hold pleasure in great scorn and offends Venus and the Amours. The other day

---

[25] Demetrius' famous encounter with Cratesipolis took place in 307 B.C.

he sustained once again before everyone that no woman was capable of provoking a single frisson in him or giving birth to the slightest desire in his flesh. He is, however, in the prime of life and his youth was stormy. Would you like to tempt him, Naïs?"

"I don't understand, Demetrius."

"I ought to say that it's Lamia who had the idea. While you were carrying off the prize, unveiling your corporeal delights before us, Polemon, it appears, was covering you with his smoldering gaze. And after the games, in praising you, he said that, except for Phryne, no other woman could show such a perfection of form. You alone, therefore, are capable of awakening his flesh. Strive to humiliate his virtue. If he succumbs to you, I shall feel as much pleasure therein as if I had won another victory. Would you like to set a carnal trap for him, to bend, soften and vanquish him? Your body is noble and polished, your mind full of resources. Will you consent to risk the adventure? My gratitude will be royal, for I shall owe you a keen enjoyment. As Polemon has known lust before, he is capable of remembering it. It is only a matter of knowing how to plunge the spur deeply into his flesh..."

"But I don't feel capable, O King..."

"Don't refuse, Naïs. I won't admit it, all the more so as I believe that you can succeed. In any case, I'll give you three days, and I'll expect you at nightfall on the fourth in order for you to announce your own victory or our common humiliation. Now, sit on my knees in order for me to taste your lips..."

I remain perplexed before that new caprice on the part of Demetrius, and I truly do not know how to go about it. I hardly know Polemon. I fear him, like all the sophists who roam around the Academy and the Lyceum, speaking abundantly and trafficking their mind. Fortunately, that one is still young. The idea of lying by his side does not revolt me, especially when I consider that he is believed to be inaccessible to amour. It is pleasant to vanquish in all contests and to collect all laurels.

I am, in any case, athirst by virtue of the memory of that divinely sculpted bowl, which might belong to me tomorrow. I know in advance where I shall place it in case of success. It will be between the two candlesticks in the middle of the bronze table, under the mirror that shines in the hand of a silver Astarte. Every time someone admires it I shall say: "Demetrius made me a gift of it, honoring the victory of amour over sagacity."

XI

When the reverberation of the sun attenuated and the evening breeze began to blow from the Phalerian sea, I put on my most beautiful attire, enlivened my complexion and my eyebrows, drank a little saffroned wine, which dilutes the eyes by communicating an indolent humidity to them, and then I headed for the Lyceum, hoping to discover Polemon among the other philosophers who gather in such places.

The sunset was glorious. The sky was softened by a pale nacreous reflection, which lent the marble figures an appearance of supernatural life. But beyond Hymetta the countryside was still enameled by gleams of emerald and gold, reminiscent of a distant Garden of the Hesperides.

There was, as always, a great flock of sophists in the enclosure. Alongside bearded old men who were carrying the beggar's wallet of the cynics, young disciples could be seen, well-dressed and elegant, each holding a sculpted staff. For the most part they had carefully curled hair, and wore a white cloak and a soft hat.

The Epicureans formed the greatest assembly. Standing near the master, they were avidly drinking in his words. The son of Neocles was talking about the voluptuousness of the body with his habitual mildness. Without looking at anyone he kept his eyes lowered and traced arabesques with the end of his staff in the dust of the pathway.

I recognized around him Athenaeus, Timocrates and two young men who had just arrived expressly from Lampsacus in order to be initiated in Epicureanism. Then there was Leontes with his wife Themista, whom is it said that he shares with the master and the ephebe Phylocles, who Epicurus ordered to cut his beautiful hair out of jealousy.

In another group there was Menander, Apollodorus and further away and apart, under the plane trees, the cynic Crates, Hipparchia and her brother Metrocles and Theodorus the God.[26] I also perceive the bizarre Pyrrho, who has a mind so distracted and so blindly attached to puerilities and stupidities that his friends are obliged to restrain him and lead him by the hand in order that he does not fall down a well or into an open ditch.

All those men, who are judged to be eminent but who appear to me to be mad, had respectful listeners in abundance and superabundance, who were bathing delightedly in their rubbish.

"There is no argument to which one cannot oppose another argument, and nothing really exists in the world," Pyrrho was saying at the moment when I passed by. "Pleasure and dolor are vain words, entirely relative, since there are animals that prosper in the burning of fire, like the phoenix of Arabia, and other that, on the contrary, perish there. Nor are there opinions common to everyone. It is sufficient to be convinced of that to think that Demophon, the steward of Alexander, was warm in the shade and cold in the sunlight. And what can one say of morality when we see that the Persians permit marriage between a father and a daughter, something of which the Greeks have a horror, and that the Massagetae practice the community of women, which we consider as a supreme immortality. The Egyptians embalm the dead, the Romans burn them, and the Paeonians throw them in pools. Everything, therefore, is illusion. Purple appears to be a different color

---

[26] The philosopher here called Théodore le Dieu [Theodorus the God} was better known as Theodorus the Atheist; he is known to have written a book entitled *On the Gods*, but it has not survived.

depending on whether it is seen in sunlight, by moonlight or by candlelight; and the same stone that two men have difficulty transporting in the air, a child can move when it is floating on the surface of water."

"Nothing exists, everything is absurd," replied a young man nearby, who appeared to be nourishing a great sadness within him. "I can demonstrate it for every particular case. In saying something, something necessarily passes through your mouth. However, when you speak about a cart, can it be said that a cart passes through your mouth?"

"Indeed," sad another, encouraged. "What you have not thrown away, one can sustain that you still have. Now, you have not thrown away horns, so you still have horns..."

I drew away, irritated by all that cackle, and I approached Hipparchia, who was standing next to Theodorus. That philosopher flatters and worships himself to the extent of claiming that he is God.

"Why, then, Hipparchia, have you abandoned the shuttle by the loom and have begun to interest yourself in the sovereign god?" I heard him say as I drew near.

"Do you not think that I have made the better choice, Theodorus?"

"I would have preferred you to continue to weave fine nightcaps."

"However, anything that Theodorus can do without attracting reproach, Hipparchia can also do without meriting criticism..."

And as the God looked at her, mockingly and without making any response, she went on: "I can take my reasoning further. If Theodorus strikes himself, he is not doing injustice to anyone and cannot be punished. Now, since Hipparchia can permit herself what Theodorus permits himself. Hipparchia can strike Theodorus without committing an injustice."

And promptly, she raised her hand in order to give him a slap; but Theodorus parried the blow and contented himself with lifting the philosopher's skirt and exposing her gangling body.

There was general laughter in the audience that was following that discussion.

At that moment, however, Leontion, who perceived me from a distance, came to extract me from the midst of the men, and, taking me aside, she said: "I'm stifling among so many hairsplitters, They exhaust me and weary me with this perpetual enervation of thought. Above all, I can't suffer any longer the yoke of that decrepit lover, that Epicurus, who, at such a high degree of old age, still permits himself to be jealous. He scolds me at the slightest opportunity and takes umbrage at everything. After eighty years, will I still have to suffer because of his stink and the filthy animal skins with which he covers himself? Let him keep for himself the beautiful sentences about the nature of things and limitless pleasure. I want him to leave me alone. Yesterday he wanted to forbid me to see the handsome Timarchus, who was the first to initiate me into the mysteries of Venus. Is it just that I distance that young man from myself, who, moreover heaps me with presents and doesn't permit anyone to taste the first fruits every years before me? Epicurus however, is furious with him. He loads him with such insults that, if you heard them, you'd believe that you were in the company of a Cappadocian rather than an Athenian philosopher!"

A few moments ago, Glycera, Menander's mistress, had come to join us, and was following our conversation.

"I agree with you," she said. "I judged all these philosophers deceptive, and I'm inconsolable that Menander, who has had so much success in the theater and who has such a sane mind, finds them pleasing. For after all, they call us corrupters of youth, we courtesans, and it's rather them who corrupt it. Only yesterday, Stilpo had the effrontery to reproach me for my profession again! 'My friend,' I replied, 'We're both equally guilty. I enfeeble the body and you spoil the mind. I don't see the difference between the ephebe who wears himself out with a girl and the one who exhausts himself with a philosopher. At least the courtesan accords him pleasure. And then, as the poet Agathon says: If woman is feeble of complexion, she has no less intelligence and activity in the soul.'"

"However," exclaimed Leontion, "These toothless and perverse old men are taking away our lovers. Consider the wan and stupid faces of those disciples surrounding Menedemus. Let's go see what grave problem is tormenting them at present."

We approached discreetly, in such a way that our arrival did not trouble their meditation. Menedemus was caressing his beard and looking at his disciples one after another as if he were waiting for a response. But they remained mute and we heard him say to them:

"In sum, we need a definition. You have said that the life of an animal is different from that of vegetables. So, I take a gourd from the garden and present it to you, asking you in what genre you classify it. What do you have to reply?"

They remained pensive for a long time. Finally, a very young man raised his dainty head and said: "It's a vegetable with a round head."

The master remained motionless, manifestly disappointed.

"It's a tree," hazarded another disciple.

"It's a plant," said a third.

"Reflect, reflect further," replied Menedemus, softly.

"The gourd is an animal," ventured my young Adonis, hoping this time to get it right.

At that moment Crates went past and, seeing them sunk in the meditation of the problem, he could not help himself, and farted tumultuously in their faces in order to create a diversion. We could not succeed in holding back our laughter. As for Menedemus, he pretended not to have heard, and addressed his pupils: "A little more effort," he said. "Don't be discouraged, you're approaching the right definition."

Four young women, recognizable as auletrides by virtue of their simple violet tunics, went past us.

"Look at those wrigglers," Leontion said to us, quivering with hatred. "Their names are Marmaria, Hedia, Erosia and

Nicidia. Where do you think they're going at that pace? They're hastening to join Epicurus, my venerable lover. I'm not sufficient, it appears, for his failing strength. By night he reposes between four young women, like some Asiatic satrap, and when I want to deliver myself from his chains he sends me Timocrates, Metrocles, Menander and the whole clan, all his favorites and all his darlings, in order to persuade me to remain faithful to him and renounce Timarchus. By Apollo, I won't put up with it!"

But I abandoned my friends to their chatter, having spotted Polemon. He was sitting next to a plane tree and looking attentively at an object that he was holding in his hand.

I went up to him and wished him a good day.

He smiled in response to my greeting, and then invited me to sit down beside him.

"I was looking at this plant," he told me, "so frail, so prettily flowering, which is called a helenium. And I was thinking, and marveling, that it's a hermaphrodite and has no need of amour. Fortunate are the plants, dear Naïs! They do not know the torments of the kiss and do not put on make-up to please their lovers. In brief, they have no need to be courtesans. Behold perfect beings!"

"You detest amour so profoundly, then, Polemon?"

"May Pallas preserve me from such unfortunate thoughts! I fear offending Venus, who would certainly punish me for them as she punished Hippolytus. No, I nourish neither hatred nor admiration for amour. I observe in its regard, rather, the same indifference as toward the Indians who live near the Ganges, or the children who are being born at this moment over the entire extent of the earth. How can I love or detest then, since I don't know them?"

"And courtesans?"

"As beautiful as you, I admire them. But on the other hand, I find them unskillful when they have been putting on make-up for three hundred Olympiads and have not yet succeeded in discovering a make-up or a manner of using it appropriately. When going through the Ceramicus I often go past

219

the priestesses of Cypris, who are lined up as naked as the nymphs of the River Eridanus, However, I always refrain from fixing my gaze upon them and fathoming the charms of their faces. They cover their eyelids with antimony, paint their lips with the juice of mulberries and plaster their cheeks with ceruse, with the result that sweat traces streams and profound meanders there. I would rather kiss a panting by Apelles while it is still fresh than such a face."

"You ought not to find me beautiful, then."

"What, you're made up too?" he replied, ironically. "I hadn't noticed."

"Listen, Polemon; I aspire precisely to correct myself, to become better, and I've come expressly to ask you for a few lessons in wisdom. I won't hide it from you, however, that coquetry is not unconnected with this step, since, once intellectually ornamented and refined, I shall appear more desirable. Like Hipparchia, Leontion and Glycera, I too want to open myself up to knowledge. I won't consent, of course, to take any other master than you. If I can rely on what you said at Demetrius' banquet, my face comes back to you, and the sight of me isn't disagreeable to you. For my part, I promise to be attentive to what you say to me. Will you accept my proposal?"

He burst out laughing, then controlled himself and said: "You also want wisdom! What egotism, and how avid you are, Naïs! You are so beautiful, and yet you don't even consent to leave the privileges of the mind to the ugly and disinherited. Well, we can try. It's sufficient for you to come to the Gardens in the morning or to the Academy after midday."

"I would have preferred you to come to my house, O Polemon. We'd be more tranquil there."

"I don't see any inconvenience in that. I'll come tomorrow, after the meal."

"I'll expect you."

Proud and content, I returned home, with a warm heart. I will win my wager. I shall see tomorrow come with impatience and great curiosity.

XII

My ideas are tangled, my reason is wandering here and there, in disorder. Amazement, the dolorous bitterness of defeat, the humiliation of my beauty vanquished and scorned, those are the sentiments that dominate me. However, I am not sad. I have discovered a superior being and sensed a master. Admiration is fomenting and soothing the numerous wounds of my vanity. That man, who departed my house victorious, made me enter into curiosity. He was able to inspire in me the delicious and furtive alarm that I experience when wandering alone in the shady and murmurous woods of Venus.

But I want to repress my confusion and try to evoke that strange day in an orderly fashion. Thus, I shall see myself with more clarity and I will be able to comprehend her.

Totally devoted since the morning to the unique thought of seduction, I prepared myself to please, prolonging my warm bath in order to accentuate the dullness of my skin, easting peppers, which heighten the cheeks like make-up, and saturating my house and my bed with heady perfumes.

But I did not ornament myself much, fearing to awaken Polemon's suspicion, and I waited for him without finery, my hair simply retained by a golden ring and my body enclosed in my long tunic from Amyclae. Made of taut crimson fabric, that tunic is decorated with a head of Medusa. The frightening and attractive beauty of the Gorgon covers it to the waist.

Polemon came at the favorable moment when it is permitted to mingle the red flame of torches with the mauve tenderness of fading daylight. He was handsome by virtue of his tall stature and the grave expression that is an ornament in him. His large eyes accorded gentleness and strength in their gaze, in the same way that his entire being, without lacking sinew or vigor, is nevertheless entirely deployed to thought.

I found myself lying cleverly on an anaclintron, my feet scarcely flexed and quivering. The tunic was narrowed at the top in order to hug and emphasize my figure, and then spread out amply in the form of a lyre, thus giving me the corporeal attitudes and appearance of the Winged Victory that Phidias represented in the little temple of the Acropolis.

I was holding a pretty papyrus in my hand, the only one there was in my house. It contains the poems of Anacreon; Philemon the comic actor left it for me after the contentment of an amorous night.

"There's a poet who incites mild wisdom," Polemon said to me, when he had inclined his head, almost touching mine, and looked at the handwriting.

Then, taking the papyrus, he chose and slowly read a gracious little ode:

"Far from me the treasures of Gyges, the monarch of Sardes. The idea of gold does not transport me and I do not have enough to make a scepter. I prefer to spread perfumes over my hair and crown my head with beautiful roses. The hour that is passing and that one must collect is my only passion, my unique concern. For I do not know whether I shall be alive tomorrow."

I looked at him, scarcely retaining my surprise. He did not have a sarcastic and somber expression, as he had the other day. His gestures were affable, his voice soft. Without any hesitation, he sat down next to me on the anaclintron.

And immediately, I thought that my ambition would be satisfied, that I would see him at my feet or feel him against my breast.

"The other day, Polemon," I said to him, "I heard related in Menander's house a certain conversation that the immortal Socrates had with the courtesan Theodota. He spoke to her agreeably about her métier, teaching her the essential and accessory aspects of it, initiating her in amorous ruses. She must certainly have profited from that lesson and become better. More than the study of the philosophy proper, what I am seeking, in my turn, is a similar amicable and substantial conversation, a little light brightly cast on the obscurity of my ideas, a delicate polishing of my thought. I do not believe, as I have already said, that another could serve as my master, but in you, everything seems pleasant and our science appears amiable."

"By Apollo, you talk well, Naïs! It would be pleasant for me to guide along the flowery paths of wisdom a woman as becoming as you. If I were more worthy of it, and the times were better, I would have liked you to become another Aspasia in my hands. But tell me first, Naïs, whether you know sensuality—for otherwise it will be difficult to bite into the fruits of knowledge. Wisdom is only a just estimation of the pleasures of this world. To appreciate them it is necessary to have known them."

I started at that demand.

"What does that speech mean, Polemon? Sensuality has never ceased for an instant to be my profession. Since the age of fourteen, insatiable and welcoming, I have embraced enjoyment in its thousand aspects."

"You want to tell me that you are a courtesan, Naïs, but I know that. Do you believe that that is sufficient to possess sensuality?

"Listen, Polemon," I said to him, estimating the moment favorable for the accomplishment of my design. "Is it sensate to assert that one knows sensuality? That cannot be enunciated, it can scarcely be proven. Shall I tell you that I always feel carnally stirred, prey to all the transports, and that the frissons emerge naturally from my body as from a profound spring? My arms are avid to embrace, and my reason is ever in debauchery. Come closer, incline your head over my breast to count the palpitations; then, see how impatient my feet are, jealous of one another, and with what fierceness the blood invades my skin, solicits it and amorously besieges it."

As I spoke, I took his hands and, looking him in the eyes, I tried to draw him toward me.

He came toward me, meekly, but in order to speak to me at closer range, not to embrace me. His hands were knotted with mine, but his gaze was untroubled. One might have thought that he was next to a friend and not a woman.

"Now, Naïs, I am sure that you are ignorant of the true essence of pleasure. I have no need of any other proof. If you have a contrary opinion it is because you are confusing sensual delirium with sensuality. You are pressed by the spurs with which Amour pricks all beings, you have entered into blind orgy, but you are still ignorant of meditative ad measured enjoyment, the ornate pleasure of thought. True sensuality, Naïs, does not flow only from the body; it needs the collaboration of the soul. And, being more demanding, it also draws in its wake the cortege of the arts, the splendor of poetry, the rhythm of music. It seems complex, conscious, refined. And, far from being avid, it gladly allies itself with satiety. In order to define it, it would first be necessary to indicate that it implies the self-fulfillment of the soul above the flesh."

"What you say there, Polemon, appears profound, although I cannot grasp its meaning clearly. But you'll talk to me about it again. Don't you believe, however, that all speech pales and is effaced before a passionate gaze, a keen and extended embrace. I am, in sum, only a woman, Polemon. While you were speaking I was thinking that a kiss from your mouth would infuse me better than your science..."

I drew nearer to Polemon negligently and put my hand on his shoulder, where the clasp of the mantle leaves a little flesh uncovered. My tunic was also disarranged and my feet emerged from its creases, round, impish and immodest.

Polemon reposed his gaze there tranquilly, and continued: "For sensuality to spring forth, therefore, I tell you, Naïs, it is necessary that the soul is tranquil and disengaged, and that it can lean over the body and gaze at it. You know the fable of Amour and Psyche. It's a pure allegory, adaptable to several meanings. Imagine that Psyche symbolizes perfect consciousness and that Amour incarnates divine desire. Their harmonious union, their hermetic assemblage, will offer you the image of perfect sensuality. Outside of that, everything is merely inferior slaking. For, in sum, pleasure, such as the vulgar conceive it, is the prerogative of all beings and does not constitute an attribute proper to humans. It animates plants, insects, and even the fish in the sea. It is by virtue of amorous solicitation that birds sing, stags bell and wild beasts roar. All of them feel that sharp constraint, all of them aspire to unite, to penetrate one another, to conjoin. The entirety of nature swells and extends. One might even say that if everything consisted of voluptuous ardor, humans would be humiliated before the superb embraces of wild pigs, the burning and consuming intercourse of cantharides and the mordant feline amours of panthers.

"But in order to equal and surpass those supreme carnal orgies, humans were endowed with the infinity of thought, the multiple decors of dream, everything that is not flesh and which can add to flesh. Only humans can fecundate their own pleasure, reflect upon it, and meditate upon its sensuality. More than that, they are capable of eroticizing dolor, of confusing the exaltation of amour with the fear of death and considering their own desire as a mirror of human desire in general.

"But now I am asking myself whether it is not too soon to talk to you about sensuality, and if it might not be preferable to talk about simpler and elementary things, about the intimate meaning of beauty, or the science of adornment. Do you even know your body? Have you fathomed its secret rhythm, its mysterious law? For every body, like every face, has a unique expression, a mind that is proper to it, and a beauty that is singular and distinct."

"Teach me, then, the law of my body, for it might be escaping me, Polemon," I said to him, smiling. "I'll render the task easier for you."

So saying, I unfastened the gold clasp at the shoulder and allowed my garments to fall. My image appeared to me in the large bronze mirror; I looked at it as if it were foreign to me and I appreciated my beauty impartially. At the same time, as if my nudity gave me a clearer consciousness of my desires, I sensed that the caresses of that man were becoming necessary to me. His words had awoken a passionate curiosity within me; his presence subjugated me. Not only Demetrius' wager, but the cry of my flesh, pushed me to his conquest.

"Yes, you are beautiful, O Naïs! I approve of your beauty and I love it, as I loved and approved of your face the first time I encountered you. How many things its lineaments say to me, and how eloquent all of your flesh is! If only you knew how to refine it, to sharpen it! You've refrained from putting on make-up today, but in exchange, you've perfumed yourself abundantly. The odor is penetrating, confused and monotonous. Do you not know, Naïs, that each member of the body has a particular essence and demands an appropriate aroma? The rose, it is said, is only for the breasts. With the violet, I would have liked the mouth to be perfumed, while the hair should be anointed with the vivid scent of rue or cinnamon, in order to intoxicate. Under the armpits, I would gladly put helenium, which has a suave and piquant odor of warm flesh and opening flowers. Over the abdomen one would spread a viscous drop of nard, which gives voluptuous dreams and emits a sort of heavy vapor, insinuating itself everywhere, like the genius the presides over orgasms."

Then, drawing away slightly in order to look at me more fully: "Your eyes are rippling, like the surface of a pool under a vesperal breeze. Part your hands slightly. One might think that it was your breasts in particular, Naïs, that enchain you to sensuality."

And, gently, his finger posed precisely on the taut skin of the breast, where I bear a kind of secret wound.

I shivered.

"I knew it, O Naïs, but don't believe that I'm a magician for that. In sum, Naïs, feminine nature is as clear as an Alexandrian papyrus for anyone who knows how to read it. The color of the skin, the perfume of the hair, the meaning of spoken words and the vivacity of movements, all take on a voice in order to recount, to whoever is able to listen, a woman's secrets."

"You are divine, like Apollo! You frighten me, but you attract me more. A caprice, a folly, summoned you to my house, but now my soul desires you and seeks you. Would you like to love me? I believe that your caress would be an even greater initiation for me than your speech. You would whisper in my ear the revelatory words that permit the fathoming of infinity. You tell me that I am ignorant of the depth of sensuality. Perhaps so, Polemon! But at least I know that humans only comprehend one another, and succeed in tearing the veils with which destiny has separated them, when they are narrowly linked, carnally mingled and confounded!"

"Yes, indeed," Polemon replied. "You have said it. Hectically enlaced, avid to penetrate one another, beings abolish death, identify one another with the imperishable essences, know and understand one another. That is why carnal amour can become the ultimate spiritual act."

"O Polemon, you find soothing and yet profound words, like the Egyptian characters that, agreeable to the sight, also hide a substantial and grave meaning. You tell the truth. It is amour that enables us to read souls. Amour alone gives knowledge. And I can now confess that I desire you and that I am worthy of you. Abandon yourself to my caresses. My strength will increase in order to embrace you, and I will have you so perfectly within me that in going away, you will not cease to belong to me."

I leaned over him, overcome by anguish and taking refuge in his bosom with the frantic disorder of a shipwreck victim. But he pushed me away gently, as if I were a child. I sensed in his movements all of his sure strength, and that sensation augmented my folly.

"I would only be insulting you, Naïs, by taking you without desiring you," he said. "You are beautiful, and no one refuses our caprices. Perhaps for the first time, you find yourself before a being who does not desire anything. That is because nothing is new for me, Naïs. You know that I have acquired a little wisdom, but you don't know that I've acquired it by means of the power of the will. My youth offered itself as prey to all the passions, my days went by in dissipation. If you ask those who knew me then—for I belong to this city and was born in the borough of Oca—they will tell you that I seemed to be in haste to enjoy and to die, to savor all beauties, to try all caresses, to sample all vices. I was so impetuous, so impatient, that I had contrived hiding places in which I placed my money, in order to be able to take it out at any moment and thus satisfy all my desires and all my fantasies promptly.

"There are no turpitudes or depravities that I have not tried, and I knew the paroxysms of amour that fraternize with death. Finally, I was weary of having scrutinized everything thus and deflowered everything, and of no longer being able to smell a perfume or taste a pleasure without knowing in advance the precise sensation that I was about to experience. It was only at that moment that I glimpsed the superior sensuality, liberated from the flesh, of which I spoke, and which one can only know with the aid of wisdom and satiety.

"One day, when I entered the school of Xenocrates, drunk and sustained by two women, I was sensible for the first time to the Word of philosophy. The voice of the master, who had received the Socratic testament from the son of Ariston's own mouth penetrated into me and worked the miracle there that the seasons operate on the embryo of a chrysalis. From that day on, I possessed something superior to carnal sensuality..."

And as, while speaking, Polemon perceived that I was clinging to his body, that I was brushing him with my breasts, he pushed me away.

"Don't you see, Naïs, that you can do nothing to me?" he exclaimed. "Your desire does not reach me. I look at you and I find you beautiful, but like a beautiful statue, and your instinct appears to me as groping and naïve as the thought of a little child. I could share your bed, and sleep beside you, but my arms would never close around your body."

Thus spoke Polemon.

Already my eyes were no longer looking at him, and my ears were not hearing his voice. I was offended, ashamed, and the idea of seeing him go away pained me and maddened me. Gradually, a sort of muffled irritation and unreflective chagrin invaded me. And suddenly I exploded into insults, desiring to humiliate him, to wound him, to do him harm, to lacerate him with him fingernails.

"Rather say that you're like an effeminate Lydian," I cried at him. "Confess that nothing of the man remains in you. Your flesh is a bruised plant, frozen by winters. All your words about sensuality make me feel pity. They are like eloquence in the mouth of a mute, like the freshness of a dried-up spring..."

But Polemon placed his hand on my shoulder, as if to calm me down, and said: "You're going to insult me because I refused you. In sum, you're acting in accordance with human logic. Know, however, that it is not my flesh, as you think, but my reason and my will that are rejecting you."

I tried to throw myself upon hum frantically. He pushed me away again, firmly gripping the hand that was clinging to him in despair. When I cried out in pain, he let me go and left.

Throughout the evening I saw the flame of the lamp aureoled with multicolored circles. My altered blood hammered in my arteries as if to force them and rupture them. Numb and breathless, I experience simultaneously the flame of desire and the mortal fatigue that follows satisfaction. And I slept late, in a leaden slumber.

XIII

Drinking my shame again, I climbed the Acropolis. It was painful for me to admit to Demetrius my complete defeat. Although I had made the resolution to keep silent about the details of the conversation with Polemon, it seemed difficult for me to omit that I had not succeeded in moving him for a single instant. I therefore climbed the great marble staircase in perplexity, and gazed at the severe statue of the Promachos. Perhaps that was what gave me courage and counseled me to simplicity.

Demetrius was in the sanctuary of Minerva, relaxing from affairs with the courtesan Demo, whom he preferred at that moment to all the others. The audacity and the great frankness of that young woman diverted him extremely.

When I went in, he was opening a superb basket enveloped in crimson and filed with fruits. There were Nicostrates grapes, the pride of Attica, noble figs from the borough of Aegila, superb violet arbutus berries and black myrtle berries.

Demo perceived me first and said, abruptly, by way of a greeting: "You've come at a good moment, Naïs, to give us your advice. I claim that Lamia is too old a lover for Demetrius."

I was frightened by that criticism, for I knew what attachment the tyrant experienced for his former mistress.

But he laughed, and turned toward Demo, saying: "It's naughty of you to remind me of Lamia's age at this moment. Don't you see how good she is to send me such delicious fruits?"

"If you consented to lodge and sleep with my mother she'd send you more," the courtesan replied, untroubled.

"Let's talk seriously, Demo." And, addressing me: "Since you're alive and still so beautiful, you've certainly only come here to bring me news of your victory, O Naïs! I'll order that the bowl be sent to your home."

"No, Demetrius, on the contrary, I've come utterly humiliated, and, to be completely frank, I ought to add that the defeat surpassed all my anticipations and all my evaluations. Instead of my seducing him, it was Polemon who succeeded in enamoring and inflaming me. I was like a child before him. Like the master of a ship who animates his hollow wood and guides it meekly through the wind and the waves, that man governed and steered me in accordance with his will."

"Then you're unlucky, Naïs," Demetrius replied to me, smiling. "But you can console yourself for it. You have only failed before the impossible, and where you have been humiliated, any other woman would certainly have no occasion to be proud. Eat this beautiful pomegranate, which conceals a treasure of fire. I give it to you in order that you can slake your thirst on it, and above all, in order that I can watch you eat it.

Your gestures have something immodest and slyly feline when you eat, and in your mouth these red seeds will be as many kisses of nymphs or satyrs."

"Do you know, my beauty, the latest epigram about Lamia?" Demo said to me, frantically pursuing the design of diminishing her rival.

"You're insupportable, Demo," said Demetrius.

"It's necessary that Naïs hears these lines, Listen, Naïs, you'll find them delightful. 'I tell you, Lamia, we're growing old. Soon will come, I warn you, the icy breath that puts amour to flight. Here come wrinkles, silver hair, a slack and graceless mouth. Your attractions are crumbling. Soon, no one will approach proud Lamia to coax her and draw her to him. No one! We shall pass before you sadly as before a tomb!'"

I saw Demetrius frown. I even thought that he was about to get annoyed. At the same moment, however, the door opened and I blushed, and then went pale, on seeing Polemon came in. Contrary to his habit of simplicity, a clasp ornamented with cornelians attached his garment at the shoulder. His beard was curled and his eyes, which reflected something akin to a distant and mysterious Orient, appeared singular to me.

"I've come in response to the summons you sent me, O King," he said, bowing to us.

"No, I don't want to see you," cried Demetrius, with a feigned irritation. "I only desire to associate and have commerce with those who 'yield to all human weaknesses,' to speak like Menander. But you, on the contrary, are a stone, a being devoid of entrails, and since you've been able to resist the charms of this divine Naïs, one ought, I believe, address to you the lofty malediction of Pindar: 'The man who can stare at the flamboyance emitted by the visage of Theoxena without being agitated by the most impetuous ardors must certainly have a black heart, forged in icy fire with the aid of diamond and iron. Let him therefore be the despicable object of the hatred of Venus, let him pursue all his life a sordid gain and, a slave of women, let him carry water to them servilely thought the streets.'"

"Those verses are beautiful," said Polemon, softly. "I blush at not meriting them. Above all, Demetrius, I do not understand how you know..."

"Have you not divined that it was me who sent Naïs, hoping to see you succumb and thus to be able to enjoy your confusions? For some time you've been annoying me with your counsels of sobriety, and the precepts of your wisdom."

"By Jupiter, O Naïs!" exclaimed Polemon, turning toward me, smiling. "Have you been able to lend yourself to this tenebrous and perfidious design?"

"I scarcely knew you, Polemon, but I've just confessed to the king not only my defeat but also my disarray. He can render testimony to that."

"She's telling the truth. Although I promised her, in case of success, this Theodorus bowl, she has deliberately confessed her humiliation and her shame."

Polemon sat down and said, in a calm voice: "Justice obliges me to declare that, on the contrary, this woman has concluded her enterprise victoriously, and that she has a right to the Theodorus bowl."

The king sat up straight, keenly intrigued, and dropped a split fig that he was holding in his hand.

I also raised my eyes, looking uncomprehendingly at that strange man.

"What do you mean?" asked Demetrius.

"I'm saying that if she ought to receive a recompense for my seduction, you can award it to her, for she had seduced me and held me in her arms at her mercy. She succeeded easily in her objectives. Verity obliges me to admit it."

"But, then Naïs…?"

"You ought not to listen to him, O King," I exclaimed, "for he's lying. Now he wants to play with me."

"I'm not lying, Naïs," Polemon said, in a voice that was still soft and imperturbable. "It is, on the contrary, the love of exactitude and the desire to be equitable that makes me speak in this way. It is true that I left your house having rejected your caresses and showing myself apparently insensible to your fiery gaze and your amorous philters. I believed myself that I was emerging victorious from that ordeal. I judged in accordance with vain appearances and in the interest of my egotism. But I was soon obliged to recognize that, deep down, your image had shaken the fortitude of my soul and that your attractions had spoken intimately to my human nature.

"When I was at home, and all the artifices of sagacity and pride vanished, I regretted my arrogant attitude. My body moaned and suffered from having refused you. Gradually, my false coldness disappeared, the fragile armor, made of an entirely intellectual chastity, fell apart. I repented of my triumph, which seemed to me to be bitter and derisory. Then your image returned to haunt me, all the memories of you that I carried away became burning. I evoked you in your superb nudity, such as you offered yourself to my sight, and I recognized how desirable and irresistible you were; you resumed and exercised over me your voluptuous empire. Since then, and until this moment, the flames that you ignited in me thus have only spread to cover me. Changing my attitude, I began to appeal to you. Mentally, I begged your naked arms to embrace me. Without resisting any longer, I aspire, on the contrary, to plunge myself into your amorous charm. That is how deceptive my apparent victory is, Demetrius, and I leave you to judge whether or not Naïs merits the bowl that you promised her."

The king was stupefied, his eyes widened in surprise, while Demo laughed stupidly, repeating: "By Jupiter! Can one see a fortune comparable to that if Naïs? She subjugates men even at a distance, and vanquishes them when they appear to resist her."

As for me, I remained perplexed. I was gazing at Polemon, I believe, with a suspicious eye, for, not understanding his conduct, I feared some secret trap, some humorous artifice.

"I do not know whether Naïs truly merits the bowl," the king finally declared. "Above all, I cannot clearly grasp the reasons why you have come here to declare yourself vanquished, Polemon!"

"It is because, in my partial defeat, I nevertheless keep intact my love of the truth. The sacrifice of my pride is of no importance to me. It would be too wretched to attach myself to vain semblances, neglecting the real foundation of things. What good does it do me to have extracted my body from the caresses of this woman, since my soul is entirely filled by her desirable image? Ataraxia, insensibility to human passions and agitations, I thought I possessed, perfectly and unassailably—and yet it was sufficient for Naïs to tempt me and for her to be resplendent in her troubling nudity for me to succumb and become the victim and the prey of carnal desire!"

"Even so, you resisted the trap," said Demo.

"But Polemon replied, slowly: "Even that appearance is deceptive. For I meditated returning to Naïs' house, and if I had not found her here, I would perhaps have gone to her home, begging for her amour."

"Since Polemon confessed himself defeated and is contrite at his defeat, I have only to send you the bowl, Naïs," the king decided. "I did not doubt, moreover, that your charms could realize the impossible." He turned to the philosopher. "My contentment is extreme," he continued, "for I desire that you change and that you emerge from the cold and virtuous continence that is like a reproof toward us all."

"I have not changed, and that is precisely what saddens me, O King," replied Polemon. "I recognize with alarm that one cannot change anything, nor bend human nature. It is an illusion to think that one is becoming better. When Socrates declared that he was born with evil and criminal sentiments, which he had succeeded in mastering and repressing thereafter, he was lying. If he lived virtuously, it is because he was originally virtuous. Originally, I too was disposed to pleasure, consecrated to sensual tumult. What I believed to be a change was merely a respite and a repose in my career of dissipation. One gesture from Naïs has sufficed to demonstrate that to me."

When we descended the Acropolis again together, while the Saronica was illuminated by the setting sun and Athens seemed as if clad in her ancient glory, I interrogated Polemon.

"Are the things that you said to Demetrius true? In the case that the account is exact, I ought to render sincerity for sincerity in confessing to you that you too have stirred the depths of my being. It is true that I began to tempt you in order to obey the king, but you quickly took real possession of me and, in wanting to subjugate you, I sensed myself becoming your slave. Now, again, I only aspire to enfold you in my warm and living arms."

I said that passionately and sincerely, for a veritable ardor bore me toward that powerful man, who had confessed himself vanquished by my charms and had permitted me to win the bowl.

Polemon seemed to sound me with his gaze then. And, fixing my eyes upon him in my turn, I understood that I finally possessed a part of his being and that a harmonious, hermetic and carnal understanding united us.

Finally, he said to me: "It's necessary that we belong to one another, Naïs. There is no point in wanting to go against destiny, for what must happen always happens." And after a pause: "Come and join me at dusk tomorrow at the baths of Thrasyllus. I'll wait for you there."

I separated from him emotional and radiant. I savored the generous pulsations of my heart. A vague spirit of delight and triumph flattered me and lightened me.

Until tomorrow...

XIV

I prepared myself at the hour of the triumphant sun, and I put a little acanthus juice on my face, even thought Polemon detested make-up, so pale with impatience and emotion did I seem when I looked at myself in my mirror.

Before crossing the threshold I made a vow to consecrate my new robe and all my golden pins to Venus if my day concluded happily.

I found Polemon emerging from the baths of Thrasyllus. He was clad in a somber and simple tunic but a strange fire was still burning in his visage. He appeared to me to be mysterious and powerful, like the statues by Harpocrates that command silence and invite meditation.

Scarcely had he seen me than he ran to press my arms in his hands. He looked me in the eyes, softly, and then said: "Would you like to spend a few hours in my house, Naïs? It is in supplication now that I ask you that, for I desire you."

"Yes, Polemon, I would like that. My desires are knotted narrowly with yours."

We went along the street of the Tripods slowly. We were walking silently, and it was thus that we arrived before the Satyr that rises up in front of the temple, smiling and hairy, on its bronze pedestal.

"It's affirmed," Polemon told me, "that Phryne, invited to choose among the works of her lover Praxiteles, and desiring to know which one was the best, imagined announcing abruptly to the artist one day that his studio had caught fire. 'As long as my Amour and my Satyr are spared!' Praxiteles replied, thus distinguishing, particularly, this excellent bronze."

"Indeed," I said, "this Satyr appears a living and active apparition. His posture seems to be that of someone reposing, and yet one might think that he is quivering with life and ready to bound."

"He is the ultimate god," Polemon went on, "the primordial breath that already fecundated things well before Olympus was populated by the generation of younger gods. Dispenser of joy and plenitude, he is the great ancestor, the original womb of creation. He incites and gives birth not only to love and hatred, but the forces and the saps that equilibrate the universe and cause it to advance and progress. We can, there-

236

fore, worship this original god, Naïs, in order for him to provide us in return with ardor and exaltation."

Meanwhile, we went past the chryselephantine statue of Alcmene, and Polemon soon introduced me into his house.

It was very simple, but entirely made of marble. A little garden of roses and jasmines in flower enlaced it in its iridescence and varied splendors.

"This house, which I bought with what remains of my paternal fortune, was never to shelter a woman," Polemon told me. "You are the first to enter it, Naïs, and in violation of my oath. But I can't feel the slightest regret for that. Since the other day, I have recognized the vanity of all efforts, and I laugh bitterly in seeing how taut and fragile by virtue was, ready to desert at the first assault."

We sat down at the entrance, near the sacrificial stone. Polemon looked at me passionately for a moment, and the sight of me seemed to draw him into long meditation.

Finally, he said, as if speaking to himself: "Inexpressible charms of desire, how powerfully you weave the veil of illusion that must cover us! The mortal and consequently imperfect image of the woman we desire is completed and perfected so delightfully within us, extracts so many new attractions in our thought, is saturated so abundantly therein with seduction that it becomes invincible and incomparable, and attains the ideal images of divinity. How will we ever be able to liberate ourselves from the trap that we create with our own substance?"

Finally, turning to me, he said: "It would be difficult for me to describe to you, Naïs, what a prosperous and miraculous florescence the seeds of desire have produced that your body and attitudes have sown within me. If I put so much vehemence into refusing you, it was because I feared the powerful poison of your caresses and the force with which they operated within me.

"What shook me above all, and conquered me, was the precise vision of the sensualities that you could provoke. I divined, I knew, with a sure science, that scarcely would I

237

have touched you than our souls would have mingled and confounded. My being would create new sensualities in order better to enlace you and seize you carnally.

"I conserved ineradicably your voluptuous attitude at the moment when, seeking to retain me when I was about to leave your house, you leaned forward, keeping your eyes avidly fixed on mine. I sensed that you were omnipotent in that instant, as powerful as the wave that overwhelms a ship, as the night that overcomes the mountain, as all invincible and occult forces.

"Such was my ardor to enclose you in my arms, and such also was my fear and disarray and sensing myself vanquished and subjugated by a woman, that I began to have ambiguous, delightful and terrible visions in which amour as mingled with death. Since that moment, you have not ceased to haunt my imagination. I rediscover you in all the spectacles that nature offers me.

"Yesterday morning, on the rocks of Piraeus, before the even respiration of the sea, I thought of the powerful elevation of bodies that sensuality agitates. Later, mounted on a Thessalian horse and riding through the countryside of Colonna, I mingled your image with the intoxication and vertigo of speed, with all the vital tumult that we experience in devouring distance. I wanted to have you there, clinging, confounded with me by the sharp anguish of a kiss, and to drink your breath, on the charger carried away by its bounds, leaps and shivers, to vary and diversify our enjoyment, associating it with all the caprices of its fervor and impetuosity.

"But I renounce, O Naïs, recounting you my obsessions. Know that I was completely yours from the moment that I drew away from your house. All my past life was engulfed in eternal forgetfulness. From then on, my existence had no goal but seeing you again and realizing the dreams and images that my desire suggested to me. Now, once again, such a mysterious attraction impels me toward you that I dread taking you in my arms. I fear the imminent hour of our union, for I believe that the joy that I shall experience therein will be mortal, ill-adapted to human nature and equivalent to death."

I did not reply to Polemon. The flame of words and the vehemence of images had gained me entirely. I did not reply to him; I drew him toward me and we went into the doma.

I shall never forget that simple and spacious place, filled with the religious horror of a sanctuary. No furniture, no ornament, except for a tiger-skin extended on the floor and strewn with rose petals. A large inclined mirror reflected the bare room and gave it a blue-tinted profundity. And all of that vacillated, darkened and was veiled, for a milky vapor of incense created a perfumed mist, separated things as if by vague shrouds, and incessantly made and unmade the forms and the lines.

Without saying anything more to me, Polemon drew me to the couch.

His ardor was silent. Until then I had seen him measured and calm. Now he was transformed and transfigured. All of his concentration, one might have thought, was mutated into a muted and valorous potency, which kneaded my body easily, as a sculptor molds social and malleable clay.

And as his amour had also communicated to me an unknown sensation, never experienced before, something more than mad joy, a sort of Dionysiac fury, I began to compete with him, to give him kiss for kiss, caress for caress. I sought him out and then I fled; I covered his head with my hair, his mouth with my lips, and his body with my agitated flesh.

The mirror repeated our beautiful dementia, the stubborn and somber fervor that made is resemble two sublime workmen occupied in digging I know not what immense tomb in order to bury themselves therein.

A time equal to eternity went by during our intercourse. I could not measure it. But I know that we forced the common limits and terrestrial conditions of sensuality. I felt like a skylark penetrated by sunlight. My eyes filled now with myriads of sparks, and in the magical stream of light images of my childhood passed back and forth, all the sweet moments of my life. Then, little by little, I believe that my thought faded away, that my senses retreated, that I was devoid of memory, devoid of past and future, light flotsam agitating in a lactescent sea strewn with roses.

When I recovered consciousness we were separated. Leaning over me, Polemon was caressing my inanimate head.

"You see, Naïs," he said, "that there is such scant difference between amour and death."

Then: "Your eyelids are covered with shadow, Naïs, and your pupils enormously dilated."

Going to the mirror, he covered it.

"Let the illusion end," he said.

I felt pure and clear, as if pleasure and its sweetness had remade a virginal innocence.

"I believe, Polemon," I said, "that you have stamped me with an indelible mark. My body has forgotten what it was before knowing you."

"I have given you my life and, for your art, you have revealed your intimate virtues to me. Your beauty and my strength know one another, are allied. Henceforth and until the end of time, somewhere, there will be our united shadow, our paired image. Sensuality has infinite echoes in time. It alone dominates immortality.

And as I left in order to go back to my house: "While I was in your arms, Naïs, I believed that the primordial attraction that had reassembled and harmonized the atoms to form my consciousness had vanished and that I was scattered in space. Now it appears to me that I am slowly being reborn, and that every wayward element is coming to resume its place. How great it is, the force of amour! There is more of the divine contained in a kiss than on the Acropolis and the temple of Eleusis combined."

As he left me on the threshold of my house, he brushed my cheek with his lips, and that caress was as immaterial as the touch of a wing.

"Until tomorrow," I said to him, "isn't it?"

He looked at me with a suddenly-altered gaze, which came, one might have thought, from the depths of his thought.

"It's frightening to talk about tomorrow, Naïs. Tomorrow is the somber prey, the obscure possession of the jealous gods."

"But can we live henceforth without one another, Polemon?"

"Leave destiny the care of uniting us. It's will is always accomplished, in spite of our words."

"Then: "Until tomorrow, perhaps," he acquiesced.

Then I saw a nocturnal bird deploying large frightened wings and flying toward the sky to my left. And I remembered that the world shelters hostile forces, and that happiness is a fleeting shadow...

XV

Sleep was approaching and I already found myself in the indecisive felicity that precedes the extinction of consciousness when someone knocked on my door.

I had promised myself that no lover would have access to my house that evening. I aspired to collect myself in the memory of Polemon's caresses. In any case, my body was exhausted, bruised by the ardent enterprises of amour. I therefore pretended not to hear it and tried to fall asleep; but the door was shaken again and a voice that was neither rude not drunken called me by name:

"Naïs! Naïs!"

I got up, half by will and half by force, and demanded to know who was knocking at such an hour.

"Me, Stagonium."

I opened up slowly, without desire, for Stagonium was still late nights and futile distractions. But the poor child came in, pale and distraught.

"Will you allow me to share your bed, Naïs?" she said. "It's because I'm dying of fatigue. I don't know where to take refuge tonight, and I'm fearful that the watch, finding me alone in the street, might mistreat me."

"Why, then, are you out of your bed and far from your sister Anthis? If you were at some dinner with your flute, why didn't you wait until morning to leave? Unless some lover..."

"Oh, I'll tell you, I'll tell you my strange adventure in a little while. But permit me first to lie down beside you."

"Lie down, lie down, Stagonium. Only refrain from embracing me, and even from touching me, for my body is weighing me down and my sensibility is capsized, so any caress would awaken torments in me."

She stretched out lightly in the bed, and when she had recovered her breath she told me her story.

"I was getting ready to accompany Anthis, who had to go to the house of Cocalus. Perhaps you know him, the fishmonger who is scornful of clients and who scarcely mutters fragments of words, saying 'bot' for turbot and 'dine' for sardine. If you reproach him for selling dear, he replies to you that the fish are not for your teeth, and if you remark that his gudgeon have rotting phosphorescent eyes he tells you that it's your nose that has infected the fish. But he's made a fortune in that thieving métier and now he gives dinners and ostentatiously offers bronze bowls to his guests in which to wash their hands."

"And you've been in Cocalus' house?"

"No, Naïs, I didn't go, for at the last minute Tychon, the young chiliarch, the one who followed the Poliorcetes to the land of the Nabataeans, informed me that he had returned and wanted to spend the night with me. I've known him for a long time and we slept in the same bed for a month in the time when Demetrius the Phalerian still governed the city. Tychon's youthful face and his manners have always pleased me, with the consequence that the spur of desire pierced me at the thought of finding myself in his arms again.

"I went out late and headed for his house, dreaming of enviable rejoicing. But I found him changed, sporting a large beard and an arrogantly turned-up moustache. He's become a

242

true military man. His bedroom, once perfumed, smells of leather and horses. He brought back bizarre weapons from his voyage—assegais brisling with human teeth, grotesque clubs, nailed and voluminous, and long silvered bows—which dishonor the walls and make them grimace. He even possesses the cadaver of a Nabataean warrior conserved in salt, and those black remains cast fear and an exhalation of death through the house.

"It was with a chill in my heart that I observed those changes.

"Tychon, who had a friend with him, barely saluted me and said: 'We were talking, dear Stagonium, about the last expedition in the land of the barbarians and the splendid fortune of our arms. My friend Geryon wanted to remember the great deeds that I accomplished personally in fighting against the Nabataeans. There's no need to interrupt him. Continue your story, Geryon. Stagonium wishes me well and it will be a pleasure for her to learn about my glory.'

"'So,' Geryon then continued in a yelping Stentorian voice, 'in an arid country where water was lacking and the food supplies had run out. We were gnawing the wood of our bucklers, and putting arrows in our mouths from time to time to stave off thirst.'

"'That's true!' Tychon exclaimed.

"'Certainly it's true,' Geryon went on. 'One day, then, we saw a multitude of camels advancing toward us. We scarcely had time to pick up our lances before the battle commenced. Tychon distinguished himself first by killing a Nabataean chief with a single blow. He struck him so vehemently that in trying to withdraw his lance thereafter he lifted both the savage and the camel off the ground, which the weapon had transpierced and spitted.'

"'That's true!' said Tychon, again.

"'Of course it's true,' Geryon went on, 'but that was only the beginning, for scarcely had the melee warmed up than Tychon saw seven warriors surrounding him, trying to assail him with their javelins. But then he gets down from his horse in order to be freer in his movements, confronts the enemies resolutely and commences making use of his sword like a club. But describe the carnage yourself, dear Tychon...'

"'I had felled one of the seven by splitting his head with my right hand, while I disemboweled a second with my left, who feel heavily, gasping. Two others were petrified, and fled. And enveloping the three that remained with my arm, I swung my word, and with a masterstroke I split and separated their miserable heads!'

"'How the blood flowed!' said Geryon.

"'That's true,' repeated Tychon, 'the blood flowed. I remember having to change my tunic when I returned to the camp.'

"'You certainly haven't forgotten, Tychon, that the chief was one-eyed, and that at a distance of thirty cubits you plucked out the remaining eye with a skillfully thrown javelin. It was blind that he plunged into death.'

"'They bleed, these barbarians, they bleed like cattle!'"

"I stood there trembling, frozen by horror. The house exhaled a nitrous and pestilential odor. The salted Nabataean seemed to be stirring, and I saw his intrepid killers dripping with black blood.

"'Bloodthirsty man!' I finally cried, addressing myself to Tychon. 'How can you embrace a woman after so many crimes, murders and decapitations? For all the gold in the world I would not let myself go into your arms. I'm still too young to soil myself next to a homicide!'

"Tychon was visibly nonplussed. 'I'll give you a mina, Stagonium,' he replied, 'and in amour you'll see that I'm as gentle as a lamb.'

"'No, my chiliarch, you have too much blood on your face for me to support your grim proximity.'

"'It's in the land of the Nabataeans that I cried out these exploits, Stagonium, and we're in Athens.'

"But I was completely gripped by repulsion and fear. I therefore wrapped myself in my mantle and went to the door. 'I'm terrified for having crossed the threshold of your house,

O Tychon, and I believe I see the room filling up with the shades of the warriors you've decapitated.'

'Why are you so fearful, Stagonium?'

'Do you take me for Clytemnestra, Medea or one of the Lemniades? Not a single drop of blood remains in my veins after that evocation of slaughter. I'm not even sure of being alive myself, and that you've spared me. It's necessary not to think of seeing me again, Tychon. It's more fitting that you continue your hecatombs rather than thinking of amour.'

"And I ran out of that lair of savages, in a panic. In vain, Geryon hurtled into the street and begged me to return, swearing that all his narrations were imaginary and that Typhon had not killed anyone. 'He remained in Upper Phrygia with a fever,' he told me. 'He's never seen the shadow of a Nabataean in his life. It's here in Athens that he bought from one of Demetrius' soldiers that baboon conserved in salt you saw in his house. In reality, Tychon is naturally mild and simple-minded. We told you those stories in the hope that you'd respect him and like him more.'

"But I wouldn't consent to return, for, although they were lies, those stories continued to frighten me and the chiliarch suddenly inspired an insurmountable dislike in me. That's why, Naïs, I've come here, having no other refuge and not wanting to venture by night as far as Piraeus, where I live. But you're very fatigued yourself."

"That's because I've had a happy day and I'm exhausted by amour. Sleep now Stagonium and try not to dream about dying Nabataeans. Know moreover, that Demetrius has made a treaty with them without a fight and, in consequence, those barbarians are still alive, procreating and prospering."

XVI

When I woke up, next to Stagonium, that day was almost half way through.

The auletride departed diligently in order to tranquilize her sister, whom she had not seen since the previous day. For myself, I had got up indolently, my body poorly relaxed and idle, when someone came to tell me that a slave was waiting at the door with tablets from Polemon.

Come at once, dear Naïs, my lover wrote. *Tomorrow I shall be far away, and you will no longer be able to reach me. Come quickly. Our day will be happy.*

"Is your master ill?" I asked the slave.

"I have reason to believe the contrary," he replied, "for he departed at dawn, in good health, for Eleusis. He gave me the order to come and find you with our mules and to take you to him, in his country house."

"Let's set forth quickly," I said to him.

"Before leaving the city it's necessary that I call in at the market. My master ordered me to buy him a fine eel."

I did not know what to think. I was feverish, and I spurred my mule, which went through the meadows insouciantly and eccentrically, at a rhythmic walk.

It was autumn. The olives had already flowed under the press, the trees were meekly shedding their leaves. There was a breath of tenderness and the vestiges of a defunct estival ardor in the air. And I thought that everything faded, that life, like amour, is a measurable and brief thing, which only triumphs in order to wither away immediately.

When we arrived at the philosopher's house, I got down promptly without seeking aid.

When I went in I saw Polemon, who was waiting for me impatiently. He seemed sensibly touched by my arrival, but did not get up from his chair.

"I dreaded finding you ill and in danger," I told him.

"Come, precious friend," he responded, smiling. "No, I'm not ill and I've never felt better; but my death is very imminent."

I ran to him and threw my arms around his neck. "What are you saying, Polemon? Can one die in the prime of life without malady?"

"Strictly speaking, yes, provided that one wants to," he replied. He continued: "Stay here by my side, Naïs, and spare me efforts and the sight of violent and disordered movement. I'm happy in gazing through the windows at the Saronica and the island of Salamina, which are turning blond in the sunlight. I don't want to miss a single particle of my quietude or my delight. Remain with me, sweet friend, give me your hair, as curly as parsley, to stroke, and listen to me.

"You recall that yesterday we were scarcely miserly in according ourselves amorous joys. As I left your house, therefore, I observed so much languor and felicity in myself, such an affluence of contentment, and, at the same time, such an absence of new desires, that I became anxious. My being had attained the perfect equilibrium, the extreme appeasement that is united, by I know not what intimate juncture, with the idea of death. And I remembered those two fortunate young men whose story Solon narrated to King Croesus. They had been victorious at the Olympic games, and they entered Argos, their native city, acclaimed and triumphant. When they were at the temple, their mother, who knew them to be sensate and prudent, prayed to the divinity that they might be accorded the best that a man can obtain after a victory. Then the two ephebes, bathed by the memory of their triumph, slipped into a durable and eternal slumber. From happiness they passed into death. And I was affirmed in the idea that after a life of plenitude and sagacity, nothing is more enviable than a rapid death in tranquility."

"But perhaps existence still reserves happy days for you, Polemon."

"They would be uniform, Naïs, and time would wear them away and diminish them, like old and obsolete coins. Days are happy when they furnish us with the new. Now, I can say that nothing of that remains for me, at least on this earth. During my life, which was attentive and perfectible, I strove to choose and appropriate that which exist of the divine in this world. I enjoyed everything sensibly, I assimilated as much as I could the marvels of measure, beauty and rhythm. But for some time, knowing that I had advanced and progressed as far as possible on the road of wisdom, I have counted on detaching myself discreetly from this uncertain life.

"Your amour, by giving me one last and vivid felicity, permitted me grave thoughts. I resolved to close my book on that pleasant and culminating page, without trusting any further in the diversities of fortune. When one has exhausted all curiosity and strung out the attractions of this world, the natural thing to do is to leave it, in the same way that when one has seen and admired the paintings in one of the galleries of the Acropolis, one has nothing to do but pass into another."

"But death is frightful!"

"Not for the sage, O Naïs! If you do not accept that at this moment, it is because, fortunately, you are still assisted by the two habitual companions of life, Desire and Ignorance. One lives while hoping for a surprise and regretting a memory. But one does nor experience either hope or regret if one has fully mediated and penetrated the monotonous play of things. In any case, either death is a passage and I shall go to participate beyond it in the society of Aspasia and Socrates, which would be new and profitable for me, or it is the entry to annihilation, and then it is rationally not worth the trouble of thinking about it or fearing it."

"There is still time, Polemon, to go back on your decision. In spite of yourself, I want to save you."

"I took the poison before you arrived, Naïs. And that poison, which comes from a physician of Pontus, is a proven and reliable friend, which never fails. Rather open the window, in order that I can hear the birds singing and that I can see the sea. Cease to beg me and to agitate yourself. I summoned you because I would like to die in your arms and attain the unknown door in the midst of pleasures. I offer you the final hours on my life, the last strength of my heart, and I want to give you as well the example of my death.

"I remember having spoken to you the other day, inexactly and conceitedly, about wisdom. In truth, wisdom consists of living one's day, without the great illusion of tomorrow, without caring about the day before, uniquely occupied in crowning with flowers the passing moment. I have had the weakness to want to differ from my fellows by means of virtue, which is as presumptuous as desiring to surpass them all in vice. You have made me repent of that error. You will recall sometimes the brief hours that we spent spinning amour together. In the midst of moderate pleasures, far from violent instants, while savoring a fine fig or seeing the blond hair of an ephebe, be sensible to my memory and think of me with benevolence. Such is my prayer, O Naïs!"

And to hide my emotion I asked him: "Why have you come to die here rather than elsewhere, Polemon?"

"Because the landscape is tranquil, and people scarce. One needs to withdraw into oneself and to review existence before desisting from all thought. Then too, I like the sea and fear the caress of the Athenian sun, which is a sorcerer and attaches one to life."

On his instruction, the table was served in order that we could take a last meal together.

"I ordered for today a eel, a fish that has always had my preference but which brings about unfortunate perturbations in my organs. Now I can eat my fill of it, sure that the eel will not reserve me a bad tomorrow."

He ate with a very good appetite and drank valiantly.

"I can say, like the soldiers of Thermopylae, that I shall sup with Pluto tonight; but I prefer to believe that I shall not sup anywhere, which is more dignified and better."

We each savored the intimate thoughts that the time brought us. Polemon said: "It's necessary not to offend human measure by feeling joy too intensely. Yesterday, in your arms, I drank sensuality in great gulps and without restraint. I therefore owe it to jealous Nemesis not to survive."

With those words, Crates and Crantor, his two best friends, came in. They came to see Polemon. He had summoned them. They did not say anything, but approached him and kissed him on the lips.

"I acted ingrately in distancing myself from you," the philosopher apologized, "but I had to. You will forgive me when I tell you that for the first time, I have the certainty of happiness. For, as Solon thought, one cannot believe oneself advantaged by fortune so long as one has a future before one. I have summoned you to inform you that the passage to death is devoid of encumbrances and torments, and that Mercury, the Conductor of Souls, comports himself as a welcoming divinity."

"Do you not think that exiting from life is an incalculable action, Polemon?" said Crantor. "The most elementary prudence ought to forbid it to you."

"On the contrary, I hold death to be the most insignificant of gestures, the only one denuded of consequences. It has no tomorrow and it entails fewer perturbations than the fall of a pebble into the sea. To live life, that is what is incalculable. And as I think sanely, I prefer to exit from existence of my own accord that to perish by some stupid accident, by means of a tortoise that one receives on the head, like Aeschylus, or a grape-seed that catches in the throat, like Sophocles, or an excessive burst of laughter, like Anacreon of Ceos. The only death that I would have preferred to mine would be that of Laïs, who died of pleasure, seized and felled in her bed by a gripping and frenzied sensuality. But such a grave and sweet death is not given to all mortals."

"On looking at funerary marbles," sad Crates, "it is difficult to judge which of the individuals represented thereon possessed felicity. Is it the one who is seen on his feet and who goes still struggling and charges with dolor in life, or the one who remains seated and who has already entered into repose."

"Whoever knows that life is a shadow can only exit from it without joy and without dolor, in the insensibility of the infant born into it," replied Crantor.

"I have only to confess one sole regret in quitting life," murmured Polemon, in a feeble voice. "That is that I am departing without knowing pertinently whether the gods exist. In the epoch of Socrates, people were almost sure of it, but since then we have made too much progress in reverse."

"Do you not believe that the dead know more about it than we do?"

"I don't believe anything," replied Polemon.

Then, after a few moments of meditation, he said: "The things that made the most impression on me during life are rare, I can only count three. Firstly, a sunset over the Mediterranean in the vicinity of the Echinades, seen from a ship that was taking me to Sicily; secondly, the strophes of a chorus of *Oedipus Rex* at the theater of Dionysus; and lastly, Naïs' breasts, which quivered and colored under caresses and gave me the illusion of being a creator. But I am wise enough not to believe that one can resuscitate and sense again any of the pleasures of the past."

Afterwards, smiling, he drew our attention to a sailing ship that was rounding the island of Salamina and passing into the Aegean.

"We are equally uncertain of our destiny, that ship which is confronting the open sea, and I, whom am abandoning myself to death. But I still have more probabilities than it has of entering into a port."

He requested that flowers be brought to him, and also strewn on the floor. Then he ordered that a Sicilian pastor hidden in the garden should begin playing his flute.

"I didn't want to summon auletrides because their songs are tumultuous. But I will hear with pleasure the Sicilian tunes with which my mother once lulled me, and which awaken distant and naïve memories in me. In that way, perhaps I shall confound my death with my birth, and I shall not know through which of the two contrary doors of life I am about to pass."

He listened to the simple tune while closing his eyes and smiling. A pallor was already tarnishing his face.

"I feel light! Come closer to me, Naïs. I feel light, but it is because my legs are quitting me. They have departed mysteriously and know already what the rest of my body still does not. Life is going away; it is in haste. One would think it were a fickle bird impatient to attain space and liberty."

251

"Would you like a drink?" asked Crantor.

"No. I shall be drinking the waters of the Cocytus in a few moments. Adieu, my friends. I would love to quit you, like Socrates, assuring you of immortality, but I do not have the courage. Dying in uncertainty myself, I do not have the effrontery to affirm anything. But if you want me to have a happy end, Naïs, read a few verses of this papyrus, covered with silk and very fatigued, in which I transcribed during life the best I have looted from the works of the poets."

I took the book and, in accordance with his choice. I read him, through my tears, the adieux of Andromache to Hector and the prayer of Ipihigenia to the light of day. The verses were so beautiful, those sublime fictions equaled so closely the solemn reality of death, that my voice failed and the last harmonies of Euripides emerged from my lips like a breath.

"There is the genius, vanquisher of death," said Polemon. "Those Olympian accents sometimes make me believe that human beings are superior to their poor destiny. It might be, in sum, my friends, that a God exists, since the poets draw from their hearts chords so elevated and so proud. Tell us now, Naïs, something more cheerful, to make us laugh. Seek, if you like, the gracious anecdote of the kiss that Sophocles gave the handsome cup-bearer of Samos..."

But I saw that our friend's eyes were veiled as if by a mist. The expression of his face undulated, obfuscated, and then brightened like a flame on the point of extinction.

I wanted to aid him to lie down, but he took my hand and squeezed it.

"I can hardly see any longer. Is that you, Naïs? Uncover your breasts, my love, in order that I might collect a beautiful image for eternity.

We were leaning over him, flowing that intimate and troubling mystery, that venerable contest of life and death, ever recommenced, ever pathetic, which, since the origins, cleans, polishes and renews the worlds.

Polemon raised his hand slightly, as if to enunciate and affirm, and was then seized by a long spasm.

"Undoubtedly," he stammered, "the Gods..."

But he interrupted himself and we never grasped what he was trying to formulate. Then he commenced against the verse of Sophocles: "Sweet light..."

His hand gripped mine more forcefully; his body stiffened.

He was dead.

And immediately, upon his face, the livid shadows and the spirits of fear descended as if they had been waiting nearby, as if they were omnipresent and nothing could resist them...

While still remaining near us, our friend was already lying in the unfathomable.

Dusk fell. There was no longer anything but a long violet peplos extending majestically over the Sea of Salamina.

Thus exited tranquilly from life the singular man that I had understood poorly but loved very much, and who left me a memory mingled with sensuality and sadness.

In accordance with his desire, we laid him down to rest near the promontory of Sunium, in order that he might be lulled eternally by the waves, and that he might be the first to perceive the beautiful ships that would bring new philosophies, young religions and as-yet-unexperienced evils to his beloved Attica.

He is buried now, but his shade floats amicably around my house, haunting me and visiting me...

And for the first time, since the distant days of my childhood, I surprise tears on my eyelids.

Adieu, dear Polemon.

XVII

Twice I went to Laurium to make libations and to spread violets on Polemon's tomb. In memory of him I refused all caresses for long months, and my door and my bed were closed to nubile young women as well as to young lovers.

Like the Arrephores weaving the veil of the goddess for the Panatheanaia, I remained chaste and suffered from my chastity. I even thought of consecrating myself entirely to the memory of my friend and, repressing my deprived and gluttonous desires, I read the dialogues of Plato, which I had bought for a price of gold in the hope of understanding them. But in vain I meditated the *Phaedo* and tried to imagine Polemon immortal. The subtleties of the Academy did not penetrate me. I can only hear the truth, it seems, spoken by a fleshy mouth, alive and ready for the kiss.

Eventually in recent days, I weakened, for, stopping by chance in the Ceramicus, I saw my name written on the part of the ship-owner Theodorus, with a offer of five mina.

I dared not disdain that regal proposition. Chances sometimes come along so exceptional that one would seem to be insulting fortune by refusing them. No consideration can permit the refusal of Prosperity. I therefore received Theodorus, who departed drunk on my embraces and will come back again this evening. He has the vigor of the prime of life. Although ugly, he charms by speaking eloquently of the lands he has visited, the hyperborean countries that extend beyond the Pillars of Hercules. He knows and frequents, so he says, thick-lipped women rouged to equal vermilion, others who consider virginity an opprobrium and others who, when married, are held in honor for regaling strangers with their bodies.

But I liked Theodorus above all, for his liberality and for the ornaments he lavished upon me. He gave me a pearl necklace, four peacocks from Samos, a writing-desk woven in gold and decorated with miniatures, and finally, a living green monkey that comes from the lands of Pontus.

That animal is clever and distinguishes himself by marvelous tricks. He grasps and holds in his hands anything that one gives him, dances to the sounds of the flute and walks on two feet like a man. Theodorus had also revealed to me a quality far more extravagant, regarding his natural lasciviousness. And yesterday, with Coronis, we were able to observe the verity of that affirmation.

Soon, my monkey will give rise to gossip in the city. Demetrius will probably want to contemplate such a phenomenon

And, seeing that the animal is expert in amour and appears to be fashioned expressly for caresses, I had a delicate thought, and this morning, I have been to take his collar as an offering to Venus.

SF & FANTASY

Adolphe Alhaiza. *Cybele*
Alphonse Allais. *The Adventures of Captain Cap*
Henri Allorge. *The Great Cataclysm*
Guy d'Armen. *Doc Ardan: The City of Gold and Lepers; The Troglodytes of Mount Everest/The Giants of Black Lake; The Abominable Snowman*
G.-J. Arnaud. *The Ice Company*
André Arnyvelde. *The Ark; The Mutilated Bacchus*
Charles Asselineau. *The Double Life*
Henri Austruy. *The Eupantophone; The Olotelepan; The Petitpaon Era*
Barillet-Lagargousse. *The Final War*
Barbot de Villeneuve.*The Naiads/Beauty & The Beast*
Cyprien Bérard. *The Vampire Lord Ruthwen*
S. Henry Berthoud. *Martyrs of Science; The Angel Asrael*
Aloysius Bertrand. *Gaspard de la Nuit*
Richard Bessière. *The Gardens of the Apocalypse; The Masters of Silence*
Chevalier de Béthune. *The World of Mercury*
Albert Bleunard. *Ever Smaller*
Félix Bodin. *The Novel of the Future*
Pierre Boitard. *Journey to the Sun*
Louis Boussenard. *Monsieur Synthesis*
Alphonse Brown. *City of Glass; The Conquest of the Air*
Émile Calvet. *In a Thousand Years*
André Caroff. *The Terror of Madame Atomos; Miss Atomos; The Return of Madame Atomos; The Mistake of Madame Atomos; The Monsters of Madame Atomos; The Revenge of Madame Atomos; The Resurrection of Madame Atomos; The Mark of Madame Atomos; The Spheres of Madame Atomos; The Wrath of Madame Atomos* (w/M. & Sylvie Stéphan); *The Sins of Madame Atomos* (w/M. & Sylvie Stéphan)
Jean Carrère. *The End of Atlantis*
Félicien Champsaur. *Homo-Deus; The Human Arrow; Nora, The Ape-Woman; Ouha, King of the Apes; Pharaoh's Wife*

Didier de Chousy. *Ignis*

Jules Clarétie. *Obsession*

Jacques Collin de Plancy. *Voyage to the Center of the Earth*

Michel Corday. *The Eternal Flame; The Lynx* (w/André Couvreur)

André Couvreur. *Caresco, Superman; The Exploits of Professor Tornada* (3 vols.); *The Necessary Evil*

Gaston Danville. *The Perfume of Lust*

Camille Debans. *The Misfortunes of John Bull*

Captain Danrit. *Undersea Odyssey*

C. I. Defontenay. *Star (Psi Cassiopeia)*

Charles Derennes. *The People of the Pole*

Georges Dodds (anthologist). *The Missing Link*

Charles Dodeman. *The Silent Bomb*

Harry Dickson. *The Heir of Dracula; Harry Dickson vs. The Spider*

Jules Dornay. *Lord Ruthven Begins*

Alfred Driou. *The Adventures of a Parisian Aeronaut*

Odette Dulac. *The War of the Sexes*

Alexandre Dumas. *The Return of Lord Ruthven; The Man who Married a Mermaid* (w/P. Lacroix)

Renée Dunan. *Baal; The Ultimate Pleasure*

J.-C. Dunyach. *The Night Orchid; The Thieves of Silence*

Henri Duvernois. *The Man Who Found Himself*

Achille Eyraud. *Voyage to Venus*

Henri Falk. *The Age of Lead*

Paul Féval. *Anne of the Isles; Knightshade; Revenants; Vampire City; The Vampire Countess; The Wandering Jew's Daughter*

Paul Féval, *fils. Felifax, the Tiger-Man*

Charles de Fieux. *Lamékis*

Fernand Fleuret. *Jim Click*

Charles-Marie Flor O'Squarr. *Phantoms*

Louis Forest. *Someone is Stealing Children in Paris*

Arnould Galopin. *Doctor Omega; Doctor Omega and the Shadowmen* (anthology)

Judith Gautier. *Isoline and the Serpent-Flower*

H. Gayar. *The Marvelous Adventures of Serge Myrandhal on Mars*

Louis Geoffroy. *The Apocryphal Napoleon*

G.L. Gick. *Harry Dickson and the Werewolf of Rutherford Grange*

Raoul Gineste. *The Second Life of Doctor Albin*

Delphine de Girardin. *Balzac's Cane*

Emmanuel Gorlier. *The Nyctalope and the Tower of Babel*

Léon Gozlan. *The Vampire of the Val-de-Grâce*

Jules Gros. *The Fossil Man*

Jimmy Guieu. *The Polarian-Denebian War* (2 vols.)

Edmond Haraucourt. *Daah, the First Human; Illusions of Immortality*

Nathalie Henneberg. *The Green Gods*

Eugène Hennebert. *The Enchanted City*

Jules Hoche. *The Maker of Men and His Formula*

V. Hugo, P. Foucher & P. Meurice. *The Hunchback of Notre-Dame*

Romain d'Huissier. *Hexagon: Dark Matter*

Jules Janin. *The Magnetized Corpse*

Gustave Kahn. *The Tale of Gold and Silence*

Gérard Klein. *The Mote in Time's Eye; Starmasters*

Fernand Kolney. *Love in 5000 Years*

Paul Lacroix. *Danse Macabre; The Man who Married a Mermaid* (w/Alexandre Dumas)

Louis-Guillaume de La Follie. *The Unpretentious Philosopher*

Jean de La Hire. *The Fiery Wheel; Enter the Nyctalope; The Nyctalope on Mars; The Nyctalope vs. Lucifer; The Nyctalope Steps In; Night of the Nyctalope; Return of the Nyctalope; The Nyctalope and the Tower of Babel*

Etienne-Léon de Lamothe-Langon. *The Virgin Vampire*

André Laurie. *Spiridon*

Gabriel de Lautrec. *The Vengeance of the Oval Portrait*

Alain le Drimeur. *The Future City*

Georges Le Faure & Henri de Graffigny. *The Extraordinary Adventures of a Russian Scientist Across the Solar System* (2 vols.)

Gustave Le Rouge. *The Dominion of the World* (w/G. Guitton) (4 vols.); *The Mysterious Doctor Cornelius* (3 vols.); *The Vampires of Mars*

Jules Lermina. *The Battle of Strasbourg; Mysteryville; Panic in Paris; The Secret of Zippelius; To-Ho and the Gold Destroyers*

Maurice Level. *The Gates of Hell*

André Lichtenberger. *The Centaurs; The Children of the Crab*

Maurice Limat. *Mephista*

Listonai. *The Philosophical Voyager*

Jean-Marc & Randy Lofficier. *Edgar Allan Poe on Mars; The Katrina Protocol; Pacifica 1, 2; Robonocchio; Return of the Nyctalope;* (anthologists) *Tales of the Shadowmen 1-14; The Vampire Almanac* (2 vols.)

Ch. Lomon & P.-B. Gheuzi. *The Last Days of Atlantis*

Charles Malato. *Lost!*

Maurice Magre. *The Marvelous Story of Claire d'Amour; The Call of the Beast; Priscilla of Alexandria; The Angel of Lust; The Mystery of the Tiger; The Poison of Goa; Lucifer; The Blood of Toulouse; The Albigensian Treasure; Jean de Fodoas; Melusine; The Brothers of the Virgin Gold*

Victor Margueritte. *The Bacheloress; The Companion; The Couple*

Camille Mauclair. *The Virgin Orient*

Xavier Mauméjean. *The League of Heroes*

Joseph Méry. *The Tower of Destiny*

Hippolyte Mettais. *Paris Before the Deluge; The Year 5865*

Louise Michel. *The Human Microbes; The New World*

Tony Moilin. *Paris in the Year 2000*

Michael Moorcock's *Legends of the Multiverse*

José Moselli. *Illa's End*

John-Antoine Nau. *Enemy Force*

Marie Nizet. *Captain Vampire*

Charles Nodier. *Trilby and The Crumb Fairy*

C. Nodier, A. Beraud & Toussaint-Merle. *Frankenstein*

Henri de Parville. *An Inhabitant of the Planet Mars*

Gaston de Pawlowski. *Journey to the Land of the 4th Dimension*

Georges Pellerin. *The World in 2000 Years*

Ernest Pérochon. *The Frenetic People*

Pierre Pelot. *The Child Who Walked on the Sky*

Jean Petithuguenin. *An International Mission to the Moon*

J. Polidori, C. Nodier, E. Scribe. *Lord Ruthven the Vampire*

P.-A. Ponson du Terrail. *The Immortal Woman; The Vampire and the Devil's Son; The Police Agent*

Georges Price. *The Missing Men of the* Sirius

René Pujol. *The Chimerical Quest*

Edgar Quinet. *Ahasuerus; The Enchanter Merlin*

Jean Rameau. *Arrival; in the Stars*

Henri de Régnier. *A Surfeit of Mirrors*

Maurice Renard. *The Blue Peril; Doctor Lerne; The Doctored Man; A Man Among the Microbes; The Master of Light*

Restif de la Bretonne. *The Discovery of the Austral Continent by a Flying Man; Posthumous Correspondence* (3 vols.); *The Fay Ouroucoucou* (2 vols.)

Jean Richepin. *The Crazy Corner; The Wing*

Albert Robida. *The Adventures of Saturnin Farandoul; Chalet in the Sky; The Clock of the Centuries; The Electric Life; The Engineer Von Satanas; In 1965*

J.-H. Rosny Aîné. *Helgvor of the Blue River; The Givreuse Enigma; The Mysterious Force; The Navigators of Space; Vamireh; The World of the Variants; The Young Vampire*

Marcel Rouff. *Journey to the Inverted World*

Marie-Anne de Roumier-Robert. *The Voyage of Lord Seaton to the Seven Planets*

Léonie Rouzade. *The World Turned Upside Down*

Han Ryner. *The Human Ant; The Superhumans*

Henri de Saint-Georges. *The Green Eyes*

Louis-Claude de Saint-Martin. *The Crocodile*

Frank Schildiner. *The Quest of Frankenstein; The Triumph of Frankenstein; Napoleon's Vampire Hunters*

Nicolas Ségur. *The Human Paradise*

Pierre de Selenes: *An Unknown World*

Norbert Sevestre. *Sâr Dubnotal: Vs. Jack the Ripper; The Astral Trail*

Angelo de Sorr. *The Vampires of London*

Brian Stableford. *The Empire of the Necromancers (1. The Shadow of Frankenstein; 2. Frankenstein and the Vampire Countess; 3. Frankenstein in London); The Wayward Muse; Eurydice's Lament; The Mirror of Dionysius; The New Faust at the Tragicomique; Sherlock Holmes and The Vampires of Eternity; The Stones of Camelot* (anthologist) *News from the Moon; The Germans on Venus; The Supreme Progress; The World Above the World; Nemoville; Investigations of the Future; The Conqueror of Death; The Revolt of the Machines; The Man With the Blue Face; The Aerial Valley; The New Moon; The Nickel Man; On the Brink of the World's End; The Mirror of Present Events; The Humanisphere*

Jacques Spitz. *The Eye of Purgatory*

Kurt Steiner. *Ortog*

Michel & Sylvie Stéphan. *The Wrath of Madame Atomos* (w/André Caroff); *The Sins of Madame Atomos* (w/André Caroff)

Eugène Thébault. *Radio-Terror*

Edmond Thiaudière. *Singular amours*

C.-F. Tiphaigne de La Roche. *Amilec*

Simon Tyssot de Patot. *The Strange Voyages of Jacques Massé and Pierre de Mésange*

Louis Ulbach. *Prince Bonifacio*

Théo Varlet. *The Castaways of Eros; The Golden Rock.; The Martian Epic* (w/Octave Joncquel); *Timeslip Troopers* (w/André Blandin); *The Xenobiotic Invasion*

Pierre Véron. *The Merchants of Health*

Paul Vibert. *The Mysterious Fluid*

Villiers de l'Isle-Adam. *The Scaffold; The Vampire Soul*

Gaston de Wailly. *The Murderer of the World*

Philippe Ward. *Artahe; Manhattan Ghost* (w/Mickael Laguerre); *The Song of Montségur* (w/Sylvie Miller)

CPSIA information can be obtained
at www.ICGtesting.com
Printed in the USA
LVOW03s2306010418
571920LV00001B/2/P